THE COUNTRY OF OTHERS

LEÏLA SLIMANI

The Country of Others

War, War, War

Translated from the French
by Sam Taylor

VOLUME ONE

faber

First published in the UK in 2021
by Faber & Faber Ltd
Bloomsbury House
74–77 Great Russell Street
London WC1B 3DA

First published in France in 2020 by Éditions Gallimard
under the title *Le pays des autres*

Typeset by Typo•glyphix, Burton-on-Trent DE14 3HE
Printed and bound by CPI Group (UK) Ltd, Croydon CRO 4YY

The right of Leïla Slimani to be identified as author of this work
has been asserted in accordance with Section 77 of the Copyright,
Designs and Patents Act 1988

Extract from *L'intention poétique* by Édouard Glissant © Éditions Gallimard, 1997
Extract from *Light in August* © William Faulkner, 1932, Penguin Random House

A CIP record for this book
is available from the British Library

ISBN 978–0–571–36161–8

MIX
Paper from
responsible sources
FSC® C020471

2 4 6 8 10 9 7 5 3 1

In memory of Anne and Atika,
whose freedom is a constant inspiration.

To my beloved mother.

The damnation of this word: miscegenation. Let us write it in giant letters on the page.

Édouard Glissant, *Poetic Intention*

But his blood would not be quiet, let him save it. It would not be either one or the other and let his body save itself. Because the black blood drove him first to the negro cabin. And then the white blood drove him out of there, as it was the black blood which snatched up the pistol and the white blood which would not let him fire it.

William Faulkner, *Light in August*

I

The first time Mathilde visited the farm, she thought: It's too remote. The isolation made her anxious. He didn't have a car back then, in 1947, so they crossed the fifteen miles from Meknes on an old cart, driven by a Gypsy. Amine paid no attention to the discomfort of the wooden bench, nor to the dust that made his wife cough. He had eyes only for the landscape. He was eager to reach the estate that his father had left him.

In 1935, after years spent working as a translator in the colonial army, Kadour Belhaj had purchased these hectares of stony ground. He'd told his son how he hoped to turn it into a flourishing farm that would feed generations of Belhaj children. Amine remembered his father's gaze, his unwavering voice as he described his plans for the farm. Acres of vines, he'd explained, and whole hectares given over to cereals. They would build a house on the sunniest part of the hill, surrounded by fruit trees. The driveway would be lined with almond trees. Kadour was proud that this land would one day belong to his son. 'Our land!' He uttered these words not in the way of nationalists or colonists – in the name of moral principles or an ideal – but simply as a landowner who was happy to own land. Old Belhaj wanted to be buried here, he wanted his children to be buried here; he wanted this land to nurture him and to be his last resting place. But he died in 1939, while his son was training with the Spahi Regiment, proudly wearing the burnous and the sirwal. Before leaving for the front, Amine – the eldest son, and now the head of the family – rented the land to a Frenchman born in Algeria.

When Mathilde asked what he had died of, this father-in-law she'd never met, Amine touched his belly and silently nodded. Later, Mathilde found out what had happened. After returning from Verdun, Kadour Belhaj suffered with chronic stomach pains that no Moroccan healer or European doctor was able to allay. So this man, who boasted of his love of reason, his education, his talent for foreign languages, dragged himself, weighed down by shame and despair, to a basement occupied by a chouafa. The sorceress tried to convince him that he was bewitched, that some powerful enemy was responsible for his suffering. She handed him a sheet of paper folded in four, containing some saffron-yellow powder. That evening he drank the remedy, diluted in water, and he died a few hours later in terrible pain. The family didn't like to talk about it. They were ashamed of the father's naivety and of the circumstances of his death, for the venerable officer had emptied his bowels on the patio of the house, his white djellaba soaked with shit.

This day in April 1947, Amine smiled at Mathilde and told the driver to speed up. The Gypsy rubbed his dirty bare feet together and whipped the mule even harder. Mathilde flinched. The man's violence towards the animal revolted her. He clicked his tongue – 'Ra!' – and brought the lash down on the mule's skeletal rump. It was spring and Mathilde was two months pregnant. The fields were covered in marigolds, mallows and starflowers. A cool breeze shook the sunflowers. On both sides of the road they saw the houses of French colonists, who had been here for twenty or thirty years and whose plantations

4

stretched gently down to the horizon. Most of them had come from Algeria and the authorities had granted them the best and biggest plots of land. Reaching out with one hand while using the other as a visor to shield his eyes from the midday sun, Amine contemplated the vast expanse. Then he pointed to a line of cypresses that encircled the estate of Roger Mariani, who'd made his fortune as a winemaker and pig farmer. From the road they couldn't see the house, or even the acres of vines, but Mathilde had no difficulty imagining the wealth of this farmer, a wealth that filled her with hope for her own future. The serenely beautiful landscape reminded her of an engraving hung above the piano at her music teacher's house in Mulhouse. She remembered this man telling her: 'It's in Tuscany, mademoiselle. Perhaps one day you will go to Italy.'

The mule came to a halt and started eating the grass that grew by the side of the road. The animal had no intention of climbing the slope that faced them, strewn with large white stones. The driver stood up in a fury and began showering the mule with insults and lashes. Mathilde felt tears well behind her eyelids. Trying to hold them back, she pressed herself against her husband, who was irritated by her sensitivity.

'What's the matter with you?' Amine said.

'Tell him to stop hitting that poor mule.'

Mathilde put her hand on the Gypsy's shoulder and looked at him, like a child seeking to appease an angry parent. But the driver grew even more violent. He spat on the ground, raised his arm and said: 'You want a good whipping too?'

The mood changed and so did the landscape. They came to the top of a shabby-looking hill. No flowers here, no cypresses, only a few stunted olive trees surviving amid the rocks and stones. The hill appeared hostile to life. We're not in Tuscany any more, thought Mathilde. This was more like the Wild West. They got off the cart and walked to a small, charmless little building with a corrugated-iron roof. It wasn't a house, just a series of small, dark, damp rooms. There was only one window, located high up to prevent vermin getting in, and it let through the barest hint of daylight. On the walls, Mathilde noticed large greenish stains caused by the recent rains. The former tenant had lived alone; his wife had gone back to live in Nîmes after losing a child, and he'd never bothered making the house more attractive. It was not a family home. Despite the warmth of the air, Mathilde felt chilled. When Amine told her his plans she was filled with anxiety.

* * *

She had felt the same dismay when she first landed in Rabat, on 1 March 1946. Despite the desperately blue sky, despite the joy of seeing her husband again and the pride of having escaped her fate, she was afraid. It had taken her two days to get there. From Strasbourg to Paris, from Paris to Marseilles, then from Marseilles to Algiers, where she'd boarded an old Junkers and thought she was going to die. Sitting on a hard bench, among men with eyes wearied from years of war, she'd struggled not to scream. During the flight she wept, vomited, prayed. In her mouth she tasted the mingled flavours of bile and salt. She was sad, not so much at the idea of dying above Africa as at appearing on the dock to meet the love of her life in a wrinkled, vomit-stained dress. At last she landed, safe and sound, and Amine was there, more handsome than

6

ever, under a sky so profoundly blue that it looked as though it had been washed in the sea. Her husband kissed her on both cheeks, aware of the other passengers watching him. He seized her right arm in a way that was simultaneously sensual and threatening. He seemed to want to control her.

They took a taxi and Mathilde was finally able to nestle close to Amine's body, to feel his desire, his hunger for her. 'We're staying in the hotel tonight,' he told the driver and, as if trying to defend his morality, added: 'This is my wife. She just arrived.' Rabat was a small city, white and solar, with an elegance that surprised Mathilde. She stared rapturously at the art deco facades of the buildings in the city centre and pressed her nose to the glass to get a better view of the pretty women who walked along the Cours Lyautey wearing gloves that matched their hats and shoes. Everywhere she looked she saw building sites, with men in rags waiting outside to ask for work. She saw some nuns walking beside two peasants, who carried bundles of sticks on their backs. A little girl, her hair cut like a boy's, laughed as she rode a donkey led by a black man. For the first time in her life, Mathilde breathed the salty wind of the Atlantic. The light dimmed, it grew pink and velvet. She felt sleepy and she was just about to lean her head on her husband's shoulder when he announced that they'd arrived.

They didn't leave their room for two days. Mathilde, normally so curious about other people and the outside world, refused to open the shutters. She never wearied of Amine's hands, his mouth, the smell of his skin, which – she understood now – was somehow connected with the air of this land. She was completely bewitched by him and begged him to stay inside her for as long as possible, even when they were falling asleep or talking.

Mathilde's mother said it was suffering and shame that brought back to us the memory of our animal condition. But nobody had ever told her about this pleasure. During the war, all those nights of desolation and sadness, Mathilde had made herself come in the freezing bed in her upstairs room. She would run up there whenever the air-raid sirens wailed, whenever she heard the hum of an aeroplane, not for her survival but to quench her desire. Every time she was frightened, she went up to her bedroom. The door didn't lock, but she didn't care if anyone walked in on her. Besides, the others liked to gather in bunkers and basements; they wanted to die huddled together, like animals. She lay on her bed, and coming was the only way she could calm her fear, control it, gain some sort of power over the war. Lying on the dirty sheets, she thought about the men crossing plains all over the continent, armed with rifles, men who were missing women just like she was missing a man. And while she rubbed her clitoris she imagined the immensity of that unquenched desire, that hunger for love and possession that had seized the entire planet. The idea of this infinite lust plunged her into a state of ecstasy. She threw back her head and, eyes bulging, imagined legions of men running to her, taking her, thanking her. For her, fear and pleasure were all mixed up, and in moments of danger this was always her first thought.

After two days and two nights Amine almost had to drag her out of bed, half dead from hunger and thirst, before she would agree to eat lunch with him on the hotel terrace. Even there, her heart warmed by wine, she thought about how Amine would soon fill the space between her thighs. But her husband's expression was serious now. Eating with his hands, he devoured half a chicken and tried to talk about the future. He didn't go back up to the room with her and grew offended when she suggested that they take a nap. Several times he absented himself to make telephone calls. When she asked him who he was talking to or when they would leave Rabat and the hotel, his answers were vague. 'Everything will be fine,' he told her. 'I'm going to arrange everything.'

A week later, after an afternoon that Mathilde had spent alone, he returned to the room looking nervous and vexed. Mathilde covered him with caresses, she sat in his lap. He took a sip from the glass of beer she'd poured for him and said: 'I have some bad news. We're going to have to wait a few months before we can move into our house. I spoke to the tenant and he refuses to leave the farm before the end of the lease. I tried to find us an apartment in Meknes, but there are still lots of refugees here and there's nothing to rent for a reasonable price.'

Mathilde was bewildered. 'So what will we do?'

'We'll live with my mother until it's ready.'

Mathilde leaped to her feet and burst out laughing. 'You're not serious?' She seemed to find the situation ridiculous, hilarious. How could a man like Amine – a man capable of possessing her as he had last night – how could he make her believe that they were going to live with his mother?

But Amine was not amused. He remained sitting, so he wouldn't have to suffer the indignity of the height difference between him and his wife, and in a cold voice, eyes fixed to the terrazzo floor, said simply: 'That's how things are here.'

She was to hear this phrase many times. It was at that precise instant that she understood she was a foreigner, a woman, a wife, a being at the mercy of others. Amine was on home soil here: he was the one who explained the rules, who decided the path they would follow, who traced the borders of modesty, shame and decorum. In Alsace, during the war, he'd been a foreigner, a man passing through, and he'd had to be discreet. When she met him in the autumn of 1944, she had been his guide and protector. Amine's regiment was stationed in her village, a few miles from Mulhouse, and they'd had to wait there a few days before they received their orders to advance eastward. Of all the girls who surrounded the Jeep on the day of their arrival, Mathilde was the tallest. She had broad shoulders and muscular calves. Her eyes were as green as the water in the fountains of Meknes and they stared steadily at Amine. During the long week that he spent in the village, she went walking with him, introduced him to her friends and taught him several card games. He was a head shorter than her and he had the darkest skin imaginable. He was so handsome that she was afraid someone would steal him away from her. Afraid that he was an illusion. She'd never felt anything like that before. Not with her piano teacher when she was fourteen. Not with her cousin Alain, who put his hand under her dress and stole cherries for her by the Rhine. But now she was here, in his homeland, she felt bereft.

* * *

Three days later they got in a truck. The driver had agreed to drive them to Meknes. Mathilde was bothered by the truck driver's smell and by the poor state of the roads. Twice they had to pull up next to a ditch so she could vomit. Pale and exhausted, staring out at a landscape in which she could find no meaning or beauty, Mathilde was submerged by melancholy. Please don't let this country be hostile, she thought. Will this world ever be familiar to me? It was dark by the time they arrived in Meknes and a hard, cold rain was rattling the truck's windscreen. 'It's too late to introduce you to my mother,' Amine explained. 'We'll sleep at the hotel tonight.'

The city appeared dark and hostile. Amine told her about the topography, which was based on the principles laid out by Marshal Lyautey at the start of the protectorate. A strict separation between the medina, whose ancestral values had to be preserved, and the European town, a laboratory of modernity where the streets were named after French cities. The truck driver dropped them further down, on the left bank of the Boufakrane wadi, at the entrance to the indigenous town. Amine's family lived there, in the Berrima quarter, opposite the Jewish mellah. They took a taxi to the other side of the river. The taxi moved up a long sloping road, passing sports fields and crossing a sort of buffer zone, a no-man's-land that split the city in two, where construction was forbidden. Amine pointed out the Poublan Camp, the military base that overlooked the Arab city, monitoring it for the slightest signs of unrest.

They found a suitable hotel and the receptionist examined their papers and their marriage certificate with bureaucratic thoroughness. There was almost a fight on the stairs leading up to their room because the bellboy insisted on speaking Arabic to Amine, who obstinately replied in French. The boy shot dubious looks at Mathilde. He had to provide the authorities with a special paper to prove that he had the right to walk in the streets of the new town at night, so he resented the idea that Amine could sleep with the enemy and circulate freely. As soon as their suitcases were in the room, Amine put his hat and coat back on. 'I'm going to see my family. I won't be long.' He left the room and slammed the door behind him before she had time to respond. She heard his footsteps hurtling downstairs.

Mathilde sat on the bed, her knees pulled up to her chin. What was she doing here? She had only her own vanity to blame. She was the one who'd wanted an adventure, whose friends had been envious of her exotic life when she embarked with such bravado on this marriage. Right now, he might be betraying her, humiliating her. Perhaps Amine had a mistress here? Perhaps he was even married! Hadn't her father told her, grimacing and blushing slightly, that the men in this country were polygamous? Or perhaps he was playing cards in a bar around the corner, laughing with his friends at how he'd managed to escape his dull wife. She started to cry. She felt ashamed at surrendering to panic like this, but it was dark outside and she didn't know where she was. If Amine didn't return she would be completely lost, with no money, no friends. She didn't even know the name of the street where they were staying.

By the time Amine came back, just before midnight, she was in a frenzy, her face red and blotchy. It took her a while to open the door and she was trembling; he thought something had happened to her. She threw herself into his arms and tried to explain her fears, her homesickness, the terrible dread that had overcome her. He didn't understand, and his wife's body, as it clung to him, seemed horribly heavy. He drew her to the bed and sat beside her. His neck was wet with tears. Mathilde calmed down, her breathing slowed. She sniffed several times and Amine took a handkerchief from his sleeve and handed it to her. He slowly stroked her back and said: 'Don't act like a little girl. You're my wife now. Your life is here.'

Two days later they moved into the house in Berrima. In the narrow streets of the old town, Mathilde kept a tight grip on her husband's arm. She was afraid of losing him in this labyrinth where shopkeepers crowded around you and vegetable vendors called out their wares. Behind the heavy, hobnailed front door, the family was waiting for her. Amine's mother, Mouilala, stood in the middle of the patio, wearing an elegant silk kaftan, her hair covered with an emerald-green headscarf. She'd taken some old gold jewellery out of her cedar chest for the occasion: ankle bracelets, an engraved brooch, a necklace so heavy that it bent her scrawny neck forward. When Amine and Mathilde entered, she threw herself at her son and blessed him. She smiled at Mathilde, who took the old lady's hands in hers and contemplated that beautiful brown face, those slightly reddened cheeks. 'She says welcome,' translated Selma, Amine's little sister, who had just turned nine. She was standing in front of Omar, a thin and silent teenager who kept his hands behind his back and his eyes to the floor.

Mathilde had to get used to this cramped and crowded life, to this house where the mattresses were infested with stink bugs and vermin, where there was no protection from the sounds of bodies and snoring. Her sister-in-law would enter her room without warning and jump on the bed, repeating the few words of French that she'd learned at school. At night Mathilde heard the cries of Jalil, the youngest brother, who

13

was locked in a room upstairs, alone with a mirror that he never let out of his sight. He smoked a sebsi pipe all the time and the smell of cannabis spread through the corridors, leaving her dazed.

All day long, hordes of bony cats paraded through the small courtyard, where a dusty banana tree struggled to stay alive. A well had been dug at the back of the patio, and the maid – a former slave – drew water from it for cleaning the house. Amine had told Mathilde that Yasmine came from Africa, maybe Ghana, and that Kadour Belhaj had bought the slave for his wife at the market in Marrakech.

In the letters she wrote to her sister, Mathilde always lied. She said that her life was like a novel by Karen Blixen or Alexandra David-Néel or Pearl Buck. In each missive she would invent adventures where she came in contact with the indigenous people, who were sometimes tender, sometimes superstitious. She described herself, wearing boots and a hat, haughtily riding an Arabian thoroughbred. She wanted Irène to be jealous, she wanted each word to be torture to her, she wanted her sister to die of envy, to be enraged. Mathilde wanted vengeance on this tall, strict, authoritarian sister who had always treated her like a child and often taken pleasure in publicly humiliating her. 'Feather-brained Mathilde', 'shameless Mathilde', Irène called her, without any love or indulgence. Mathilde had always felt misunderstood by her sister, a prisoner of her tyrannical affection.

When she'd left for Morocco, when she'd left behind their village, their neighbours and the future that had been promised to her, Mathilde's first feeling had been one of triumph. To begin with, she wrote enthusiastic letters describing her life in the house in the medina. She emphasised the mysteriousness of Berrima's alleys, exaggerated the filthiness of the streets, the noise, the stink of the donkeys transporting men and merchandise. One of the nuns at the school gave her a little book about Meknes, with reproductions of engravings by Delacroix.

She put this book with its yellowed pages on a table and tried to steep herself in it. She memorised certain especially poetic passages by Pierre Loti and marvelled at the thought that the writer had slept only a few miles from there, that his eyes too had seen the walls and pools of the Agdal Basin.

She told her sister about the embroiderers, the boiler-makers, the woodturners who sat cross-legged in their underground shops. She told her about the processions of guilds and associations in Place El-Hedim and the parade of seers and healers. In one of her letters she devoted almost a whole page to a description of a bonesetter's shop that sold hyena skulls, dried crows, hedgehog feet and snake venom. She thought this would impress Irène and Georges, their father, and that they, upstairs in their bourgeois house, would envy her for having sacrificed boredom to adventure, comfort to exoticism.

Everything in this landscape was unexpected, different from what she had known before. She would have needed new words, a whole vocabulary freed of the past, to express her feelings, the light so bright that you lived life through squinting eyes, to describe the awe she felt, day after day, when faced with so much mystery, so much beauty. Nothing here was familiar: not the colour of the trees or the sky, not even the taste that the wind left on her tongue and lips. Everything had changed.

During the first months in Morocco, Mathilde spent a lot of time behind the little desk that her mother-in-law had put in their room. The old woman was touchingly deferential towards her. For the first time in her life, Mouilala was sharing her home with an educated woman; whenever she saw Mathilde bent over her brown writing paper, she felt an immense admiration for her daughter-in-law. She told her family to be quiet in the corridors and forbade Selma from running in the house. She also refused to let Mathilde spend her days in the kitchen because she believed it was not a suitable place for a European woman capable of reading newspapers and novels. So Mathilde stayed in her room and wrote. But it rarely gave her much pleasure because, each time she started describing a landscape or recounting a lived experience, she felt cramped by her own vocabulary. She kept bumping against the same dull, heavy words, and perceived in a vague way that language was a limitless playground whose vast panoramas frightened and overwhelmed her. There was so much to say, and she wished that she were Maupassant so she could describe the yellow that covered the walls of the medina, so she could bring to life the young boys who played in the streets or the women who glided past like ghosts, enveloped in their white haiks. She summoned an exotic vocabulary that she felt certain would please her father. She wrote about razzias, fellahs, djinns and multicoloured zellige tiles.

But what she wanted was a way of expressing herself with no barriers or obstacles at all. To be able to say things as she saw them. To describe the kids with their heads shaved because of ringworm, all those boys who ran from street to street, yelling and playing, and who stopped when they saw her and – with dark eyes that seemed older than the boys themselves – observed her. One day she was stupid enough to hand a coin to a little boy, not even five years old, who wore shorts and a fez too big for his head. He was no taller than those jute bags filled with lentils or couscous that the grocer would leave outside their door, into which Mathilde always fantasised about plunging her arm. 'Buy yourself a ball,' she told him, all puffed up with pride and joy. But the little boy shouted and children appeared suddenly from all the neighbouring streets and swarmed around Mathilde like a cloud of insects. She heard them invoking the name of God, heard a few words in French, but she didn't understand and in the end she had to run away, under the mocking stares of passers-by who thought: That'll teach her to give away her money. She wished she could observe this beautiful world from afar, that she could be invisible. Her height, her whiteness, her status as a foreign woman all combined to keep her at a distance from the heart of things, from the silence that lets you know you are home. In the narrow streets she tasted the smell of leather, of firewood and fresh meat, the mingled odours of stagnant water and overripe pears, of donkey dung and sawdust. But she had no words for all this.

When she was tired of writing or rereading novels that she knew by heart, Mathilde lay on the roof terrace where laundry was washed and meat hung to dry. She listened to the conversations on the street, the songs of the women in those private labyrinths reserved for them. She watched them as they moved along walls that separated one terrace from another like tightrope walkers, sometimes almost falling and breaking their necks. The girls, the maids, the wives all shouted, danced, swapped secrets on those terraces of varying heights that they deserted only at night or at noon, when the heat of the sun grew too intense. Hidden by a small wall, Mathilde worked on her accent by repeating the few insults she'd learned, and the passers-by looked up and insulted her in return. 'Lay atik typhus!' they called. 'May God give you typhus!' They probably thought it was a little boy making fun of them, some young rascal bored from trailing behind his mother's skirts all day. Her ears were always pricked and she absorbed the local vocabulary with a speed that took everyone by surprise. 'Just yesterday she didn't understand a word!' Mouilala exclaimed. From then on, people were more careful what they said in her presence.

It was in the kitchen that Mathilde learned Arabic. In the end she insisted on being allowed in there and Mouilala let her sit and watch. The women winked at her, smiled at her, sang. First she learned how to say tomato, oil, water and bread. She learned hot, cold, the lexicon of spices, then words related to the climate: drought, rain, ice, hot wind, even sandstorm. With this vocabulary, she could also talk about the body, about love. Selma, who was learning French at school, acted as her interpreter. Often, when she came downstairs for breakfast, Mathilde would find Selma asleep on a bench in the living room. She would scold Mouilala, who didn't care about her daughter's education, shrugging at bad reports, never encouraging her to work hard. She let Selma sleep as long as she wanted; she thought it cruel to wake her early just so she could go to school. Mathilde would try to convince Mouilala that education could provide her daughter with the means to gain her independence, her freedom. But the old woman would only frown. Her expression, normally so affable, would darken, and she'd grow angry with the nassrania – the Nazarene – for preaching to her. 'Why do you let her miss school? You're endangering her future.' What future was this Frenchwoman talking about? What did it matter if Selma spent her days at home, if she learned to stuff intestines and sew them back up instead of covering the pages of an exercise book with ink? Mouilala had

had too many children, too many worries. She'd buried a husband and several babies. Selma was her gift, her respite, her last chance in life to be tender and indulgent.

For her first Ramadan, Mathilde decided to fast too, and her husband was grateful for this show of respect for their rites. Every evening she drank the harira, although she didn't like the taste, and every morning she was up before the sun to eat dates and drink sour milk. During the holy month Mouilala never left the kitchen, and Mathilde, with her gourmand's desires and her weak will, found it hard to understand how anyone could deprive themselves of food while spending their days amid the aromas of tajines and baking bread. From dawn until dusk, the women rolled marzipan and dipped fried cakes in honey. They kneaded the fat-soaked pastry and stretched it out until it was as thin as parchment. Their hands had no fear of hot or cold and they would often place their palms on burning metal. Fasting made them pale and Mathilde wondered how they could resist temptation, in this overheated kitchen where the smell of soup made your head spin. She herself could think of nothing, during these long days of abstinence, but what she would eat when night fell. She would lie on one of the damp benches in the living room, eyes closed, letting the saliva slosh around her mouth. She warded off headaches by imagining freshly baked bread, fried eggs with smoked meat, gazelle horns soaked in tea.

Then, when they heard the call to prayer, the women set the table with a carafe of milk, hard-boiled eggs, the bowl of steaming soup, the dates that they would open with their fingernails. Mouilala paid attention to everyone; she stuffed raïs with meat, adding chilli to the ones for her youngest son, who liked it when his tongue burned. She squeezed oranges for Amine, whose health was a source of worry to her. Standing in the doorway of the living room, she would wait for the men – faces still creased after their nap – to break the bread, peel a boiled egg and lean back against a cushion before she would finally return to the kitchen and start eating. Mathilde could not understand this at all. 'It's slavery!' she said. 'She spends all day cooking and then she has to wait until you've eaten! I can't believe it.' Selma, sitting on the kitchen window-sill, laughed at this and Mathilde took offence.

She roared out her anger at Amine and she did it again after Eid al-Adha, the feast that would give rise to a terrible argument. The first time, Mathilde remained silent, as if petrified by the spectacle of the butchers in their blood-splattered aprons. From the roof terrace, she observed the silent alleys of the medina where these men moved, accompanied by young boys who came and went between the houses and the oven. Streams of hot, bubbling blood trickled from house to house. The smell of raw flesh filled the air and the woolly skins of sheep were hung from iron hooks on front doors. This would be a good day to murder someone, thought Mathilde. On the other terraces, in the domain of women, the activity was relentless. They cut, gutted, flayed, quartered. They shut themselves in the kitchen to clean the entrails, removing the stink of shit from the intestines before stuffing them, sewing them back up and browning them for a long time in a spicy sauce. They had to separate the fat from the flesh and cook the animal's head, because even the eyes would be eaten by the oldest son, who would poke his index finger into the sockets and pull out the glistening white balls. When she told Amine that it was a 'feast of savages', 'a cruel rite', when she told him that the raw meat and the blood made her want to throw up, her husband would raise his shaking hands above his head and the only reason he held back from smashing them against his wife's mouth was that it was a sacred day and he had a duty to God to be calm and understanding.

* * *

At the end of each letter Mathilde asked Irène to send her books. Adventure novels, short story collections set in cold, distant countries. She didn't admit that she no longer went to the bookshop in the centre of the European town. She hated that neighbourhood – it was full of busybodies, the wives of colonists and soldiers – and she felt ready to kill somebody whenever she set foot in those streets, with all their bad memories. One day in September 1947, when she was seven months pregnant, she had found herself on the Avenue de la République, which most of the locals called simply 'the Avenue'. It was hot and her legs were swollen. She was thinking about going to the Empire cinema or having a cold drink on the terrace of the Roi de la Bière. Just then, two young women pushed past her. The dark-haired one started laughing: 'Look at her. She's pregnant by an Arab!' Mathilde turned around and grabbed the woman's sleeve, but she yanked it free. If it hadn't been for her big belly and the oppressive heat, Mathilde would have gone after her. She'd have stuffed those words back down her throat. She'd have returned all those blows that she'd received throughout her life. As an insolent little girl, as a lustful teenager, as a disobedient wife, she'd been slapped and bullied many times by angry men who wanted to turn her into a respectable woman. Those two young women would have paid for the life of domestication that Mathilde had endured.

As strange as it may seem, it never crossed Mathilde's mind that Irène or Georges might not believe her, and it certainly never occurred to her that they would one day come and visit. After finally moving to the farm, in the spring of 1949, she felt free to lie about her life as a landowner. She didn't admit that she missed the bustle of the medina, that she now longed for the lack of privacy she'd once cursed. Often she wrote 'I wish you could see me' without realising that this was, in fact, a confession of her immense solitude. She was saddened by all these first times that interested nobody but her, by this hidden existence. What was the point of living, she thought, if not to be seen?

Her letters ended with phrases such as 'I love you' or 'I miss you', but she never mentioned her homesickness. She didn't surrender to the temptation to tell them that the flight of the storks, which arrived in Meknes at the start of winter, plunged her into a deep melancholy. Neither Amine nor any of the people on the farm shared her love of animals, and when one day she mentioned Minet, the cat she'd had as a child, in front of her husband, he rolled his eyes at her sentimentality. She collected cats, which she tamed with milk-soaked bread, and when the Berber women looked at her resentfully, because they considered it a waste to give good bread to cats, she thought: These cats need love – they haven't had any for so long.

What good would it have done to tell Irène the truth? To admit that she spent her days working like crazy, with her two-year-old on her back? What poetry could she wring from her long nights spent sewing Aïcha clothes that looked new, or from the blistered thumb that this work gave her? In candlelight, sickened by the smell of the cheap wax, she cut patterns from old magazines and, with remarkable devotion, knitted little woollen knickers. Through the scorching month of August, she sat on the concrete floor dressed in overalls, and made a dress for her daughter. Nobody saw how beautiful it was, nobody noticed the delicacy of the gathered stitches, the little bows above the pockets, the red lining. It was killing her, people's indifference to the beauty of things.

Amine was rarely mentioned in her letters. Her husband was a secondary character, a vague presence in the background. She wanted to give Irène the impression that their love was so passionate that it could not be shared or put into words. Her silence was thick with insinuation; she wanted her omissions to be seen as an act of modesty – or even delicacy – on her part. Because Irène, who had fallen in love and got married just before the war, to a German man with scoliosis, had been widowed after only three months. When Amine had arrived in the village, Irène had watched, sick with envy, as her sister's body trembled in the African's hands. Little Mathilde, her neck covered in black love bites.

How could Mathilde admit that the man she'd met during the war was no longer the same? Weighed down by all his worries and humiliations, Amine had changed, his personality had darkened. How many times, walking with him in town, had she felt the oppressive stares of passers-by? The touch of his skin seemed to burn her then, and she was unable to prevent a frisson of disgust when she perceived her husband's foreignness. It struck her that it would take a vast amount of love – more love than she imagined herself capable of feeling – to endure the contempt of others. It would require a solid, huge, unshakeable love to bear the shame she felt when French people called him *tu* instead of *vous*, when policemen asked to see his papers, when they apologised upon seeing his war medals or noting his perfect mastery of French. 'But with you, my dear friend, it's not the same.' And Amine would smile. In public, he gave the impression that he had no problem with France after almost dying for its honour. But as soon as they were alone, Amine would shut himself away in silence and brood over his cowardice, his betrayal of his people. He went into the house, opened the cupboards and flung everything to the floor. Mathilde had a temper too: once, in the middle of an argument, when he yelled, 'Shut up! You make me ashamed!', she opened the fridge and picked up a bowl of overripe peaches, which she'd been planning to turn into jam, and threw them at Amine's face, unaware that Aïcha was watching them and that she would never get over the sight of her father in that state, his hair and neck dripping with sticky juice.

Amine didn't talk to her about work. The labourers, his anxieties, the price of wheat, weather forecasts. When family members visited the farm, they sat in the parlour and, after asking about his health three or four times, just sat there in silence and drank their tea. Mathilde found their company sickening; there was a baseness, a triviality to them that hurt her more than homesickness or loneliness. She wished she could talk about her feelings, her hopes, the anxieties that swarmed inside her meaninglessly, like all anxieties. Doesn't he have an inner life at all? she wondered, watching Amine as he ate in silence, gazing vacantly at a tajine of chickpeas prepared by the maid, cooked in a fatty sauce that disgusted Mathilde. Amine was only interested in the farm and in work. Never in laughing, dancing, relaxing, talking. People didn't talk here. Her husband was as dour as a Quaker. He spoke to her as if to a little girl who needed educating. She learned good manners at the same time as Aïcha, and she had to nod when Amine explained: 'You can't do that' or 'We can't afford that.' When she had come to Morocco, she'd still looked like a child, and she'd had to learn – in the space of a few months – to endure the loneliness of domestic life, to bear the brutality of a man and the foreignness of a country. She had gone from her father's house to her husband's house but she felt as if she had no more independence or authority than before. She could barely even exercise her domination over Tamo, the young maid, because Ito – Tamo's mother – was always watching, and Mathilde didn't dare raise her voice in front of her. She didn't know how to be patient when teaching her daughter. She would switch from sweet hugs to hysterical anger in a second, with nothing in between. Sometimes, watching Aïcha, the fact of her motherhood struck her as monstrous, cruel, inhuman. How could a child raise other children? Her young body had been torn open and out of it they had pulled an innocent victim that she didn't know how to defend.

When Amine had married her, Mathilde had only just turned twenty. At the time, this hadn't worried him. In fact he found his wife's youth charming, her big eyes thrilled and surprised by everything, her voice still fragile, her way of speaking mild and sweet like a little girl's. He was twenty-eight, which wasn't much older, but later he had to acknowledge that age had nothing to do with the unease that he sometimes felt when he looked at his wife. He was a man and he had been to war. He came from a country where God and honour were conflated, and he no longer had a father, which forced him into a certain gravity. What had charmed him when they were still in Europe now started to annoy him. Mathilde was capricious, frivolous. Amine was irritated by her thin skin, her lack of toughness. He didn't have the time or the ability to console her. And her tears! How many tears had she shed since arriving in Morocco? She wept at the slightest setback. She was constantly bursting into sobs and it exasperated him. 'Stop crying. My mother lost children and became a widow at forty, and she's cried less in her whole life than you have in the last week. Stop it, stop!' It was in the nature of European women, he thought, to reject reality.

She cried too much and she laughed too much. When they'd first met, they'd spent afternoons lying in the grass beside the Rhine. Mathilde would tell him about her dreams, and he encouraged her, without thinking about the consequences or the vanity of such conversations. She amused him. He'd never been able to laugh freely; he always covered his mouth when laughing, as if he considered happiness the most shameful and immodest of all the passions. In Meknes everything was different: the few times he accompanied her to the Empire, he would leave the cinema in a bad mood, angry at his wife who'd giggled too much and tried to cover him with kisses.

Mathilde wanted to go to the theatre, to listen to loud music, to dance in the parlour. She dreamed of pretty dresses, parties, tea dances, dinners under the palm trees. She wanted to go to the Saturday-night dance at the Café de France, to the Vallée Heureuse on Sundays, to invite friends over for tea. Sinking into nostalgia, she would remember parties that her parents had thrown. She was afraid that time would pass too quickly, that poverty and work would drag on forever, and that, when there was finally time to rest, she would be too old for pretty dresses and palm tree shade.

One evening, just after they'd moved to the farm, Amine walked through the kitchen dressed in his Sunday best while Mathilde was feeding Aïcha. She looked up in shock at her husband, unsure whether to be excited or angry. 'I'm going out,' he said. 'Some old friends from the garrison are in town.' He was bending down to plant a kiss on Aïcha's forehead when Mathilde stood up. She called out to Tamo, who was cleaning the courtyard, and handed her the child. In a confident voice, she asked: 'Should I change or isn't it necessary?'

Amine was speechless. Then he mumbled something about it being a night out with friends, that it wasn't suitable for a woman. 'If it's not suitable for me, I don't see how it could be suitable for you.' And without understanding what was happening, Amine let Mathilde follow him outside after leaving her jacket on the back of a kitchen chair and pinching her cheeks to give herself some colour.

In the car Amine didn't say a word. He just stared sullenly at the road as he drove, furious at Mathilde and at his own weakness. She chatted and smiled, acting as if she didn't realise that she'd gone too far. She was sweet, mischievous, carefree, convinced as she was that if she could just remain light-hearted, he would eventually start to relax. But his lips were still pursed when they arrived in town. Amine parked and hurried out of the car, walking quickly towards the café terrace. It was hard to tell whether he was hoping he might lose her in the streets of the European town or whether he simply wanted to avoid the humiliation of arriving on his wife's arm.

She caught up to him so quickly that he didn't have time to provide an explanation to the other men. They stood up and shyly, deferentially, greeted Mathilde. Omar, her brother-in-law, gestured to a chair next to his. All the men were dressed elegantly: they'd put on jackets, slicked back their hair. They ordered drinks from the jovial Greek who'd run this café for twenty years. It was one of the few unsegregated cafés in the city, where Arabs could drink alcohol at a table with Europeans, where women other than prostitutes could brighten the evenings. The terrace, on a street corner, was protected from public view by bushy bitter orange trees. Sitting there, you felt safe and sheltered from the world. Amine and his friends clinked glasses but they didn't say much. There were long silences punctuated by quiet laughter or the telling of an anecdote. It was always like this, but Mathilde didn't know that. She couldn't believe that this was what Amine's nights out with his friends were really like, those evenings that had caused her so much jealousy and concern. She thought it was her fault that the evening had been ruined. She wanted to tell a story to liven things up. The beer gave her courage and, in a timid voice, she talked about a memory from her native Alsace. She was trembling slightly, struggling to find the right words, and her story turned out to be boring. Nobody laughed. Amine stared at her with such contempt that she felt heartbroken. Never in her life had she felt so out of place.

On the opposite pavement the streetlamp flickered and then died. The terrace, lit only by a few candles, suddenly appeared more charming and Mathilde calmed down as her presence was forgotten. She dreaded the moment when Amine would cut short the evening, end the awkward tension, when he would say: 'Time to go.' There was bound to be a scene afterwards: some shouting, a slap, her forehead crushed against a window. So she savoured the tranquil sounds of the city, she listened to the conversations around the table and she closed her eyes to better hear the music at the back of the café. She wanted it all to last a bit longer; she wasn't ready to go home yet.

The men relaxed. The alcohol did its work and they began speaking Arabic. Perhaps because they thought she wouldn't be able to understand. A young waiter, his face covered with acne, placed a large plate of fruit on the table. Mathilde bit into a slice of peach, then into a crescent of watermelon. The juice dribbled on to her dress and stained it. She trapped a black pip between her thumb and her index finger and let it slide through the pressed flesh. It shot out like a bullet and hit the face of an obese man in a fez who was sweating in his frock coat. The man waved at it with his hand as if shooing away a fly. Mathilde picked up another pip and this time she aimed at a tall, very blonde man who'd put his feet up and was jabbering away enthusiastically. But she missed her target and the pip hit the back of a waiter's neck, almost making him spill the plate he was carrying. Mathilde giggled, and in the hour that followed she machine-gunned the men around her, sending them into convulsions. It looked as if they'd caught some strange disease, like those tropical fevers that drive their sufferers wild with the urge to dance and have sex. The customers complained and the bar owner burned incense sticks to ward off this invasion of flies. But the attacks didn't cease and soon all the men had headaches from the mixture of incense and alcohol. The terrace emptied, Mathilde said goodbye to the others, and as soon as they were home Amine slapped her. At least I had fun tonight, she thought.

During the war, while his regiment was advancing eastward, Amine had thought about his domain the way other men thought about wives or mothers left behind. He was afraid that he would die before he had time to honour the promise he'd made to fertilise that land. In the war's long moments of boredom the men would play cards or read novels or look through stacks of letters covered in stains. As for Amine, he would open a book about botany or a specialist magazine on new irrigation methods. He'd read that Morocco was going to become like California, that American state filled with sunlight and orange trees, where the farmers were millionaires. He confidently told Mourad, his aide-de-camp, that the kingdom was about to go through a revolution, to escape these dark times when farmers feared razzias or preferred to raise sheep rather than plant wheat because sheep could run away if someone attacked them. Amine fully intended to turn his back on the old methods and make his farm a model of modernity. He'd recently been bowled over by the account of a certain H. Ménager, a former soldier who, after the end of the First World War, had planted eucalyptus trees in the barren plain of Gharb. This man had been inspired by the report of a mission to Australia, ordered by Lyautey in 1917, and he'd compared the qualities of the earth and the region's rainfall totals to those of that faraway continent. Of course, he'd been mocked.

This pioneer, who wanted to plant vast fields with ugly grey trees that gave no fruit, had been laughed at by Frenchmen and Moroccans alike. But H. Ménager managed to convince the Department of Rivers and Forests and soon everyone had to acknowledge that he was right: the eucalyptus trees put an end to the sandstorms; they allowed the purification of cesspools where parasites proliferated; and their deep roots could draw sustenance from the water table that would otherwise have been inaccessible to the simple peasants. Amine wanted to be part of that wave of pioneers for whom agriculture was a mystical quest, an adventure. He wanted to walk in the footsteps of those wise, patient men who had carried out experiments in hostile soils. All those farmers denounced as madmen had steadfastly planted orange trees from Marrakech to Casablanca, and they were going to turn this dry, sterile country into a land of plenty.

Amine returned to Morocco in 1945, aged twenty-eight, victorious and married to a foreign woman. He fought to regain possession of his domain, to train his labourers, to sow, harvest, to 'see far and wide', as Marshal Lyautey had once said. At the end of 1948, after months of negotiations, Amine got his land back. First he had to renovate the house: make new windows, create an ornamental garden, pave a courtyard behind the kitchen for washing and hanging laundry. The terrain to the north sloped downward and he had to build some pretty stone steps and an elegant French window that opened on to the dining room. From there they could admire the magnificent outline of the Zerhoun mountain and the vast wild expanses that had for centuries been trampled and grazed by passing animals.

During the farm's first four years they would encounter every imaginable disappointment and life would begin to feel almost biblical. The colonist who'd rented the property during the war had lived on a small plot of cultivable land, but all the rest needed a huge amount of work. First they had the exhausting job of ridding the earth of dwarf palms. Unlike the colonists on the neighbouring farms, Amine had no tractors, so his labourers had to spend months digging into the hard earth with pickaxes to dislodge those vicious, tenacious little trees. Next they spent weeks clearing away stones, before ploughing the rockless soil. They planted lentils, peas, beans and whole acres of barley and wheat. Then the farm was attacked by a plague of locusts. A rattling, reddish-brown cloud swooped down on their fields and devoured all their crops, all the fruit from their trees. It was like something from a nightmare. Amine grew angry at his labourers, who did nothing more to frighten away the parasites than hitting tin cans with sticks. 'You ignorant fools! Is that all you can think to do?' he yelled at them, before teaching them to dig ditches and fill them with poisoned bran.

The following year there was a drought. The harvest was a time of mourning, because the ears of wheat were as empty as the peasants' bellies would be for months to come. In the douars the workers prayed for rain – the same prayers that had been muttered for centuries without any evidence of their effectiveness. But they prayed anyway, in the hot October sun, and nobody cursed God's deafness. Amine ordered a well dug: this necessitated a huge amount of work and swallowed up part of his inheritance. But the tunnels kept filling up with sand and the peasants couldn't pump water for irrigation.

Mathilde was proud of him. And even though she raged at his absences and blamed him for leaving her alone in the house, at least she knew he was honest and hard-working. Sometimes she thought that all her husband lacked was luck and a certain instinct. Her father had been blessed with those gifts. Georges was less serious and determined than Amine. He drank until he forgot his name and all the basic rules of decency and decorum. He played cards until dawn and fell asleep in the arms of large-breasted women who smelled of butter. He fired his accountant on an impulse, forgot to hire another one, and let the letters pile up on his old wooden desk. He invited the bailiffs to have a drink with him and they ended up rubbing their bellies and singing old songs together. Georges had a remarkable sixth sense, an instinct that never failed him. That was just how it was; even he couldn't explain it. He understood people and there was something in his character – a sort of tender, benevolent pity for mankind (himself included) – that always aroused the sympathy of strangers. Georges never negotiated out of greed but purely as a game, and if he ever conned anybody it wasn't deliberate.

Despite the failures, despite the arguments and the poverty, Mathilde never thought that her husband was lazy or incompetent. Every day she saw Amine wake at dawn and leave the house with a look of determination, and every evening she saw him come home, his boots covered with earth. Amine walked miles and never got tired. The men of the douar admired his endurance, even if they were sometimes annoyed with their brother for his contempt towards the old ways of farming. They watched him crouch down, feeling the earth with his fingers, placing his hand on the bark of a tree as if he hoped that nature was going to reveal its secrets to him. He wanted it to happen quickly. He wanted to succeed.

Around this time, in the early fifties, the nationalist fever was on the rise and the colonists were widely hated. There were kidnappings, killings, farms set on fire. The colonists responded by forming white defence organisations and Amine knew that their neighbour, Roger Mariani, belonged to one of these groups. 'Nature doesn't care about politics,' Amine said one day, to explain the visit he was planning to make to his inflammatory neighbour. He wanted to find out the secret behind Mariani's stunning prosperity, learn what types of tractors he used, what irrigation system he'd opted for. Amine also imagined that he might be able to sell cereals to Mariani for the colonist's pig farm. The rest didn't matter to him.

One afternoon Amine crossed the road that separated their two properties. He walked past large warehouses filled with modern tractors, past stables filled with fat, healthy pigs, past the wine cellar where the grapes were processed using the same methods as in Europe. Everything here radiated hope and wealth. Mariani was standing on the front steps of his house, holding two fierce yellow dogs on a leash. Occasionally he would be jerked forward, losing his balance, and Amine couldn't tell if the dogs really were stronger than him or if Mariani was just pretending they were to demonstrate the threat they posed to any unwelcome visitors. Amine, nervous, stammered as he introduced himself. He pointed towards his property. 'I need advice,' he said, and the colonist smiled as he eyed this timorous Arab.

'First let's have a drink, neighbour! We have plenty of time to talk business later.'

They walked through a luxuriant garden and sat in the shade on a terrace with a view of the Zerhoun. A thin man with black skin put some bottles and glasses on the table. Mariani poured his neighbour an anisette and when he saw Amine hesitate – because of the heat and the work that awaited him – he burst out laughing. 'Oh, you don't drink?' Amine smiled and took a sip of the whitish liquid. Inside the house the telephone rang but Mariani ignored it.

The colonist didn't let him get a word in. It struck Amine that his neighbour was a lonely man and that this was, for him, a rare opportunity to confide in someone. With a familiarity that made Amine ill at ease, Mariani complained about his workers; he'd trained two generations of them but they were still as lazy and filthy as ever. 'My God, the filth!' From time to time he looked up with rheumy eyes at his handsome guest and added with a laugh: 'I'm not saying this about you, of course.' And without giving him a chance to respond, he went on: 'They can say what they like, but this place will be a shithole once we're no longer here to make the trees bloom, to turn over the earth, to water it with our sweat. What was there here before we arrived, eh? Nothing. There was nothing at all. Look around you. Centuries of human beings and not one who could be bothered to cultivate this land. Too busy fighting. We've been through hunger here, we've buried people. We've sown fields, dug graves, built cradles. My father died of typhus in this dump. I ruined my back from days and days spent sitting on my horse, surveying the plain, negotiating with the local tribes. My spine was so messed up I couldn't lie on a bed without screaming out in pain. But I have to tell you: I owe this place a lot. It took me to the heart of things, it reconnected me with the vital life force, with brutality.' Mariani's face turned red and his speech grew slower as the alcohol took effect. 'In France, I would have had a queer's life, a narrow little existence with no ambition, no triumph, no grandeur. This country gave me the chance to live a man's life.'

Mariani called the servant, who came trotting along the terrace. He scolded him in Arabic for his slowness and slammed his fist on to the table so hard that it knocked over Amine's glass. The colonist spat on the ground as he watched the old servant disappear into the house. 'Watch and learn! I know these Arabs! The workers are morons; how can you not want to give them a good thrashing? I speak their language, I know them inside out. I've heard all the talk about independence, but no bunch of troublemakers is going to steal years of sweat and hard work from me.' And then, laughing, he picked up some of the little sandwiches that the servant had left, and repeated: 'I'm not saying this about you, of course!' Amine almost gave up then; he almost got to his feet and walked away, forgetting the idea of making this powerful neighbour his ally. But Mariani, whose face was strangely similar to those of his dogs, turned to him and – as if sensing that Amine felt hurt – said: 'You want a tractor, right? That could be arranged.'

II

It was very hot the summer before Aïcha started school. Mathilde hung around the house in faded overalls, one strap falling from her shoulder, her hair glued with sweat to her forehead and temples. In one arm she held Selim and with her free hand she fanned herself with a newspaper or a piece of cardboard. She always walked around barefoot, despite the protests of Tamo, who said it was bad luck. Mathilde still did all her chores but she moved more slowly and laboriously than usual. Aïcha and her brother Selim, who had just turned two, were both exceptionally well behaved. They had no appetite, no desire to play, and they spent the days naked, lying on the tiled floor, too weary to talk or invent games. At the start of August the chergui came and turned the sky white. This wind from the Sahara was every mother's fear, and the children were forbidden to go outside. How many times had Mouilala told Mathilde the story of children who'd died of the fever that the chergui brought with it? Her mother-in-law said it was dangerous to breathe that contaminated air; she said if you swallowed it you might burn your insides, might dry up like a withered plant. When that cursed wind blew, the night-time brought no respite. The light faded and darkness covered the countryside, the trees all disappeared, but the heat kept beating down as if a black sun now burned invisibly above them. The children grew fretful. Selim started screaming. He wept with rage and his mother took him in her arms and consoled him. For hours she held him against her body, their torsos soaked with sweat, both of them exhausted. The summer was endless and Mathilde felt terribly lonely. Her husband still spent his days in the fields despite the oppressive heat. He went with his labourers to the harvests, which turned out to be disappointing. The ears of wheat were dry, they kept working day after day, and everyone worried that they would starve to death in September.

One evening Tamo found a black scorpion under a stack of saucepans. She shrieked and Mathilde and the children came running into the kitchen. The room gave on to a small court-yard where meat and laundry were hung to dry, where dirty bowls piled up and Mathilde's beloved stray cats roamed. Mathilde insisted that the door to the kitchen always be kept shut since she feared snakes, rats, bats and even jackals (there was a pack of them near the lime kiln) might come into the house. But Tamo was a daydreamer and she must have forgotten to close the door. Ito's daughter was still only sixteen. She was cheerful and strong-willed; she liked to be outside, to take care of the children, to teach them the names of animals in the Shilha language. But she didn't like Mathilde's attitude towards her. The Frenchwoman was harsh, curt, domineering. She'd decided to teach Tamo what she called good manners, but she had no patience with the girl. After trying to teach her the rudiments of Western cuisine, she was forced to accept that Tamo simply didn't care: she barely listened and when she was supposed to stir the crème pâtissière she just stood there with the spatula hanging limply from her hand.

When Mathilde went into the kitchen that evening, the Berber girl buried her face in her hands and started intoning some kind of prayer. Mathilde didn't understand what had put her in this state. Then she saw the creature's black pincers poking over the top of a frying pan that she'd bought in Mulhouse just after her wedding. She picked up Aïcha, who was also barefoot. In Arabic, she ordered Tamo to pull herself together. 'Stop crying,' she repeated. 'Get rid of the scorpion and tidy up those pans.' She carried her children through the long corridor that led to her bedroom and said: 'Tonight, my angels, you're sleeping with me.'

She knew that her husband would be angry. He didn't like the way she was raising the children, her indulgence towards their feelings. He accused her of making them weak, spoiled whiners, especially their son. 'That's no way to educate a man. You have to give him the resources he'll need to deal with the realities of life.' In this remote house, Mathilde was afraid. She missed their early years in Morocco, when they'd lived in the medina in Meknes, surrounded by people, noise, bustle. When she opened up to her husband about this he laughed at her. 'You're safer here, believe me.' By this time – late August 1953 – he wouldn't even let her go into town because he feared an insurrection. After the announcement that Sultan Sidi Mohammed Ben Youssef had been exiled to Corsica by the French government, the people rose up in revolt. In Meknes, as in all the other cities of the kingdom, the atmosphere was combustible, on edge: the slightest incident could lead to a riot. In the medina the women wore black and their eyes were red with hate and tears. 'Ya Latif, oh my God!': in every mosque Muslims prayed for the sovereign's return. Secret organisations were formed to lead the armed struggle against the Christian oppressor. In the streets, from dawn until dusk, people chanted: 'Yahya el Malik, long live the king!' But Aïcha knew nothing about politics. She didn't even know it was 1953, that men were polishing their weapons, some ready to rise up for their independence, others to prevent it. Aïcha didn't care. All she thought about that summer was school, and it terrified her.

Mathilde put her children on the bed and told them not to move. She returned after a few minutes, carrying a pair of white sheets soaked in ice water. The children lay down on the cool, wet sheets and Selim fell asleep quickly. Mathilde hung her swollen feet over the edge of the bed. She stroked her daughter's hair and Aïcha whispered: 'I don't want to go to school. I want to stay with you. Mouilala can't read, and nor can Ito or Tamo. Why does it matter?' Mathilde was shocked out of her drowsiness. She sat up and put her face close to Aïcha's. 'Your grandmother and Ito had no choice.' In the darkness the little girl couldn't see her mother's face but she could hear the gravity in her voice and it worried her. 'I never want to hear you spout that kind of nonsense again, you understand?' Outside, some cats were fighting, yowling like banshees. 'I envy you, you know,' Mathilde went on. 'I wish I could go back to school. Learn so many things, make friends for life. That's when real life starts. You're a big girl now.'

The sheets had dried and Aïcha couldn't sleep. Eyes wide open, she dreamed about her new life. She imagined herself in a cool, shady courtyard, holding hands with another little girl who would be her soulmate. Real life, Mathilde had said . . . So that meant this wasn't real life: this white house, alone on its hill. Wandering around all day following the farm labourers wasn't real life. Didn't they have a real existence, then, all those men who worked in her father's fields? Didn't it count,

44

the way they sang and sweetly welcomed Aïcha to picnic with them in the shade of the olive trees? A half-loaf of bread baked that morning on the canoun, the women sitting in front of it for hours inhaling the black smoke that would end up killing them.

Until then, Aïcha had never thought of this life as existing in parentheses. Except perhaps when they went up to the European town and she found herself trapped amid the noise of cars, street vendors, teenagers rushing into cinemas. When she heard music bursting from cafés. The click of heels on concrete. When her mother pulled her along the pavement, apologising to the other pedestrians. Yes, in those moments, she'd seen that there was another life, a denser, faster life that seemed tensed towards a certain goal. Aïcha suspected that their existence here was only a shadow, a devotion, a life of hard labour unseen by others. A life of servitude.

The first day of school arrived. Sitting in the back seat of the car, Aïcha was paralysed with fear. There was no doubt about it now – whatever her parents might say, the reality was that they were abandoning her. Abandoning her in the most terrible, cowardly way. They were just going to leave her here, in this unknown street: Aïcha, the wild little girl who knew nothing but the vastness of the fields, the silence of the hill. Mathilde made conversation, she laughed idiotically, and Aïcha sensed her mother's unease beneath the feigned cheer. The doors of the school appeared and her father parked the car. On the pavement mothers held hands with girls in their Sunday best. They were wearing new dresses, perfectly tailored, in discreet colours. They were city girls, used to strutting about. The mothers in their hats chatted to one another while the children hugged. They were already friends. For them, thought Aïcha, this was just a continuation of the world they'd always known. She started to tremble. 'I don't want to,' she yelled. 'I don't want to get out!' The other parents and schoolchildren turned to stare. Aïcha, normally so calm and timid, had lost all self-control. She curled up in a ball in the middle of the back seat and emitted a deafening, heartbreaking wail. Mathilde opened the door: 'Come on, darling, it's all right, don't worry.' She looked imploringly at her daughter, a look that Aïcha recognised. It was the same look the labourers gave the animals before killing them. 'Come here, it's all right, come on' – and then they were penned in, beaten, slaughtered. Amine opened the other door and both parents tried to catch hold of her. Her father managed to pull her out and she clung to the door with surprising strength, her face a picture of rage.

A small crowd had formed. They complained about Mathilde, who, living on the very edge of civilisation, surrounded by natives, had raised savages. That yelling, that hysteria, it was just how the local people behaved. 'Did you know that when their women want to express despair, they scratch their faces until they bleed?' No one here was friends with the Belhaj family, but they all knew about them: living on the road to El-Hajeb, fifteen miles from the city centre, on a remote farm. Meknes was so small, and the people there were so bored, that this odd couple were the subject of endless speculation during the sweltering afternoons.

* * *

At the Palace of Beauty, where young women had their hair curled and their toenails painted, Eugène the hairdresser made fun of Mathilde, the tall, green-eyed blonde who was a good four inches taller than her dirty Arab husband. Eugène made everyone laugh by pointing out their differences: Amine, with his dark hair that grew so low on his forehead that he always looked like he was frowning; and Mathilde, who was fretful in the way that girls of twenty often are, but who also had something else in her character, something masculine and violent, a sort of indecency that had driven Eugène to refuse to serve her. The hairdresser described the young woman's long, solid legs, her strong chin, the hands she made no effort to care for, and then those huge feet, so large and swollen that she had to wear men's shoes. The white woman and the darkie. The giantess and the dwarf. Under their hood hairdryers, the customers snorted. But when they remembered that Amine had fought in the war, that he'd been wounded and decorated, the laughter faded. The women felt obliged to be respectful, and that just made them more bitter. As spoils of war went, they thought, Mathilde was a strange reward. How had that soldier managed to convince the tough Alsatian woman to follow him to his homeland? What had she wanted to escape so badly that she was prepared to come here?

* * *

Now, outside the school, they crowded around the child, dispensing advice. A man roughly shoved Mathilde out of the way and tried to reason with Aïcha. With his arms raised, he invoked Our Father and the fundamental principles of a good education. Mathilde was pushed and elbowed as she tried to protect her child. 'Don't touch her! Get away from my daughter!' She was devastated. It was torture to see her cry like that. She wanted to take Aïcha in her arms, to gently rock her and confess her lies. Yes, she'd invented all those idyllic memories of eternal friendship and devoted teachers. In reality her teachers had not been kind at all. What she retained from her school years were memories of cold water splashed on her face in the dark dawn, of being beaten, of the awful food, of her stomach churning every afternoon with hunger and fear and the desperate desire for some shred of tenderness. Let's go home, she wanted to yell. Let's forget the whole thing. Let's go home and everything will be fine, I can teach her myself. Amine glared at her. She coaxed and cajoled her daughter, offered her treats if she would only calm down. After all, it had been her idea to enrol Aïcha here, in this French-run school with its church tower and its prayers to a foreign god. Finally Mathilde swallowed her tears and clumsily, unconvincingly, reached out to her daughter. 'Come on, darling . . . Come to me, my little one.'

She was so concentrated on her daughter that she didn't notice people mocking her. She didn't notice the eyes staring down at her big, faded leather shoes. The mothers whispering behind their gloved hands. Some of them appalled, others laughing. Then, suddenly aware they were still at the gates of the Notre-Dame School, they remembered that they were supposed to be compassionate because God was watching.

Amine grabbed his daughter by the waist. He was furious. 'I've had enough of this nonsense! Let go of that door now! Behave properly! This is shameful!' The girl's skirt was hitched up to her waist, exposing her underwear. The school caretaker watched anxiously. He didn't dare intervene. Brahim was an old Moroccan man with a round, friendly face. He wore a white crocheted hat over his bald head. His navy-blue jacket was too big for him but neatly ironed. These parents seemed unable to calm down their little girl, who was acting as if possessed. The opening ceremony would be ruined and the Mother Superior would be angry when she heard about this farce being played out in front of her venerable institution. She would demand an explanation. She would blame him for it.

The old caretaker approached the car and, as gently as possible, attempted to detach the girl's fingers from the metal door. He spoke in Arabic to Amine: 'I'll grab her and you drive away, okay?' Amine nodded, then gestured with his chin for Mathilde to return to the passenger seat. He didn't thank the old man. As soon as Aïcha let go of the door, her father set off. The car sped into the distance and Aïcha didn't even know if her mother had given her a second glance. So there it was: they'd abandoned her.

She found herself on the pavement. Her blue dress was crumpled and she'd lost a button. Her eyes were red and the man who was holding her hand was not her father. 'I can't go inside with you,' he said. 'I have to stay here, at the gates. That's my job.' He put his hand on the child's back and pushed her through the doorway. Aïcha nodded obediently. She was ashamed. She always wanted to be as discreet as a dragon-fly, but here she was now, the centre of attention. She walked through the courtyard to where the nuns were waiting, lined up outside the classroom in their long black robes.

In the classroom the other girls were already sitting behind desks. They grinned as they stared at her. Aïcha was so frightened that she wanted to sleep. Her head was filled with a humming sound. If she closed her eyes she felt sure she would instantly fall into the deepest sleep. A nun gripped her shoulder. Holding a sheet of paper, she asked Aïcha what her name was. Aïcha looked up, confused. The nun was young and the little girl liked her pale, pretty face. The nun repeated her question and crouched down next to Aïcha so their faces were on the same level. At last Aïcha whispered: 'My name is Mchicha.'

The nun frowned. She nudged up the glasses that had slid down her nose and examined the list of pupils again. 'Mademoiselle Belhaj. Mademoiselle Aïcha Belhaj, born 16 November 1947.'

The child turned and looked behind her, as if she didn't understand who the nun was talking to. She didn't know who these people were and a sob caught in her chest. Her chin started to quiver. She dug her fingernails into the flesh of her arms. What was happening to her? What had she done to deserve this? When would Mama come back? The nun found it hard to believe, but in the end she had to admit it: this child didn't know her own name.

'Mademoiselle Belhaj, sit over there, near the window.'

For as long as she could remember, Mchicha was the only name she'd ever been called. It was the name that her mother yelled from the front steps when she wanted her daughter to come in for dinner. It was the name that flew between the trees, that climbed up the hill in the mouths of the peasants who searched for her and finally found her, curled up and fast asleep inside a tree trunk. 'Mchicha', she always heard, and what other name could she have, since that was the one blown about on the wind, the one that made the Berber women laugh as they hugged her as if she were their very own child. That name was the one her mother hummed to her at night as she made up nursery rhymes. It was the last sound she heard before falling asleep, and ever since birth it had echoed in her dreams. 'Mchicha' – little kitten. Old Ito, who'd been there on the day she was born, had mentioned to Mathilde that her baby's cries were like little miaows, and the name had stuck. Ito had taught Mathilde to tie the baby to her back with a large cloth. 'That way, she can sleep while you work.' Mathilde had thought this very funny. She'd spent her days like that, her baby's mouth gummed to the back of her neck, her heart filled with tenderness.

Aïcha sat down in the chair the teacher had indicated, next to the window, behind beautiful Blanche Colligny. The other pupils were all watching her and Aïcha felt threatened by this sudden attention. Blanche stuck out her tongue at her, then laughed and elbowed the girl beside her. She imitated the way Aïcha kept scratching because of the cheap wool that her mother had used to knit her knickers. Aïcha turned to the window and buried her face in the bend of her elbow. Sister Marie-Solange walked over to her.

'What's the matter, mademoiselle? Are you crying?'

'No, I'm not crying. I'm taking a nap.'

Wherever she went, Aïcha carried around a heavy burden of shame. She was ashamed of her clothes, which her mother sewed for her. Ashamed of the greyish blouses that Mathilde would sometimes brighten up with a little added detail – flowers on the sleeves, blue edging around the collar – but which never looked new. None of the clothes ever seemed truly hers; they all looked second-hand. She was ashamed of her hair too. In fact her hair was what bothered her the most: that shapeless, frizzy mass, impossible to style, which – almost as soon as Aïcha arrived at the school – would escape from the clips that Mathilde used to pin it in place. Mathilde didn't know what to do with her daughter's hair; she'd never had to deal with anything like it before. The individual hairs were so fine that clips broke them and irons burned them, but the mass itself was so dense that it could not be combed. She asked Mouilala for advice, but her mother-in-law just shrugged. No woman in her family had ever before been cursed with such kinky, unruly hair. Aïcha had her father's hair. But Amine always kept his hair cut short, like a soldier. And because he went to the hammam so often, and sprayed his hair with hot water, the bulbs had atrophied and his hair had stopped growing.

Aïcha was cruelly taunted because of her hair. In the middle of the courtyard she stood out like a sore thumb, with her slender figure, elfish face and enormous hair – an explosion of coarse blonde strands that shone like a golden crown in the sun. How many times did she dream that she had hair like Blanche's? In front of the mirror in her mother's bedroom she would hide her hair with her hands and try to imagine what she would look like with Blanche's long, silky tresses. Or with Sylvie's brown curls. Or Nicole's neat locks. Her uncle Omar teased her. He told her she would struggle to find a husband because she looked like a scarecrow. And it was true, thought Aïcha: her hair was like a clump of hay. She felt ridiculous in her second-hand clothes, with her impossible hair.

The weeks passed, all of them identical. Every morning Aïcha would wake at dawn and kneel in the dark at the foot of her bed, praying to God not to let her be late for school. But there was always something. Black smoke pouring from the oven. An argument with her father. Shouting in the corridor. Her mother finally arriving and stopping to adjust her hair, her scarf, then wiping away a tear with the back of her hand. Mathilde wanted to look dignified, but sometimes she would just turn around and start screaming that she had to get out of this place, that she'd made the worst mistake of her life, that she was a stranger here. She yelled that if her father knew the truth, he would beat up her bully of a husband. But her father didn't know the truth. Her father lived far away. So Mathilde surrendered to her fate, and took out her frustrations on little Aïcha, who was waiting patiently outside the door, biting her lip so she wouldn't yell at her mother: 'Please hurry up! Just for once, I'd like to get there on time!'

Aïcha cursed her father's van. He'd bought it from the American army for a reasonable sum. Amine had tried to scratch the painted flag off the bonnet but he'd been afraid of damaging the metal, so a few flaking stars and part of a red stripe were still visible on the bodywork. The van was not only ugly, it was also unreliable. When it overheated, grey smoke would pour from the bonnet and they would have to stop and wait for the engine to cool down. In winter it wouldn't start. 'It has to warm up,' Mathilde would always say. Aïcha blamed that vehicle for all her troubles and she even cursed America, a country that everyone else seemed to revere. Those Americans are just a bunch of thieves and incompetent fools, she thought. Thanks to that old banger, she was constantly mocked by her schoolmates – 'Your parents should buy you a donkey instead: you'd get to school faster!' – and told off by the Mother Superior.

Amine had managed to fit a small seat in the back, with the help of one of his labourers. Aïcha would sit there surrounded by tools and by crates of fruit and vegetables that her mother was taking to the market in Meknes. One morning, still half-asleep, the child felt something move against her tiny calf. She screamed and Mathilde almost swerved off the road. 'I felt something,' Aïcha said. Mathilde didn't want to stop, in case the van wouldn't start again afterwards, so she just grumbled, 'You're imagining things again', as Aïcha put her hands under her soaking armpits. When the van came to a halt outside the school gates and Aïcha jumped on to the pavement, the dozens of little girls crowded around the entrance began to scream. They gripped their mothers' legs and some started running towards the courtyard. One of them fainted, or pretended to. Mathilde and Aïcha looked at each other, completely baffled, and then they noticed Brahim, who was pointing at something and laughing. 'Look what you've brought with you,' he said.

A long grass snake had escaped from the back of the van and was lazily following Aïcha, like a faithful dog being taken for a walk.

When the wintry weather began in November, they also had dark mornings to contend with. Mathilde would hold her daughter's hand and lead her into the driveway, between the frozen almond trees, and Aïcha would shiver. In the black dawn they could hear nothing but their own breathing. No animal sounds, no human voices broke the silence. They'd get into the damp van and Mathilde would turn the key in the ignition, but the engine would just cough. 'Don't worry, it just needs to warm up.' The poor vehicle, numb with cold, would hack and hawk like a consumptive. Sometimes Aïcha would have a meltdown. She'd cry, kick the wheels, curse the farm, her parents, the school. She'd get a slap. Mathilde would get out of the van and push it down the driveway to the gates at the end of the garden. In the middle of her forehead, a vein would throb. Her purplish face would frighten Aïcha. At last the engine would start, but they'd still have to climb a steep hill. The old van would whine and growl ever louder, and often it stalled.

One day, despite her exhaustion and the humiliating prospect of having to ring the school's doorbell again because they were even later than normal, Mathilde started to laugh. It was a December morning, cold but sunny. The sky was so clear that they could see the Atlas Mountains like a watercolour floating above the horizon. In a stentorian voice, Mathilde shouted: 'Dear passengers, please fasten your seatbelts. We're about to take off!' Aïcha laughed and leaned back in her seat. Mathilde made loud noises with her mouth and

Aïcha held on to the door, ready for the van to roar into the air. Mathilde turned the key, pressed down on the accelerator, and the engine purred before wheezing asthmatically. Mathilde gave up. 'We're very sorry, dear passengers, but it would seem that the engines aren't powerful enough and the wings are in need of repairs. We will not be able to take off today, so we'll just have to continue on the ground. But have faith in your pilot: in a few days, I promise, we will fly!' Aïcha knew a van couldn't fly and yet for years she was unable to approach that steep incline without her heart pounding, without thinking: This is the day! Despite the improbability of such an event, she couldn't help hoping that, just this once, the van would soar up into the clouds, carrying them to new places where they could laugh like hyenas, where they would see their remote little hill from another angle altogether.

Aïcha hated that house. She'd inherited her mother's sensitivity, and Amine concluded that women were all the same, fearful
and impressionable. Aïcha was afraid of everything. Of the owl
in the avocado tree, whose presence, according to the labourers,
foretold death. Of jackals, whose howling stopped her falling
asleep, and of the stray dogs with their jutting ribs and infected
teats. Her father had warned her: 'If you go out walking, take
some stones with you.' She doubted she'd be able to defend herself, to scare off those fierce animals. All the same, she filled her
pockets with rocks and they clicked together as she advanced.

Most of all, Aïcha was afraid of the dark. Of the deep, dense,
infinite dark that surrounded her parents' farm. In the evenings,
when she'd been picked up from school, her mother's car would
drive along the country roads, the lights of the city would fade
behind them, and they would enter an opaque, dangerous world.
The car moved through darkness like someone entering a cave
or sinking into quicksand. On moonless nights, they couldn't
even see the thick silhouettes of the cypresses or the haystacks.
The blackness swallowed up everything. Aïcha held her breath.
She muttered Our Fathers, Hail Marys. She thought about
Jesus, who had been through such terrible sufferings, and she
repeated to herself: I could never do that.

Inside the house, the lighting was feeble and Aïcha lived in
permanent dread of a power cut. Often she had to grope her

way along the corridor like a blind person, hands patting the walls, cheeks wet with tears, calling out, 'Mama! Where are you?' Mathilde, too, dreamed of brightness and she nagged her husband about it. How could Aïcha do her homework if she ruined her eyes trying to read in this gloom? How could Selim run and play when he was shivering with fear? Amine had got hold of a generator that could recharge batteries, but he also used it at the other end of the farm to pump drinking water to the animals and irrigate the fields. In its absence the batteries soon died and the light bulbs flickered and dimmed. When that happened Mathilde would light candles and pretend to find the light they gave beautiful and romantic. She told Aïcha stories about dukes and marquesses, about masked balls in magnificent palaces. She laughed but the truth was that she was thinking about the war, about the blackouts when she had cursed her people, the sacrifices she'd made, the way her first seventeen years of life had flown past in a blur. The house was heated by coal and consequently Aïcha's clothes were impregnated with the smell of soot, which made her retch and amused her classmates. 'Aïcha stinks of smoked meat!' shouted the other girls in the courtyard. 'Aïcha lives like the Shilhas in their country shacks!'

In the house's west wing, Amine had his office. He called it 'my laboratory' and on its walls he'd pinned up pictures whose titles Aïcha knew by heart. 'On the culture of citrus fruit', 'How to prune vines', 'The application of botany to tropical agriculture'. These black-and-white images meant nothing to her and she thought of her father as a sort of wizard, capable of influencing the laws of nature, of speaking to plants and animals. One day, when she was yelling because she was afraid of the dark, Amine put her on his shoulders and carried her into the garden. It was so dark she couldn't even make out the end of her father's shoe. A cold wind lifted up her nightshirt. Amine took an object from his pocket and handed it to her. 'It's a torch. Shake it at the sky and point the light at birds' eyes. If you can, they'll be so frightened that they'll be paralysed and you'll be able to pick them up in your hands.'

Another time he asked his daughter to go with him into the little ornamental garden that he'd created for Mathilde. There was a young lilac there, a rhododendron bush and a jacaranda that had never flowered. Beneath the living room window grew a tree whose misshapen branches sagged under the weight of oranges. Amine showed Aïcha the lemon tree branch he was holding and, pointing with his permanently soil-stained index finger, he indicated the two large white buds that had formed on it. With a knife, he dug a deep notch in the trunk of the orange tree. 'Now watch carefully.' Amine delicately inserted the end of the lemon tree branch, which had been carved into a bud shield. 'I'm going to ask one of the men to stick it in place with putty and string. But what I want *you* to do is think of a name for this strange new tree.'

Sister Marie-Solange loved Aïcha. She was fascinated by this child for whom she secretly nursed great ambitions. The girl had a mystic soul, and while the Mother Superior suspected her of being slightly hysterical, Sister Marie-Solange believed that Aïcha had been called by God. Every morning before class the girls went to the chapel, which was located at the end of a narrow gravel path. Aïcha was often late, but as soon as she came through the school gates her entire attention was focused on the house of God. She gave herself to it with a determination and a seriousness unusual in one so young. A few feet before the door she would sometimes kneel and then move forward in that position, arms crossed, face impassive as the gravel dug into her flesh. Whenever she saw this the Mother Superior would roughly lift the girl to her feet. 'I do not approve of such self-indulgence, mademoiselle. God knows when someone's heart is sincere.' Aïcha loved God and she said this to Sister Marie-Solange. She loved Jesus, who welcomed her, naked, in the freezing mornings. She'd been told that suffering brought you closer to God and she believed it.

One morning, as Mass was ending, Aïcha fainted. She couldn't speak the last words of the prayer. She shivered in the ice-cold chapel, her bony shoulders covered by an old shawl. Nothing – not the singing, nor the smell of incense, nor Sister Marie-Solange's powerful voice – could warm her. Her face turned pale, she closed her eyes, and she collapsed on to the stone floor. Sister Marie-Solange had to pick her up and carry her. The other girls were annoyed by this. Aïcha, they said, was a sanctimonious little goody-two-shoes who would probably end up a religious fanatic.

Sister Marie-Solange lay her down in the small room that served as the infirmary and kissed her cheeks and forehead. She wasn't really worried about Aïcha's health. Her fainting was simply proof that a dialogue had begun between this puny little girl and Our Lord, the depth and beauty of which Aïcha herself could not yet comprehend. Aïcha sipped the warm water but pushed away the sugar cube that the nun offered to let her suck. She said she didn't deserve such a treat. Sister Marie-Solange insisted and Aïcha stuck out her pointed tongue then crunched the sugar cube between her teeth.

She asked to go back to class. She said she felt better, that she didn't want to be late. She sat at her desk, behind Blanche Colligny, and the rest of the morning passed calmly and uneventfully. Aïcha stared at the back of Blanche's neck, which was plump and pink and covered with light blonde down. Blanche wore her hair in a bun, high on her head, like a ballerina. Every day Aïcha would spend hours contemplating that neck. She knew it by heart. She knew that whenever Blanche leaned down to write, a little roll of fat would appear just above her shoulders. During the heat of September, Blanche's skin was covered in little red patches that itched. Aïcha would observe the girl's ink-stained fingernails scratching until they drew blood. Drops of sweat trickled from the roots of her hair down her back, soaking the collars of her dresses, which gradually turned yellowish. In the sweltering classroom her neck would twist like a goose's as her attention wavered, as tiredness overpowered her, and sometimes Blanche would fall asleep in the middle of the afternoon. Aïcha never touched her classmate's skin. Occasionally she wanted to reach out and stroke the bumps of Blanche's vertebrae with the back of her hand, to caress the strands of blonde hair that escaped her bun and reminded Aïcha of a chick's soft feathers. She had to force herself not to move her nose close to that neck so she could breathe in its aroma, to stick out her tongue so she could taste the sweaty skin.

That day, Aïcha saw the neck shudder suddenly and pale little hairs rise up like the fur of a frightened cat. She wondered what could have provoked such a reaction. Or was it just the cool breeze blowing through the window that Sister Marie-Solange had opened? Aïcha could no longer hear the teacher's voice or the squeak of chalk on slate. That patch of pink skin was driving her wild. She couldn't hold back. She grabbed her compass and stabbed the point into Blanche's neck, withdrawing it almost immediately and smearing a drop of blood between her index finger and her thumb.

Blanche cried out. Sister Marie-Solange turned around and almost fell off the rostrum. 'Mademoiselle Colligny! Why on earth are you yelling like that?'

Blanche threw herself at Aïcha. She pulled her hair. Her face was deformed with rage. 'It was her! It was this little bitch! She pinched my neck!' Aïcha didn't move. She just lowered her head, hunched her shoulders and kept silent. Sister Marie-Solange grabbed Blanche by the arm and dragged her to her desk with a brutality that shocked the other pupils.

'How dare you accuse Mademoiselle Belhaj? As if Aïcha would ever do such a thing! You're jealous of her, aren't you?'

'No! I swear!' Blanche shouted, putting her hand to the back of her neck and examining her palm in the hope of finding a trace of blood. But there was nothing, and Sister Marie-Solange ordered her to write lines: *I will not accuse my classmates of imaginary crimes.*

At break time Blanche stared daggers at Aïcha. 'You'll get what's coming to you,' that look said. Aïcha regretted that the attack with the compass had not had the effect she'd been hoping for. She'd imagined Blanche's body bursting like a pricked balloon, leaving only a limp flap of skin. But Blanche was still alive. She was jumping around in the schoolyard, making her friends laugh. Leaning against the classroom wall, face turned to the winter sun that warmed her bones and calmed her, Aïcha watched the little girls playing in the patch of ground bordered by plane trees. The Moroccan girls put their hands around their mouths and whispered secrets. Aïcha thought them beautiful with their long, dark, braided hair held in place with a thin white headband on the forehead. Most of them boarded at the school, and on Fridays they would travel back to their families in Casablanca, Fez or Rabat, cities Aïcha had never been to and which seemed as distant to her as her mother's homeland, Alsace. There were two camps in the school – the whispering natives and the hopscotch-playing Europeans – and Aïcha belonged to neither of them. She didn't know what she was, so she stayed on her own, her back to the hot wall. To Aïcha, the day seemed to drag on forever. She longed to see her mother again.

That evening, the little girls ran yelling to the school gates. The Christmas holidays had begun. Polished shoes crunched gravel and white dust clung to imitation suede coats. Aïcha was elbowed and shoved by the buzzing swarm of girls. She walked through the gates, waved goodbye to Sister Marie-Solange and stopped on the pavement. Mathilde wasn't there. Aïcha watched as her classmates walked away, rubbing against their mother's legs like cats. An American car slowed to a halt in front of the school and a man got out, wearing a red fez. He circled the vehicle, looking for one particular little girl. When he spotted her he put his hand on his chest and lowered his face in a gesture of respect. 'Lalla Fatima!' he said to the approaching schoolgirl, and Aïcha wondered why that child, who drooled over her schoolbooks every time she fell asleep in class, was being addressed like a lady. Fatima disappeared into the huge car and some other students waved at her and shouted: 'Have a good holiday!' Then the girlish twittering faded and ordinary life took over the street once again. Some teenagers were playing with a ball in the wasteland behind the school and Aïcha heard them insulting each other in Spanish and French. Passers-by shot her furtive glances, looking around for some explanation of why this child, who was clearly not a beggar, was standing there alone, as if forgotten. Aïcha looked away. She didn't want anyone to feel sorry for her or try to console her.

Night fell and Aïcha leaned against the gate, praying that she would disappear into a breath, a ghostly puff of steam. It felt as if she was standing there for eternity, arms and ankles freezing, her entire being reaching out for her mother who didn't come. To keep warm, she rubbed her arms and jumped from foot to foot. By now, she thought, her classmates would be safe in warm kitchens, their mouths full of hot pancakes and honey. Some would be doing their homework on mahogany desks in bedrooms that Aïcha imagined overflowing with toys. Car horns started to honk, men in hats and overcoats came out of offices, and Aïcha blinked in the glare of headlights. The rhythm of the city sped up to a frenetic dance. Those men walked confidently to heated rooms, happy at the thought of the night they would spend drinking or sleeping. Aïcha began to pace around like a jammed watch mechanism, praying to Jesus and the Virgin Mary, hands joined so tightly that her fingers turned white. Brahim didn't say a word because the Mother Superior had forbidden him to speak to the school-girls, but he reached out a hand to her and Aïcha held it tightly. Standing by the gates, they both stared at the crossroads until Mathilde finally appeared.

She leaped out of the old van and swept her daughter up in her arms. She thanked Brahim in Alsatian-accented Arabic, then began patting the pocket of her dirty coat, presumably in search of a coin to hand to the caretaker. But the pocket was empty and Mathilde blushed. Inside the van Aïcha didn't answer her mother's questions. She said nothing about the hate that Blanche and the other girls felt for her. Three months earlier Aïcha had wept outside the school because a girl had refused to hold hands with her. Her parents had told her not to worry about it, that it didn't matter, and Aïcha had been hurt by their indifference. But that night, unable to sleep, Aïcha had heard her parents arguing. Amine had raged at that Christian school where his daughter didn't belong. Mathilde, sobbing, had cursed their isolation. So now Aïcha didn't tell them any-thing. She never mentioned Jesus to her father. Her love for that bare-legged man who gave her the strength to master her anger had to remain a secret. And she never admitted to her mother that she hadn't eaten anything at school since discovering a tooth in the mutton-and-bean stew. It had not been a small, white, pointy milk tooth like the ones she'd lost that summer and put under her pillow for the tooth fairy to take in return for a praline. No, it had been a large, black, hollow tooth that looked like it had fallen straight from some old man's rotten gums. Every time she thought about this, she felt sick.

Back in September, while Aïcha was starting school, Amine had decided to buy a combine harvester. After all the money he'd spent on the farm, the children and the house, he had so little left that he went to see a crafty old scrap merchant who promised him an exceptional machine straight from an American factory. Amine silenced the man with a brusque hand gesture. He didn't want to listen to his sales patter. Anyway, this machine was all he could afford. He spent whole days perched on the harvester, unwilling to let anyone else use it. 'They'd mess it up,' he explained to Mathilde, who watched anxiously as her husband lost weight. His face was worn with fatigue and sun; his skin was now as dark as the African infantrymen he'd once fought alongside. He worked relentlessly, monitoring every movement his labourers made. Until nightfall he would stand there, supervising the loading of the bags, and often they would find him asleep behind the wheel of his van, too tired to make it back to the house.

For months now, Amine had not been sleeping in the conjugal bed. He ate standing up in the kitchen, while talking to Mathilde in terms that she didn't understand. There was something crazed about him, his eyes bloodshot and bulging from their sockets. He obviously wanted to tell her something, but all he could do was wave his arm strangely, as though throwing a ball or preparing to stab someone to death. His anguish grew all the more painful because he didn't dare talk to anyone about it. Admitting that he'd failed would have killed him. The problem wasn't the machines or the climate, or even the incompetence of his farmworkers. No, what ate away at him was the fact that his own father had been wrong. This earth was good for nothing. Only a thin layer of it was cultivable; below that it was tuff, the solid, impenetrable rock against which all his ambitions shattered.

Sometimes he was so oppressed by exhaustion and worry that he wanted to curl up in a ball on the ground and sleep for weeks. He wanted to cry like an overtired child. Perhaps the tears would loosen the vice around his heart. The endless sun and the sleepless nights were going to drive him insane, he thought. Darkness filled his soul, where memories of the war mixed with fears of impending poverty. Amine remembered the era of the great famines. He'd been ten or eleven when he saw all those families coming from the south with their animals, so skinny and starved that they couldn't make a sound. Heads ravaged by ringworm, they were migrating towards the cities with their silent supplications, burying their children by the roadside as they went. It seemed to him that the whole world was suffering, that hordes of the hungry were pursuing him, and that he could do nothing about it because soon he would be one of them. This nightmare haunted him.

* * *

But Amine did not give up. After reading an article, he decided to start cattle farming. One day, on her way back from school, Mathilde spotted him by the side of the road, more than a mile from the farm. He was walking beside a thin man dressed in a filthy djellaba and a pair of cheap sandals that made his feet bleed. Amine smiled and patted the man's shoulder. They looked like old friends. Mathilde stopped the car and got out, smoothed down her skirt and walked towards them. Amine looked embarrassed, but he introduced them. The man's name was Bouchaib and Amine had just made a deal with him. He seemed so proud as he told her that he planned to use their few remaining savings to buy four or five oxen, which the peasant would lead to pasture on the Atlas Mountains to fatten them up. Once the animals were sold, the two men would share the profits.

Mathilde stared at the man. She didn't like him: there was something sneaky about his smile, and when he laughed it sounded like a man having a coughing fit. She was repulsed by the way he kept rubbing his face with his long, dirty fingers. Not once did he look her in the eye and she knew it wasn't just because she was a woman or a foreigner. That man was going to swindle them, she felt sure. That evening she spoke about it to Amine. She waited until the children were asleep and her husband was relaxing in an armchair. She tried to convince him not to go into business with the peasant. She felt a little ashamed of her own arguments, ashamed that she was saying all of this only out of some sixth sense, a bad feeling, the peasant's unprepossessing appearance. 'You're just saying that because he's black. Because he's an uneducated hick who lives in the mountains and isn't used to city manners. You know nothing about people like that. You can't possibly understand.'

The next day Amine and Bouchaib went to the animal market together. The souk was at the end of a road, between some trees and the ruins of a wall that had once protected people from tribal razzias. The mountain people had laid some rugs down near the trees. It was stiflingly hot and Amine was stunned by the smell of cattle, of shit, and of the peasants themselves. Several times he lifted his sleeve to his nose because he feared he was going to vomit or faint. The skinny animals stared placidly at the ground. The donkeys, the goats and the few cattle seemed aware of how little the human beings cared about their feelings. They chewed listlessly at the yellow grass, a few dandelions, odd bunches of bakkoula. They waited, calmly resigned, to be passed from one cruel master to another. The peasants moved around, shouting out the animals' weights, prices, ages, uses. In this poor and arid region it was a struggle to grow anything, to harvest anything, to take care of the animals. Amine stepped over the large jute bags on the ground, taking care not to walk in the turds that were drying in the sun, and went directly to the western side of the market, where a herd of oxen was gathered.

He greeted the owner, an old man with a bald head covered by a white turban, and interrupted – a little abruptly for Bouchaib's tastes – the blessings that the man gave him. Amine spoke about the animals like a scientist. He asked technical questions that the old man couldn't answer. Amine was making it clear that they were not from the same world. The man became irritated and started chewing at the stem of a wildflower, making the same noises as the cattle he was selling. Bouchaib took matters in hand: he stuck his fingers in the animals' nostrils and stroked their rumps. Then, patting the man's shoulder, he asked him about quantities of grain and excrement and congratulated him on the good care he had taken of these animals. Amine took a few steps back. With difficulty, he concealed his anger and impatience. The negotiation went on for hours. Bouchaib and the owner exchanged so many empty words. They would agree on a price then one of them would change his mind and threaten to walk away, and then there would be a long silence. Amine knew that this was how deals were done here, that it was a game, a ritual, but more than once he wanted to yell at them to cut short these ridiculous traditions. It was late afternoon and the sun was starting to vanish behind the Atlas Mountains. A cold wind blew through the market. They touched hands with the peasant, who had sold them four healthy oxen.

Bouchaib was very friendly as he prepared to leave his business partner and take the cattle up to his village in the hills. He complimented Amine on his manners and his nego- tiating skills. He gave a long speech about the meaning of honour among the mountain tribes, about the importance of a man's word. He insulted the French, who were mistrustful people, obsessed with rules. Amine thought of Mathilde and nodded. He was exhausted by the day and now all he wanted to do was go home and see his children.

In the weeks that followed, Bouchaib would regularly send a messenger to the farm: a young shepherd with scabies on his calves, his eyes so ringed with pus that they attracted clouds of flies. The boy, who had probably never had a full belly in his life, spoke in poetic terms about Amine's oxen. He said that the grass up in the mountains was so fresh and thick that the animals were fattening up before their eyes. As he uttered these words, he saw Amine's face light up and felt happy at having brought some joy to this house. He came a few more times after that and slurped greedily at the tea into which Mathilde had, at his request, poured three spoonfuls of sugar.

Then the boy stopped coming. Two weeks passed and Amine started to worry. When Mathilde asked him about this, he flew into a rage. 'I already told you to mind your own business. That's just how things work here. You really think you can teach me how to run a farm?' But doubt tortured him. At night he couldn't sleep. Exhausted and wild with anxiety, he sent one of his labourers to ask for news, but the man came back shaking his head. He had not been able to find Bouchaib. 'It's a very big mountain, Si Belhaj. Nobody's heard of him.'

One evening Bouchaib returned. He stood at the front door, red-eyed and miserable. When he saw Amine coming towards him he slapped his head with both hands, scratched his cheeks and howled like a hunted beast. He struggled to catch his breath and Amine found it impossible to understand what he was saying. Bouchaib repeated: 'Thieves, thieves!' and his eyes filled with terror. He explained that a gang of armed men had come in the night, that they'd beaten the guards then tied them up, loaded the entire herd into the back of a truck and driven off. 'There was nothing the shepherds could do. They're good men, good workers, but what can a few boys do against men with weapons and a truck?' Bouchaib collapsed into a chair. He put his hands on his knees and sobbed like a child. He said he was eternally humiliated, that he would never recover from the shame. After drinking a mouthful of tea – with five spoonfuls of sugar in it – he sighed: 'This is a terrible misfortune for us.'

'We're going to the police.' Amine said.

'The police!' The man started crying again. He shook his head despairingly. 'The police can't do anything. Those thieves, those devils, those sons of bitches are already far away. How could the police find them now?' And he went into a long litany on the hardships of the mountain people, who lived so far from everything, at the mercy of violence and the seasons. He sank into self-pity, then raged against drought, disease, corrupt officials, women who died in childbirth. He was still sobbing when Amine grabbed his arm and lifted him to his feet.

'We're going to the police.' Amine was shorter than the peasant, but he was a strong man, young and determined, his muscles strengthened by working in the fields. Bouchaib knew Amine had gone to war, that he'd been an officer in the French army and had been decorated for heroism. Amine held the sleeve of Bouchaib's djellaba in his fist, and the peasant offered no resistance. They got into the car and were enveloped in darkness. There was a long silence. Despite the cold night, Bouchaib was sweating. Amine kept glancing at him. He watched the peasant's hands, barely illuminated by the dim glow of the headlights, afraid that the man might attack him in a fit of madness or despair.

The police barracks appeared on the horizon. Bouchaib started speaking again, less tragic and more sarcastic now. 'Do you really think those bumbling idiots can help us?' He shrugged, as if Amine's naivety was the most ridiculous thing he'd ever seen. They came to a halt in front of the entrance and Bouchaib remained in his seat. Amine walked around the car and opened the passenger door. 'You're coming with me,' he said.

It was dawn when Amine got home. Mathilde was sitting at the kitchen table. She was trying to braid Aïcha's hair and the little girl was biting her lip to stop herself crying. Amine looked at them. He smiled without a word and headed towards his room. He didn't tell Mathilde that the police had greeted Bouchaib like an old friend. They'd laughed as they listened to his story of the thieves in the mountains. In a mocking tone they'd asked: 'And the truck, what was it like? Oh, and those poor shepherds, I hope they weren't too frightened! Maybe they could come here to make a statement? Tell us about the thieves again, go on! This is the funniest story I've ever heard!' Amine had had the impression that it was really *him* they were laughing at. This Moroccan who thought he was a big landowner, who swaggered around like a colonist and yet had been conned by a smooth-talking peasant. Bouchaib would spend a few months in prison, but that was no consolation to Amine. It wouldn't help pay his debts. Ultimately the peasant had been right: it had been pointless, going to the police. All it had done was add to his humiliation. Amine should just have punched that stupid peasant in the face. He should have beaten that piece of shit until he was dead. Who would have complained? Did that lowlife have a wife somewhere, a child, a friend who'd have come in search of him? No, everyone who'd known Bouchaib would have been relieved that he was dead. Amine could have left the corpse for the jackals and the vultures. At least that way he'd have felt avenged. Going to the police . . . What an idiot.

III

Aïcha felt elated when she woke up on the first day of the Christmas holidays. She prayed as she lay in bed under the wool blanket. She prayed for her parents, who were so unhappy, and she prayed for herself because she wanted to be good and to save them. Since moving to the farm her parents had fought non-stop. The previous night, her mother had ripped two of her own dresses into pieces. She'd said she couldn't bear to wear these miserable rags any more, and that if her husband refused to give her money for new clothes she would go around naked. Aïcha pressed her hands together even harder and begged Jesus to make sure her mother did not walk in the street with no clothes; she begged the Lord to save her from such a humiliation.

In the kitchen Mathilde held Selim in her lap and adoringly caressed his curls. She looked wearily at the sun-soaked court-yard and the line sagging under the weight of laundry. Aïcha asked her mother to make her a little basket of food. 'We could go with you on your walk, don't you think? Why don't you wait for us?' Aïcha glared at her lazy, whiny brother. She didn't want anyone following her. She knew exactly where to go. 'They're expecting me. I have to go.' Aïcha ran to the door, gave a cursory wave and left.

She kept running all the way to the douar, which was half a mile away, on the other side of the hill, behind the fields of quince trees. Running made her feel that she was out of everyone's reach. She ran and the rhythm in her body made her blind and deaf, enclosed her in a happy solitude. She ran, and when her torso filled with pain, when her throat tasted of dust and blood, she recited an Our Father to give herself courage. *'Thy kingdom come, thy will be done . . .'*

She was out of breath when she got to the douar, her legs stung red by nettles. *'On earth as it is in heaven.'* The douar consisted of five miserable shacks, with hens and children hopping about in front of them. This was where the farmworkers lived. Clothes were drying on a line hung between two trees. Behind the buildings a few mounds of white stones were a reminder that ancestors had been buried here. This dusty path, this hill with its view of passing flocks, was all they'd ever seen, even after death. It was here that Ito lived with her seven daughters. The all-female brood was famous for miles around. Of course, there had been laughter and jeers at the birth of the fifth daughter: the neighbours had made fun of Ba Miloud, the girls' father, taunting him for the poor quality of his sperm, claiming he'd been cursed by some former lover. Ba Miloud had been angry. But when the seventh daughter was born everything changed, and the people all around believed that Ba Miloud was blessed, that there was something magical about that family. He was known as 'the man with seven maidens' and that name filled him with pride. Other men might have lamented their fate: how difficult, how worrying, to have seven girls wandering the fields, to be lusted after and impregnated by men! How expensive, all these girls who would have to be married off, sold to the highest bidder! But easy-going, optimistic Ba Miloud felt as if he were haloed with glory. He was happy in this house filled with femininity, where the voices of his children were like the twittering of birds at the start of spring.

For the most part, they had inherited their mother's high cheekbones and pale hair. The first two were redheads and the next four blondes, and each of them had a henna tattoo on her chin. They braided their long hair, and those long braids hung down to the base of the spine. They covered part of their broad foreheads with a coloured ribbon, bright yellow or carmine pink, and they wore earrings so heavy that their lobes were strangely elongated. But what everyone noticed – what made them so unusual – was the beauty of their smiles. They had tiny little teeth, as white and shiny as pearls. Even Ito, who was older now and who drank her tea very sweet, still had a sparkling smile.

One day Aïcha had asked Ba Miloud how old he was. 'I'm at least a hundred years old,' he'd replied in perfect seriousness, and Aïcha had been impressed. 'Is that why you only have one tooth?' Ba Miloud had burst out laughing and his lash-less eyes had shone. 'Oh, that's because of the mouse,' he'd said. He'd whispered mysteriously into the little girl's ear as Ito and his daughters giggled outside. 'One night I worked so hard in the fields that I fell asleep in the middle of dinner. I still had a piece of bread in my mouth, soaked in sweet tea. I fell into a sleep so deep that I didn't feel the little mouse as it climbed over me, ate the bread in my mouth and stole all my teeth. When I woke up I only had one left.' Aïcha had cried out in shock and the women in the house had laughed. 'Don't scare her, ya Ba! Don't worry, my girl, there are no little mice like that at your farm.'

* * *

79

Since starting school, Aïcha had had less time to come here. Today Ito welcomed her into her home with yelps and laughter. She loved the master's daughter, with her huge pile of straw hair, her shy ways and her little basket. Aïcha felt like her daughter too, in a way, since Ita had seen her emerge from her mother's vagina, and since Tamo – the eldest of her seven daughters – had worked at the farm since Aïcha's family moved there. Aïcha looked around for the children, but there was nobody in the large central room where they ate and slept, where Ba Miloud rode his wife without worrying about the presence of all those girls. The house was cold and damp and Aïcha found it hard to breathe because of the smoke coming from the canoun. Ito was crouching in front of the stove, poking a piece of cardboard. With her other hand she broke an egg and fried it on the charcoal, adding a pinch of cumin. She handed it to Aïcha: 'This is for you.' And while the child ate with her fingers, sitting on her heels, Ito gently stroked her back, laughing as the yolk ran on to the collar of the little blouse that Mathilde had spent two nights making.

Rabia arrived, her cheeks purple from the effort of running. She was only three years older than Aïcha but she wasn't really a child any more. Aïcha saw her as an extension of her mother's arms. Rabia could peel vegetables with the same dexterity, she could clean noses covered with dried snot, she could find mallows near the roots of trees, chop them up and cook them. With her hands, which were as slender as Aïcha's, Rabia could knead bread and knock olives from trees into wide nets at harvest time. She knew not to climb the wet branches of the trees because they were too slippery. When she whistled, stray dogs would run away, tails down, hind legs trembling with fear. Aïcha admired Ito's daughters, whose games she watched without always understanding them. They would run after each other and pull each other's hair, or sometimes jump on each other and the one on top would perform a strange up-and-down movement that made the one underneath giggle. They liked to dress Aïcha up and play with her. They would attach a rag doll to her back, wrap a dirty scarf around her head, clap their hands and tell her to dance. Once, they tried to convince Aïcha to get a tattoo like theirs and to cover her hands and feet with henna, but Ito intervened before that could happen. They called her 'Bent Tajer', the master's daughter, with mocking deference and said: 'You're not better than us, are you?'

One day Aïcha told Rabia about the school and left her in a state of shock. How terrible the girl made it sound! Rabia imagined the school as a sort of prison where adults yelled in French at the petrified children. A prison where you couldn't enjoy the passing of the seasons, where you spent all day sitting at a desk, at the mercy of the grown-ups' cruelty.

The girls ran through the countryside and nobody asked them where they were going. Thick, sticky mud clung to their shoes and they found it harder and harder to keep moving. They had to use their fingers to remove the clay from their soles, and the feel of it made them laugh. They sat at the base of a tree, tired out, and wearily dug little holes with their index fingers, discovering large earthworms that they crushed between their fingers. They always wanted to know what was inside things: in the bellies of animals, in the stems of flowers, in the trunks of trees. They wanted to cut the world open in the hope of revealing its mystery.

81

That day, they talked about running away, going on an adventure, and they laughed at the thought of such vast freedom. But then they felt hungry, the wind grew cold and the sun began to set. Aïcha begged her friend to walk with her; she was afraid of going home alone and she held Rabia's elbow on the narrow rocky path. They weren't too far from the house when Rabia spotted an enormous pile of hay just under the barn that the labourers had not taken to the stables. 'Come on,' she said. Aïcha didn't want to look like a coward, so she followed Rabia up an old orange ladder on to the roof of the barn. Then Rabia, her little torso shaking with laughter, said, 'Watch!' And she jumped.

For a few seconds there was no sound at all. It was as if Rabia's body had vanished, as if she'd been kidnapped by a djinn. Aïcha stopped breathing. She moved to the very edge of the roof, bent down and, in a tiny voice, called out: 'Rabia?' After a moment she thought she heard a moan or a sob. She was so frightened that she hurtled down the ladder and ran into the house. She found Mathilde sitting in her chair, with Selim at her feet. Her mother stood up and started to scold her daughter, to tell her that she'd been worried sick, but Aïcha threw herself at her mother's legs. 'I think Rabia is dead!'

Mathilde summoned Tamo, who was dozing in the kitchen, and they ran to the barn. Tamo started screaming when she found her sister in the bloodstained hay; her eyeballs bulged as she screamed. To calm her down, Mathilde slapped her so hard that she fell to the ground. Mathilde leaned over Rabia, whose arm had been deeply wounded by a pitchfork hidden in the hay. She picked her up and carried her to the house. While stroking the fainted girl's cheek, she tried to call the doctor, but the telephone was out of order. Her jaw trembled and this scared Aïcha, who thought that if Rabia died the whole world would hate her. It was all her fault and tomorrow she would have to face the anger of Ito and Ba Miloud, the curses of the entire village. She hopped from foot to foot, with pins and needles in her legs.

'Stupid phone, stupid farm, stupid country!' Mathilde threw the telephone against the wall and asked Tamo to lay her sister down on the living room sofa. They lit candles around Rabia; she didn't move, and in that light she looked like an adorable corpse, ready to be buried. The only reason Tamo and Aïcha said nothing – the only reason they didn't hurl themselves down on the ground and weep – was because they feared and admired Mathilde, who was now rummaging around in her medicine cabinet. She leaned over Rabia and time stopped. There was no sound but the saliva that she swallowed, the scissors she used to cut the gauze and thread. Rabia moaned slightly as Mathilde placed a cloth soaked with cologne on her forehead and said: '*Voilà.*' Aïcha had been asleep for a long time, her heart crushed by fear, when Amine came home. Mathilde started crying and screaming. She cursed this house and said she couldn't go on living this way, like savages. She refused to put her children's lives in danger for one minute longer.

* * *

The next day Mathilde woke at dawn and went into her daughter's room. Aïcha was sleeping next to Rabia. She delicately lifted the bandage that covered the child's wound then kissed both their foreheads. On her daughter's desk she saw the advent calendar with 'December 1953' spelled out in gilt lettering. Mathilde had made it herself: she'd cut out twenty-four little windows, and they had all – she noticed now – remained unopened. Aïcha claimed that she didn't like sweets. She never asked for any treats at all, and she refused to eat the fruit jellies or the cherries preserved in eau de vie that Mathilde kept hidden behind some books. She was annoyed by her daughter's seriousness. She's as grim as her father, Mathilde thought. Her husband had already left for the fields and she sat at the table facing the garden, wrapped in a blanket. Tamo brought her tea, leaning over her to place it on the table. Mathilde sniffed. She hated the smell of the maid. She couldn't stand the way she laughed, her curiosity, her lack of hygiene. She called her a pig and a moujik.

Tamo gasped admiringly. 'What's that?' she asked, pointing at the calendar. The gold stars were starting to peel off. Mathilde slapped Tamo's fingers.

'Don't go near that. It's for Christmas!'

Tamo shrugged and went back to the kitchen. Mathilde bent down towards Selim, who was sitting on the rug. She licked her finger and stuck it in the sugar bowl that Tamo had left. Selim, who knew how to enjoy himself, sucked her finger and said thank you.

For weeks Mathilde had been saying that she wanted to have a Christmas like the ones she remembered from Alsace. When they still lived in Berrima, she hadn't protested about the absence of a tree or presents or lights. She hadn't made a fuss because she understood that it was impossible, in that dark and silent house, in the middle of the medina, to impose her own god and her own rites. But Aïcha was six now and Mathilde dreamed of giving her daughter an unforgettable Christmas. She knew that the children at school boasted about the gifts they were going to receive, the dresses that their mothers had bought for them, and she refused to let Aïcha be deprived of those little joys.

Mathilde got in her car and started along the road that she knew by heart. From time to time she waved her left arm through the window to greet the labourers who put their hands on their hearts. When she was alone she drove fast, and someone had told Amine about this. He'd forbidden her to take such risks. But she liked speeding through the countryside, raising clouds of dust; it made her feel that she was getting somewhere in life, as quickly as possible. She arrived in Place El-Hedim and parked near an alley. Before getting out of the car she put a djellaba on over her clothes and tied a headscarf around her hair, letting it fall over her face. A few days earlier her car had been attacked with stones. Her children, terrified, had screamed in the back seat. She hadn't told Amine because she was afraid he'd forbid her to leave the house. He said it was dangerous for a Frenchwoman to walk around the medina. Mathilde didn't read newspapers and barely listened to the radio, but her sister-in-law Selma had told her, eyes glinting mischievously, that the Moroccan people's victory was at hand. Laughing, she'd said that a young Moroccan boy had been punished for not following the boycott of French goods by being forced to eat a packet of cigarettes. 'One of our neighbours had his lips cut with a razor because he was smoking and offending Allah.' Outside Aïcha's school, in the European town, the mothers liked to talk in loud, severe voices of the Arabs' betrayal, after the French had treated them with such

85

deference and respect. They wanted Mathilde to hear these tales of Frenchmen kidnapped, held hostage and tortured by the mountain people, because they regarded her as complicit in such crimes.

With her face and body covered, she got out of the car and headed towards her mother-in-law's house. She was sweating under the layers of cloth and occasionally she moved the scarf away from her mouth so she could catch her breath. It felt strangely intoxicating, going out in disguise like this. She was like a little girl, pretending to be someone else. She went unnoticed, a ghost among ghosts, and nobody could guess that, beneath those veils, she was a foreigner. She passed a group of young boys selling peanuts from Boufakrane and stopped in front of a little cart to run her fingertips over some fleshy orange medlars. In Arabic, she negotiated a price and the vendor – a thin, laughing peasant – let her have a kilo for a modest sum. She wanted to lower her veil then, show her face, her big green eyes, and tell the old man that she'd fooled him. But on second thoughts this seemed like a bad idea, and she sacrificed the pleasure of mocking the naivety of the people around her.

Eyes lowered and veil raised over her mouth again, she felt herself disappear and she didn't really know what to think about this. The anonymity protected her, even thrilled her, but she felt as if she were advancing into a dark pit, losing more of her name and identity with each step, as if by masking her face she was also masking some essential part of herself. She was becoming a shadow, a nameless, genderless, ageless being. The few times she'd dared to speak to Amine about the condition of Moroccan women, about how poor Mouilala never left the house, her husband had cut short the discussion. 'What are you complaining about? You're a European – nobody stops you doing anything. So mind your own business and leave my mother in peace.'

But Mathilde was naturally contrary and she couldn't resist the temptation to argue with him. Some evenings, when Amine came home exhausted after a day in the fields, hollowed out by worries, she would speak to him about Selma's future, about Aïcha, about all those young girls whose fate was not yet sealed. 'Selma should study,' she would tell him. If Amine kept calm, she would go on. 'Times have changed. Think about your daughter too. Don't tell me that you intend to raise Aïcha as a submissive woman!' Then Mathilde would quote, in her Alsace-accented Arabic, the words of Lalla Aïcha in Tangier, in April 1947. They had named Aïcha in tribute to the sultan's daughter, and Mathilde liked to remind him of this. Didn't the nationalists themselves make a direct link between the desire for independence and the need for women's emancipation? More and more Moroccan women were educating themselves, wearing a djellaba or even European clothes. Amine would nod and grunt but make no promises. Out on the dirt paths, surrounded by his labourers, he would sometimes think back to these conversations. Who would want a degenerate wife? he'd wonder. Mathilde doesn't understand. Then he'd think about his mother, who had spent her entire life locked indoors. As a little girl, Mouilala had not been allowed to go to school with her brothers. And then Si Kadour, her late husband, had built the house in the medina. He'd made a concession to custom with that single high window, the blinds always kept closed, which Mouilala was forbidden to approach. Kadour had been a modern man in many ways – he kissed Frenchwomen's hands and sometimes used a Jewish prostitute in El Mers – but his modernity did not extend to his wife's reputation. Sometimes, when Amine was a child, he would see his mother peeking through the gaps in the blind at the street outside. When she noticed him standing there, she would put her finger to her lips to seal the secret between them.

For Mouilala, the world was criss-crossed with impassable borders – between men and women; between Muslims, Jews and Christians – and she believed that if people were to get along, it was better that they didn't come into contact too often. Peace would last as long as everyone knew his place. To the Jews in the mellah she entrusted the repair of braziers and the making of baskets; she also had certain dry goods, essential for the running of her house, delivered to her by a thin Jewish dressmaker with hairs on her cheeks. Kadour had boasted of being a modern man and had liked to wear frock coats and darted trousers, but she had never met any of his European friends. And she'd asked no questions when, one morning, she was cleaning her husband's private salon and discovered lipstick traces on the rim of a glass and several cigarette stubs.

Amine loved his wife. He loved and he desired her so passionately that sometimes he would wake up in the middle of the night with the urge to bite her, devour her, possess her absolutely. But then he would start to have doubts. What madness was this? How could he have thought he'd be able to live with a European woman as emancipated as Mathilde? Thanks to her and her contrary nature, he felt as if his life were governed by a pendulum, swinging him from one hysterical crisis to another. Sometimes he felt a violent, cruel need to return to his culture, to love his god, language and country with all his heart, and Mathilde's incomprehension drove him crazy. He wanted a wife like his mother, who would understand him instinctively, who shared the patience and abnegation of his people, who spoke less and worked more. A woman who would wait for him in the evenings, silent and devoted, and who would feel fulfilled, all her ambitions met, when she watched him eat the meal she'd prepared. Mathilde was turning him into a traitor and a heretic. Occasionally he wanted to unroll a prayer rug, press his forehead to the ground, to hear in his heart and in his children's mouths the language of his ancestors. He dreamed of making love in Arabic, of whispering sweet nothings into the ear of a golden-skinned woman. At other times – when he went home and his wife threw herself at him, when he heard his daughter singing in the bathroom, when Mathilde invented games and made jokes – he was filled with joy and felt himself raised above other men. He had the impression that he'd been pulled from the common herd and he had to admit that the war had changed him and that modernity had its advantages. He was ashamed of himself and his fickleness and it was Mathilde, he knew, who paid for that.

* * *

When Mathilde reached the old hobnailed door, she grabbed the knocker and banged it twice, very hard. Yasmine opened it – she'd lifted up her skirts and Mathilde could see that her black calves were covered in curly hairs. It was almost ten in the morning but the house was quiet. She could hear the purring of

89

the cats stretched out in the courtyard and the slop of the wet mop that the maid was using to clean the floor. Yasmine watched in astonishment as Mathilde took off her djellaba, tossed her headscarf on to a chair and ran upstairs. Yasmine coughed so hard that she spat a thick, greenish wad of mucus into the well.

Upstairs, Mathilde found Selma asleep on a bench. She was very fond of this capricious, rebellious girl who'd just turned sixteen. Selma had no manners but she did have a certain grace; unfortunately Mouilala was content to give her nothing but food and love. When Mathilde had mentioned this to Amine, he'd said: 'That's quite a lot, you know.' Yes, it was a lot, but it wasn't enough. Selma's life was caught between her mother's blind love and her brothers' brutal vigilance. Since developing hips and breasts, Selma had been declared fit for combat and her brothers often sent her hurtling into walls. Omar, who was ten years older than her, said he could sense something rebellious and untameable in his sister's soul. He was envious of the protection she enjoyed, the tenderness that his mother had never shown to him. Selma's beauty made her brothers as nervous as animals before an approaching storm. They beat her pre-emptively, imprisoning her before she did anything stupid, because if they waited then it would be too late.

Selma's beauty had increased through the years, and now it was irritatingly obvious, the kind of beauty that made people uneasy and seemed to foretell some terrible calamity. When Mathilde looked at her, she wondered how it must feel to be so beautiful. Did it hurt? Did beauty have a weight, a taste, a texture? Was Selma even aware of the nervousness that her presence provoked, of the irresistible attraction that men felt when they saw the perfect features of her adorable face?

Mathilde was a wife, a mother, but oddly she felt like less of a woman than Selma. The war had left its traces on Mathilde's body. She'd turned fourteen on 2 May 1939, and her breasts had been late in developing, as if stunted by fear and hunger. Her dull blonde hair was so thin that her scalp was visible. Selma, on the other hand, radiated sensuality. Her eyes were as dark and shiny as the olives that Mouilala marinated in salt. Her thick brows, her lush hair, the faint brown fuzz on her upper lip made her look like Carmen, a vision of Mediterranean sultriness. A vibrant fever dream of a brunette, capable of driving men wild. Despite her youth, Selma had the raised chin, bee-stung lips and swaying hips of a heroine from some romantic novel. Women hated her. At school her female teacher picked on her remorselessly and was constantly telling her off and punishing her. 'She's an insolent, rebellious girl. Would you believe that I am afraid to turn my back on her? Knowing that she's there, sitting behind me, plunges me into a state of irrational terror,' she'd confided to Mathilde, who had decided to oversee her sister-in-law's education.

* * *

In 1942, when Amine had been taken prisoner in Germany, Mouilala had left behind the familiar backstreets of Berrima for the first time in her life. With Omar and Selma she travelled to Rabat, where she had been summoned by the general staff, and where she hoped to be able to send a package to her beloved firstborn. Mouilala got on the train, enveloped in a large white haik, and she felt frightened when the machine moved away from the station in a cloud of smoke and whistling. For a long time, she watched the men and women who remained standing on the platform, their hands waving vainly. Omar ushered his mother and his little sister to a first-class compartment where two Frenchwomen were sitting. The women started to whisper. They seemed surprised that a woman like Mouilala – with her ankle bracelets, henna-dyed hair and long, callused hands – could sit next to them on a train. First class was for Europeans only and they were outraged by the stupidity and impertinence of these illiterate Arabs. When the ticket inspector boarded the carriage, they couldn't contain a frisson of excitement. Ah, now this farce will be over, they thought. The old fatma will be put in her place. She thinks she can sit wherever she wants, but there are rules, you know.

Mouilala reached into her haik and pulled out the train tickets along with the letter from the army informing her of her son's imprisonment. The inspector examined the letter and rubbed his forehead, embarrassed. '*Bon voyage*, madame,' he said, raising his cap. And he disappeared into the corridor.

The two Frenchwomen couldn't believe it. The journey was ruined. They couldn't bear the sight of this woman in her veil. They were sickened by the spicy smell of her skin, by the idiotic way she stared through the window. They were annoyed, most of all, by the little slattern who was with her. A girl of six or seven whose bourgeois clothes were not enough to mask her poor education. Selma, who was travelling for the first time in her life, could not keep still. She climbed into her mother's lap, said she was hungry, then stuffed herself with cakes, her fingers sticky with honey. She talked in a loud voice to her brother, who was pacing up and down the corridor. She hummed Arab songs. The younger and angriest of the two Frenchwomen glared at the little girl. 'She's very pretty,' she said. Without knowing why, she was exasperated by Selma's beauty. She had the impression that the child had stolen that gracious face, that she'd taken it from someone else who deserved it more than her and who would, undoubtedly, have taken better care of it. The girl was beautiful and indifferent to that beauty, which made her even more dangerous. The warm orange sunlight came through the window and, despite the thin curtains, which the Frenchwomen had drawn, made Selma's hair glow, made her copper-toned skin look even softer and creamier. Her huge eyes were like the eyes of a black panther that the younger Frenchwoman had once seen at the zoo in Paris. Nobody, she thought, has eyes like that. 'She's wearing make-up,' she whispered to her friend.

'What did you say?'

The younger woman leaned towards Mouilala and, clearly articulating each syllable, said: 'You shouldn't put make-up on children. That kohl, on her eyes? It's not good. It's vulgar. Do you understand?'

Mouilala stared at the Frenchwoman without understanding what she was saying. She turned to Selma, who burst into laughter and handed a box of cakes to the two women. 'She doesn't speak French.'

The Frenchwoman was put out. She'd lost a good opportunity to underline her superiority. If this native didn't understand, there was no point trying to educate her. And then, as if she'd suddenly gone mad, she seized Selma's arm and pulled the girl towards her. She took a handkerchief from her bag, spat on it, and roughly rubbed it against Selma's eyes. Selma cried out and Mouilala pulled her away, but the Frenchwoman wouldn't let go. She looked at the strangely clean handkerchief then rubbed even harder, to prove to herself and her travelling companion that this girl was a floozy in the making, a little whore. Yes, she knew all about those sorts of girls, those fearless brunettes that drove her husband wild. She knew them and she hated them. Omar, who was smoking in the corridor, heard his sister crying and burst into the compartment. 'What's going on?' The Frenchwoman was frightened by this teenage boy in his glasses and she left the compartment without a word.

The next day, on the way back to Meknes, happy that he'd been able to send letters and oranges to Amine, Omar slapped his sister. She cried. She didn't understand. Omar said: 'Don't even think about wearing make-up when you're older, you understand? If I ever catch you in lipstick, I'll give you something to smile about!' And with the tip of his index finger, he drew a long, macabre smile across the child's face.

* * *

Waking up now, Selma wrapped her arms around Mathilde's neck, then covered her face with kisses. Ever since they'd first met, Selma had acted as her sister-in-law's guide, interpreter and best friend. Selma had explained to her the local rites and traditions, she'd taught her how to be polite. 'If you don't know how to reply, just say Amen and you'll be fine.' Selma had taught her how to pretend, how to stay calm. Whenever they were alone, Selma showered Mathilde with questions. She wanted to know everything about France, about travelling, about Paris and the American soldiers that Mathilde had seen during the Liberation. She was like a prisoner questioning a man who has managed, at least once, to escape.

'What are you doing here?' Selma asked.

'I'm going Christmas shopping,' Mathilde whispered. 'Do you want to come with me?'

Mathilde accompanied her sister-in-law to her bedroom and watched her undress. Sitting on a cushion on the floor, she observed Selma's slim hips, her slightly rounded belly, her dark-nippled breasts that had never been constrained by an underwired bra. Selma put on an elegant black dress, the round neckline highlighting the slenderness of her neck. She took a pair of gloves from a box – the white fabric yellowed with age and covered in little stains of mould – and put them on with ludicrous delicacy.

Mouilala was worried.

'I don't want you walking around the medina,' she told Mathilde. 'You don't understand how envious people are. They'd give an eye to take both of yours. Two pretty girls like you . . . No, you can't do it. The people in the medina will curse you and you'll come back with a fever or worse. If you want to go for a walk, go to the new town. You won't be in danger there.'

'What's the difference?' asked Mathilde, amused.

'Europeans don't look at you the same way. They don't know about the evil eye.'

The two girls left laughing and Mouilala remained behind the door for a long time, trembling and speechless. She didn't understand what was happening to her. Was it anxiety or joy she felt at seeing the two of them go out into the street like that?

Selma was sick of Mouilala's ridiculous old superstitions and backward beliefs. She had stopped listening to her mother. It was only out of respect for her elders that she didn't shut her eyes

and plug her ears with her fingers every time Mouilala started going on about djinns, bad luck and ancient curses. Her
mother had nothing new to say. Her life went round in circles
as she carried out the same tasks over and over with a docility, a
passivity, that made Selma want to vomit. The old woman was
like those stupid dogs that chase their tail for so long that they
end up collapsing on the floor with dizziness. Selma couldn't
bear her mother's constant presence any longer. Whenever
she heard a door creak, her mother would say: 'Where are you
going?' And she was always asking if Selma was hungry, if she
was bored, and going out on to the roof terrace to spy on her.
Selma felt oppressed by Mouilala's solicitude, her tenderness.
It was like a form of violence. Sometimes the teenager wanted
to yell in her mother's face – and in Yasmine's too. For Selma,
both women – the mistress of the house and the servant – were
slaves, and it really made little difference that one of them had
bought the other at a market. Selma would have given anything
for a locked door, a place where she could keep her dreams and
secrets. She prayed that fate would smile on her and that one
day she could escape to Casablanca and reinvent herself. Like
the men in the street shouting, 'Freedom! Independence!', she
shouted the same words, but nobody heard her.

She begged Mathilde to take her to Place de Gaulle. She
wanted to 'do the Avenue', as all the boys and girls in the new
town called it. She was desperate to be like them, to live for
being seen, to parade up and down the Avenue de la République on foot or in a car, as slowly as possible, windows open
and the radio playing full blast. She wanted to be seen like the
girls here, to be voted the prettiest girl in Meknes, to sashay
past rows of boys and photographers. She would have given

anything to kiss a man's neck, to taste his nakedness, to see the way he looked at her. Selma had never been in love, but she had no doubt that it would be the most beautiful thing in the world. The old times – the days of arranged marriages – were over. Or at least that was what Mathilde had told her, and she wanted to believe it.

* * *

Mathilde agreed to Selma's request, less because she wanted to please her sister-in-law than because she had shopping to do in the European quarter. Selma was almost a woman now, but she spent a long time outside the toy shop, and when she placed her gloves against the window one of the salesmen yelled: 'Hands off the glass!' People stared at her suspiciously in her European outfit, her hair tied in a cowardly bun at the base of her neck. She kept tugging at her white gloves and smoothing down her skirt, smiling at passers-by in the naive hope of reassuring them. Outside a café, three boys wolf-whistled when they saw her and Mathilde was irritated by the smile that Selma gave them. She had to take her hand and walk faster because she was afraid that someone would spot them and report this embarrassing incident to Amine. They hurried towards the covered market and Mathilde said: 'I have to buy food for dinner. Don't wander off.' At the entrance to the market some women were sitting on the ground, waiting to be hired as servants or babysitters. All but one of them wore a veil over her face, and that woman's toothless smile frightened Selma, who found it hard to imagine anyone possibly wanting to hire such a hag. The teenager walked slowly, dragging her black ballet shoes along the wet street. She would have liked to stay in town, to eat an ice cream and admire the skirts in the shop windows and the women driving cars. She would have liked to belong to those groups of young people who danced to American music every Thursday afternoon. There was an automated figure in the window of the café: a black man with a flat nose and thick lips who nodded his head. Selma stood in front of this robot and for a few minutes she nodded in time with it, like a mechanical doll. In the butcher's shop, she laughed at a drawing of a cockerel on a poster under these words: 'Credit we'll bestow, when you hear this cock crow.' She insisted on showing the poster to Mathilde, who grew annoyed. 'Everything's a joke to you! Can't you see that I'm busy?' Mathilde was worried. She rummaged in her pockets. Frowning, she counted the change that the shopkeepers gave her. Money had become a subject of perpetual dispute. Amine accused her of being an irresponsible spendthrift. Mathilde had to argue, nag, sometimes even beg to be given the money she needed for the school, the car, Aïcha's clothes, visits to the hairdresser. Amine doubted her word. He accused her of buying books, make-up, useless fabrics to make dresses that nobody cared about. 'I'm the one who has to earn all this money!' he would yell sometimes. Then, pointing at the food on the table, he would add: 'Do you know how hard I worked to pay for that, and that, and that?'

As a teenager it had never occurred to Mathilde that it was possible to be free on her own. As a woman with no education, it struck her as inevitable that her fate should be intimately linked to that of a man. She realised her mistake far too late and – now that she'd developed some discernment and courage – it had become impossible to leave. The children were her roots and they attached her to this earth. Without money, there was nowhere for her to go. No matter how much time passed, she never seemed to get over it: her dependence, her submission, was like a rotting organ inside her body, something that left her disgusted with herself. Every time Amine slipped a banknote into her hand, every time she bought herself a chocolate out of desire rather than need, she wondered if she really deserved it. And she feared that, one day, when she was an old woman in this foreign land, she would own nothing and would have accomplished nothing.

When he got home on the night of 23 December 1953, Amine was dazzled. He walked on tiptoe into the parlour, where Mathilde had left a few candles lit on a wreath of leaves that she'd made herself. On the sideboard a cake was covered by an embroidered cloth. Red tinsel, decorated with glass balls and velvet bows, hung from the walls.

Mathilde had become the mistress of her domain. After four years of life on the farm, she had proved her ability to make the most of what little she had; to decorate the tables with bouquets of flowers picked from the fields, to dress the children like their bourgeois counterparts, to make meals despite the smoking cooker. She had overcome her fears: she crushed insects with her sandals now, and impassively butchered the dead animals that the peasants brought her. Amine was proud of her and he liked to watch her, sweating and red-faced, her sleeves rolled up to her armpits, when she cleaned the house or cooked. He was moved by his wife's unflagging energy, and when he kissed her he called her 'my love', 'my darling', 'my little soldier'.

If he could, he would have given her a real winter with snow, and she'd have believed she was back in her native Alsace. If he could, he'd have built a wide, noble fireplace in the cement wall, and she'd have been warmed by it, as she had been in her childhood home. He couldn't give her fire or snowflakes, but that night, instead of joining her in bed, he woke two labourers and made them follow him across the fields. The peasants asked no questions. They walked obediently and as they disappeared into the countryside, as the darkness and the sounds of animals surrounded them, they wondered if they were being lured into a trap, if the master was about to punish them for some crime they couldn't remember committing. Amine had told them to bring an axe, and as they walked he kept turning around and whispering: 'Faster! We have to get it done before daybreak.' One of the labourers, whose name was Achour, pulled at his master's sleeve. 'This isn't our land any more, Sidi. We're on the widow's property.' Amine shrugged him off. 'Shut up and keep going,' he snapped, then pointed his torch through the dark and said: 'There!' Amine looked up; he stayed like that for several seconds, his throat exposed, eyes riveted to the treetops. He seemed happy. 'That tree. We're going to cut it down and take it back to the house. Quickly. And silently.' For nearly an hour, the men took turns swinging the axe against the trunk of a young cypress with leaves as blue as the night. When they'd chopped it down, the three of them picked up the tree – one at the top, another at the roots, the third keeping it balanced in the middle – and carried it across the Mercier widow's estate. If anyone had witnessed this scene, they would probably have thought that they'd gone mad, because the tree's leaves concealed the men's bodies and it looked as though the tree was moving on its own, advancing horizontally towards an unknown destination. The labourers carried their victim unprotestingly, but they had no idea what was going on. Amine had a reputation as an honest man, yet here he was suddenly transformed into a thief, a poacher, deceiving a woman. And anyway, if he was going to steal something, why not animals, crops, machines? Why this skinny tree?

Amine opened the door and for the first time in their lives the labourers went inside the master's house. Amine put a finger to his lips and took off his shoes. His men copied him. They put the tree in the middle of the living room. It was so tall that the top of it bent against the ceiling. Achour wanted to get a ladder and cut it off but Amine became annoyed. That man's presence in his living room embarrassed him, and he sent him outside without another word.

When he woke the next morning, worn out from his brief sleep and his sore shoulder, Amine stroked his wife's back. Mathilde's skin was hot and damp; saliva trickled from her half-open mouth, and he felt a violent desire for her. He nuzzled her, ignoring the words she stammered, then took her like an animal, blind and deaf. He scratched her breasts, he dug his black-nailed fingers into her hair.

Mathilde had to stifle a cry when she found the tree in the middle of the living room. She turned to Amine, who was just behind her, and she understood that he had taken his reward that morning, that the rough sex had been a way of celebrating his victory. She walked around the cypress and picked off a few needles which she rubbed in her palm and held to her nose. She breathed in that familiar scent. Aïcha, who'd been woken by her father's groans, watched the scene uncomprehendingly. Her mother was happy, and this surprised her.

That day, while Mathilde and Tamo were plucking the enormous turkey that one of the labourers had brought them, Amine went to the Avenue de la République. When he went into the chic boutique owned by an old Frenchwoman, the two sales assistants sniggered. Amine lowered his eyes and regretted not changing his shoes. They were covered in mud from his adventures in the night and he hadn't had time to get his shirt ironed. The shop was packed with customers. There was a line of ten people at the cash registers, all holding packages. Elegant women tried on hats or shoes. Amine slowly approached some glass display cabinets on the wall; inside were various styles of women's shoes. 'What do you want?' asked one of the young saleswomen, her smile at once mocking and lewd. Amine almost told her that he'd come to the wrong shop. He was silent for a few seconds, wondering what attitude to adopt, and the young woman opened her eyes wide and tilted her head. 'What's up, Mohamed, don't you understand French? Can't you see we're busy here?'

'Do you have my size?' he asked.

The saleswoman turned to the display that Amine was pointing to and frowned.

'That's what you want? A Father Christmas costume?'

Amine bowed his head like a naughty child that's been caught red-handed. The woman shrugged. 'Wait here.' She walked across the shop and went into the storeroom. This man, she thought, didn't look like a servant, more like a weird master who has to wear that kind of stuff to amuse his children. No, actually, he looked more like those young nationalists who were always being arrested in the cafés of the medina and with whom she fantasised about sleeping. But she found it hard to imagine one of them wearing a white beard and a ridiculous red hat.

Amine tapped his toes impatiently beside the till. With the package under his arm he felt like he was committing a crime, and he started to sweat as he imagined an acquaintance finding him here. On the way back home he drove fast, thinking how happy the children would be.

He put on his costume in the car and entered the house like that. When he opened the door to the dining room, he cleared his throat noisily and, in a warm, deep voice, called the children's names. Aïcha couldn't believe it. She kept turning to look at her mother and the laughing Selim. How could Father Christmas have come all the way here? The old man in the red hat patted his belly and guffawed, but Aïcha noticed that he wasn't carrying a sack over his shoulder and felt disappointed. There was no sign of a sleigh or reindeer in the garden either. She looked down and noticed that Father Christmas was wearing the same shoes that her father's labourers wore: grey rubber boots, covered in mud. Amine rubbed his hands. He didn't know what to do or say and he suddenly felt silly. But he turned to Mathilde and his wife's enchanted smile gave him the courage to go on. 'So, children, have you been good?' he asked in a cavernous voice. Selim went pale. Pressing his little body against his mother's skirt and lifting his arms up to her, he burst into tears. 'I'm scared!' he cried. 'Mama, I'm scared!'

Aïcha was given a rag doll that Mathilde had made herself. For the hair, she'd used brown wool that she wet and then soaked with oil and braided. The body and the face were made from an old pillowcase on which Mathilde had sewn asymmetrical eyes and a smiling mouth. She'd even perfumed it with her own scent. Aïcha loved that doll. She also received a jigsaw puzzle, some books and a packet of sweets. Selim was given a toy car with a big button on top that, when you pressed it, lit up and made a loud noise. To his wife, Amine gave a pair of pink mules. He handed her the package with an embarrassed smile and Mathilde, after tearing off the wrapping paper, stared at the mules and pursed her lips to stop herself crying. She didn't know if it was because the slippers were so ugly or too small or if it was simply the awful banality of them that threw her into such a state of sadness and rage. She said, 'Thank you', then locked herself in the bathroom, held the pair of shoes in one hand and smacked the soles against her forehead. She wanted to punish herself for having been so stupid, for having expected so much from this holiday when Amine didn't understand anything about it. She hated herself for not having given up on the idea, for lacking the selflessness of her mother-in-law, for being so obsessed with pointless, trivial things. She wanted to cancel the Christmas dinner, to hide under the sheets and sleep until tomorrow. The whole charade seemed ludicrous now. She'd made Tamo wear a black-and-white maid's costume. She'd worn herself out cooking dinner and now she felt sickened at the thought of eating the turkey that she'd spent so long stuffing, burying her hands inside the bird's belly, exhausting herself over these invisible, thankless domestic tasks. She walked to the table like a prisoner walking to the scaffold and she stared at Amine with wide-open eyes to push the tears back and make him believe that she was happy.

IV

In January 1954 it was so cold that the almond trees froze and a litter of kittens died in the kitchen doorway. At the school, the nuns agreed to make an exception to their usual routine and they kept the stoves in the classrooms lit all day long. The little girls kept their coats on during their lessons and some of them wore two pairs of tights under their dresses. Aïcha was starting to get used to the monotony of school and in a notebook that Sister Marie-Solange had given her she listed all the things that made her sad and happy.

Aïcha did not like: her classmates, the cold in the corridors, the food at lunch, the interminable classes, the warts on Sister Marie-Cecile's face.

She liked: the peacefulness of the chapel, the music they played on the piano on certain mornings, the physical education classes when she ran faster than the others, climbing to the top of the rope before her classmates had even touched the bottom.

She didn't like afternoons because she was always sleepy, or mornings because she was always late. She liked it when there were rules and people followed them.

When Sister Marie-Solange complimented her on her work, Aïcha would blush. During prayers Aïcha would hold the nun's rough, cold hand. Her heart filled with joy whenever she saw Sister Marie-Solange's face, with its clear, homely features and its skin damaged by cold air and bad soap. It looked as though the nun spent hours cleaning her cheeks and eyelids, because her skin was almost translucent, and her freckles – which would normally have given her some charm – were practically erased. Perhaps she was striving to rid herself of all spark, all femininity, all prettiness and, consequently, all danger. Not once did Aïcha think that her teacher was a woman, that beneath her habit was a living, pulsating body, a body like her mother's, capable of yelling with anger, moaning in ecstasy or bursting into tears. When she was with Sister Marie-Solange, Aïcha left this earthly domain, she left behind the pettiness and ugliness of men, and floated through an ethereal universe in the company of Jesus and the apostles.

The pupils all closed their books at the same time and it sounded as if they were applauding. They started chatting. Sister Marie-Solange told them to calm down, but her words had no effect. 'Stand in line! You won't be leaving this classroom, ladies, until you do.' Aïcha rested her head on her hand and stared dreamily out at the schoolyard. She tried to see as far as she could, beyond the tree that had lost its leaves, beyond the wall, beyond the workman's hut where Brahim was allowed to take a break when it was cold. She didn't want to go outside, didn't want to hold hands with a little girl who would sneakily dig her fingernails into Aïcha's flesh and start giggling. She hated the city, and the idea of going through it – through that swarm of strangers – made her anxious.

Sister Marie-Solange stroked Aïcha's back and told her that they would walk together, leading the class, and that there was nothing to worry about. Aïcha stood up, rubbed her eyes and put on the coat that her mother had made, which was too tight around the armpits and made her walk in a strange, rigid way.

The little girls gathered outside the school gates. They tried to stay calm, but it was obvious that this legion of school-children was in a state of hysterical excitement, that a riot might break out at any minute. Nobody had listened to Sister Marie-Solange's lesson that morning. Nobody had heeded the warning that she'd concealed in her religious discourse. 'God,' she'd said, in her fragile voice, 'loves all children. There is no such thing as an inferior race or a superior race. Men are all equal before God, even if they are different.' Aïcha didn't know what the nun meant by this either, but those words had made a strong impression on her. What she drew from them was this: only men and children are loved by God. It seemed clear to her that women were excluded from this universal love and she began to worry about what would happen when she became one. This destiny struck her as horribly cruel and she thought again about Adam and Eve, who had been exiled from Paradise. When the woman inside her hatched out, she would be con-demned to this arid existence, deprived of divine love.

'Forward, ladies!' Sister Marie-Solange made an expansive gesture with her arm, inviting the children to follow her to the bus parked in the street. On the way she gave them a history lesson. 'This country,' she explained, 'which we all love so much, has a very old history. Look around you, ladies: that pond, those walls, those doors are the products of a glorious civilisation. I have already told you about Sultan Moulay Ismail, who was a contemporary of our Sun King. Remember his name, girls.' The children laughed because their teacher had insisted on pro-nouncing the Moroccan king's name with the guttural sounds of Arabic. But nobody said anything because they all remembered how angry Sister Marie-Solange had been that day when Ginette said: 'Oh, are you teaching us to speak like darkies now?' The look in her eyes had been so scary that the little girls had thought Ginette was going to get slapped. But presumably the teacher had remembered that Ginette was only six and that she needed to show patience in educating her. One evening Sister Marie-Solange had confided in the Mother Superior, who listened as she ran her rough tongue along her lips before nibbling off pieces of dry skin. Marie-Solange told her that she'd had a vision – yes, an illumination – while she was walking to Azrou, under some cedars that grew beside a mountain stream. Watching the women walk carrying their children on their backs, colourful shawls covering their hair; watching the men leaning heavily on their wooden staffs, guiding their families and their flocks, she had seen Jacob, Sarah and Solomon. This country, she'd exclaimed, offered scenes of poverty and humility worthy of Old Testament engravings.

* * *

The class stopped outside a dark building. Impossible to tell what it was for or what lay inside. A man in a navy-blue suit was waiting for them outside the 'door', a hole dug into the wall. The guide held his hands tightly together in front of his crotch. He looked anxious – terrified, even – when he saw the swarm of schoolgirls approaching him. In his high-pitched, quavering voice, he tried to make himself heard above the hum of other voices, but in the end the nuns had to shout at the children to make them shut up. 'We're going to go downstairs. It's dark and the floor is slippery. I would ask you to be very careful.' As soon as they entered what appeared to be a cave, the girls fell silent, rendered mute by fear, the icy cold that emanated from the earthen walls and the place's gloomy, subterranean atmosphere. One of the girls – nobody could tell which one, in that dim light – made a sinister howl, imitating a ghost or a wolf. 'Show some respect, please, ladies. Many Christian brothers suffered terrible torture in this place.' They walked in silence through a maze of corridors.

Sister Marie-Solange told the young guide that he could speak now. He was surprised by the youth of his audience and couldn't think what to say to such impressionable souls. Several times he stammered over his words, backtracked, apologised, wiping his forehead with a frayed handkerchief. 'This place is known as the Christians' prison.' He pointed to the wall facing them and they cried out when they saw the inscriptions left there by prisoners centuries earlier. After a while he turned his back on the schoolgirls and forgot their presence to the point where his words flowed more confidently and eloquently. He told them about the sufferings of those men – 'almost two thousand of them by the end of the seventeenth century' – imprisoned here by Moulay Ismail, and he emphasised the genius of this 'sultan and builder' who had ordered the construction of miles of underground tunnels through which the slaves were dragged, dying, blinded, trapped. 'Look up,' he told them with what sounded almost like real authority, and the little girls silently lifted their faces. A hole had been dug in the rock above them; it was through this hole that food had been tossed down to the prisoners, in meagre quantities barely sufficient to keep them alive.

Aïcha pressed her face to Sister Marie-Solange's body. She breathed in the smell of her dress and her fingers gripped the rope that the nun used as a belt. When the guide described for them the system of matmouras, the subterranean silos in which the prisoners were locked and would sometimes suffocate to death, she felt tears well in her eyes. 'Inside these walls,' the man went on, now taking perverse pleasure in scaring the young children, 'there are skeletons. The Christian slaves, who also built the high walls that protect the city, sometimes collapsed with exhaustion, and when that happened their masters would wall them in.' The man's voice took on the timbre of a prophet, a voice from beyond the grave that sent shivers down the girls' spines. 'In all the walls of this glorious country, in all the ramparts of the imperial cities, if you scratch beneath the stone you will find the bodies of slaves, heretics, undesirables.' Aïcha thought about this constantly during the days that followed. Everywhere she seemed to see through to the skeletons curled up in their hiding places, and she prayed passionately for those damned souls.

A few weeks later Amine found his wife on the floor by their bed, face down, her knees pressed against her chest. Her teeth were chattering so hard that he was afraid she would bite off her tongue and swallow it, as had happened to some epileptics in the medina. Mathilde moaned and Amine picked her up. He felt her muscles contract against his hands and he gently stroked her arms to reassure her. He called Tamo and, without looking at the maid, put her in charge of his wife. 'I have to work. Take care of her.'

When he came back that evening Mathilde was delirious. She twitched as if imprisoned by the drenched sheets and called out for her mother in her native Alsatian dialect. Her temperature was so high that her body kept convulsing, as if she were being electrocuted. At the foot of the bed, Aïcha was weeping. 'I'm going to fetch the doctor,' Amine announced early the next morning. He took the car and went, leaving Mathilde in the care of the maid, who seemed unfazed by her mistress's illness.

As soon as she was alone with the patient, Tamo set to work. She made a mix of plants, meticulously measuring each ingredient, then poured boiling water on top of it. Watched by the dumbstruck Aïcha, she kneaded the aromatic paste and said: 'We have to drive away the evil spirits.' She undressed Mathilde, who did not react at all, and plastered this mixture over her long and dazzlingly white body. She could have drawn a malign pleasure from dominating her mistress in this way. She could have sought vengeance on this harsh, hurtful Christian woman who treated her like a savage and told her she was as filthy as the cockroaches that crawled around the jars of olive oil. But Tamo, who had wept a great deal the previous night in the solitude of her room, massaged her mistress's thighs, put her hands to her mistress's temples and prayed for her with sincere devotion. After an hour Mathilde grew calm. Her jaw relaxed and her teeth stopped grinding. Sitting against the wall, her fingers stained with green, Tamo repeated endlessly the same prayer, whose melody Aïcha followed by watching her lips.

When the doctor arrived he found Mathilde half-naked, her body covered with a greenish paste whose smell reached all the way to the corridor. Tamo was sitting at the patient's bedside and when she saw the man come in with Amine she covered her mistress's lower half with the sheet and left the room, head lowered.

'Did the fatma do that?' the doctor asked, pointing at the bed. The green paste had stained the sheets, the pillows, the bedspread; it had run on to Mathilde's favourite rug, which she'd bought when she first arrived in Meknes. Tamo had left fingerprints on the walls and the bedside table, and the room looked like a painting by one of those degenerate artists who mistake melancholy for talent. The doctor raised his eyebrows, then closed his eyes for a couple of minutes that seemed to Amine to drag on forever. He wanted the doctor to rush over to his patient, make a diagnosis, find a cure. Instead of which he paced around the bed, tucking in a corner of the sheet, straightening a book on the shelf and performing various other pointless, absurd actions.

The doctor took off his jacket and folded it carefully before placing it on the back of a chair. Then he gave Amine a brief, scathing look, like a teacher reprimanding a naughty pupil. At last he leaned over the patient, put his hand under the sheet to examine her, and – as if just remembering that there was a man in the room, observing him – turned around and told Amine to leave.

Amine obeyed.

'Madame Belhaj, can you hear me? How do you feel?'

Mathilde turned her tired face towards him. She found it hard to keep her eyes open and she looked disorientated, like a child waking up in an unfamiliar room. The doctor thought she was going to cry, to ask for help. It broke his heart to see this tall blonde woman, this woman who was probably beautiful when she made an effort, when she was given the opportunity to show her good manners. Her feet were dry and callused, her nails long and thick. He held Mathilde's arm and took her pulse, careful not to get the green paste on his skin, then slid his hand under the sheet to palpate her abdomen. 'Open your mouth and say, "Aaaah".' Mathilde did what she was told.

'It's malaria. Quite common around here.' He walked up to the chair at Mathilde's little desk and contemplated Uncle Hansi's engravings, depicting Colmar in the 1910s, then noticed the book on the history of Meknes. A few sheets of cheap writing paper lay on the table: scrawled words, crossed out. He took a prescription slip from his leather bag and filled it out, then opened the bedroom door and looked for the husband. The only person in the hallway was a young girl, very thin, with unbrushed hair. She was leaning against the wall, holding a doll covered in stains. Amine arrived and the doctor handed him the prescription.

'Go to the pharmacist and get this.'

'What is it, Doctor? Is she any better?'

The doctor looked irritated.

'Be quick.'

He closed the bedroom door and sat down beside the bed. He felt as if he ought to protect this woman, not from the disease but from the situation into which she'd got herself. Looking at this naked, exhausted white woman, he imagined the intimacy she shared with that tempestuous Arab. He could imagine it all the better after glimpsing the disgusting fruit of that union, and he felt sick with repulsion at the memory of the girl in the hallway. Of course, he knew that the world had changed, that the war had overthrown all the rules, all the codes, as if the world's population had been poured into a jar and shaken up, bringing together bodies that, in his view, should never have come into contact. This woman slept in the arms of that hairy Arab. The lout possessed her, gave her orders. All this was unfair, indecent, it was not how things were supposed to be. Such miscegenation created disorder and unhappiness. Half-bloods heralded the end of the world.

Mathilde asked for something to drink and he raised a glass of cold water to her lips. 'Thank you, Doctor,' she said, squeezing his hand.

Emboldened by this intimate gesture, he said: 'Excuse me, madame, if this is indiscreet, but I am curious. How the devil did you end up here?'

Mathilde was too weak to speak. She wanted to scratch

his hand. Deep within the chasms of her mind, a thought was struggling to emerge, to make itself heard. A revolt was germinating, but she didn't have the strength to give birth to it. She wished she could think of a parry, a cutting riposte to the term that had so enraged her. 'End up', as if her life were no more than an accident, as if her children, this house, her entire existence were merely a mistake, a wrong turn. I have to think of a response, she told herself. I have to build a protective shell out of words.

All through the days and nights that her mother stayed in her bedroom, Aïcha worried. If her mother died, what would happen to her? She moved frantically around the house, like a fly trapped under a glass. She questioned the adults with her eyes, although she had no faith in the answers they gave. Tamo hugged her and spoke tender words. She knew that children are like dogs: they understand when something is being hidden from them and they can smell death before it comes. Amine, too, looked lost. The house was sad without Mathilde's games, the idiotic pranks that she liked to pull. She would put little buckets of water on the tops of doors or sew the sleeves of Amine's jacket closed. He would have given anything for her to suddenly jump out of bed and organise a game of hide-and-seek in the garden. For her to tearfully tell him an Alsatian folk tale.

* * *

While her neighbour was ill, the Mercier widow often went to check on her and to lend her novels. Mathilde had no explanation for this sudden friendship. Before, they'd been on no more than nodding terms: a brief wave as they passed in adjoining fields, a gift of fruit when the harvest had been plentiful and it would otherwise just rot in a crate. Mathilde didn't know that on Christmas Day the widow had got up at dawn and bitten into an orange, alone in her freezing bedroom. She unpeeled citrus fruits with her teeth and she liked the bitter taste that the zest left on her palate. That morning, she had opened the back door and, despite the frost that had paralysed all the plants, despite the icy wind that was blowing across the plain, gone out barefoot into the garden. She had a peasant's feet: soles callused from treading the burning earth, skin thickened against the sting of nettles. The widow knew her domain by heart. She knew how many rocks there were, how many rose bushes were in flower, how many rabbits were scratching at the earth under their hutches. That Christmas morning, she gazed at the row of cypresses and gave a little cry. The beautiful row of trees that marked the border of her property now looked like a smiling mouth with a single tooth missing – pulled out, secretly, during the night. She summoned Driss, who was drinking his tea in the house. 'Driss, come here. Quickly!' The labourer, who served as her substitute business partner, son and husband, came running, still holding his glass. She pointed at the missing tree and Driss took a few moments to understand. She knew that he would talk about evil spirits, that he would warn her of a curse that someone had put on her, because Driss could only explain extraordinary events by invoking magic. The old woman, whose craggy face was etched with deep furrows, placed her fists on her narrow hips. She pressed her forehead against Driss's and looked into his grey eyes. 'What do you know about Christmas?' she asked. The man shrugged, as if to say: 'Not much.' He'd seen generations of Christians pass through this land, from poor farmers to wealthy landowners. He'd seen them turning over the earth, building huts, sleeping under tents, but he knew nothing about their private lives and beliefs. The widow patted his shoulder and started laughing. Her laughter was open and glittering, like silver coins raining down on the silent countryside. Driss scratched his head and looked puzzled. This story made no sense. The tree must have been stolen away by a djinn who had taken against the old woman. He remembered the rumours about his mistress. It was said that she'd buried stillborn children on her property and even foetuses that her dry womb had miscarried. That one day a dog had arrived in the douar with a baby's arm dangling from its mouth. Some claimed that men came in the night, seeking comfort between those withered thighs, and even though Driss spent all his days here, even though he saw how ascetic the old woman's life truly was, he couldn't help hearing such slander and worrying. She had no secrets from him. When her husband had been mobilised, then taken prisoner, and when he'd died of typhus in a POW camp, it was to Driss she had gone to share her distress, her grief. He admired her courage and it had shocked him to see her crying, this woman who drove a tractor, looked after the animals and gave orders to the labourers with resounding authority. He was grateful to her for standing up to their neighbour Roger Mariani, who had come here from Algeria in the 1930s, just before the widow and Joseph, her husband, and who treated his workers harshly, never satisfied until the men's burnouses were soaked with sweat.

The widow crossed her arms and stood there, silent and motionless, for several minutes. Then she turned quickly and in perfect Arabic told Driss: 'Let's just forget it, all right? Go on, now, get to work.' In the days that followed, every time she thought about the missing tree her frail body shook with laughter. She conceived a secret affection for Mathilde and her husband. And after the holidays, which she spent alone on her property, she decided to pay a visit to her neighbours. There, she found Mathilde laid low by malaria. The old woman asked what she could do, before glimpsing – on the sofa where Mathilde spent her days – some novels with well-thumbed pages. The widow offered to lend her a few books and the Alsatian woman, eyes shining with fever, squeezed her hand and thanked her.

One day, while Mathilde was still recovering from the disease, a gleaming car driven by a chauffeur in a cap stopped outside the gates of the estate. Amine saw a tall, stately man get out. The man walked up to him and in a strong accent asked: 'May I see the owner?'

'I am the owner,' Amine replied, and the man looked delighted. He wore elegant, polished shoes and Amine couldn't stop staring at them. 'You'll get your shoes dirty.'

'Oh, that is not important, believe me. What interests me is this beautiful property of yours. Would you agree to show me around?'

Dragan Palosi asked Amine lots of questions. He asked him how he'd bought his land, what types of farming he was planning to develop, what his revenues were and his expectations for the coming years. Amine gave very brief replies because he was suspicious of this man with his strange accent, dressed in clothes too smart for walking the fields. Amine started to sweat and he watched from the corner of his eye as his visitor wiped his round face with a handkerchief. It occurred to Amine that he hadn't even thought to ask the man his name. When he did at last ask – and the man told him his name – Amine gave an involuntary grimace.

The visitor burst out laughing. 'It's Hungarian. Dragan Palosi. I'm a doctor. I have an office on Rue de Rennes.'

Amine nodded, although he still didn't understand. What was a Hungarian doctor doing here? Was this some kind of racket? Suddenly Dragan Palosi stopped and looked up. He stared attentively at the row of orange trees in front of him. The trees were still young but their branches were heavy with fruit. Dragan also noticed that there was a branch from a lemon tree on one of them and that its yellow fruit was mixed up with the huge oranges.

'Amusing,' said the Hungarian as he walked up to the tree.

'Oh, that? Yes, it makes the children laugh. It's a little game we're playing. My daughter calls it the "lemange". I grafted a pear tree branch on to a quince tree too, but we haven't found a name for that one yet.'

Amine fell silent then. He didn't want the doctor to think him a dilettante.

'I would like to offer you a deal,' Dragan said. He took Amine's arm and led him towards a shady corner near one of the trees. He explained that for years he had dreamed of exporting fruit to Eastern Europe. 'Oranges and dates,' he told Amine, who had no idea what countries he was talking about. 'I'll take care of transporting the oranges to the port in Casablanca. I'll pay your workers for the harvest and I'll pay you rent for your land. Do we have a deal?' Amine shook his hand.

Later that day, when he brought Aïcha back from school, they found Mathilde sitting on the steps that led down to the garden. The little girl ran into her mother's open arms and thought that her prayers had not been in vain. Mathilde was going to live. *Hail Mary.*

* * *

Once she had recovered, Mathilde was happy about the weight she'd lost. In the mirror she saw her pale face, her drawn features, the bags under her eyes. She got into the habit of laying a sheet on the grass in front of the house's French window and spending her mornings in the sun with the children while they played. She was thrilled by the arrival of spring. Every day she observed new buds flowering on the branches. She crushed the fragrant orange-tree flowers between her fingers, she leaned in close to the fragile lilac. Before her the uncultivated fields were completely covered in blood-red poppies and orange wildflowers. Here there was nothing to prevent the birds flying freely. No telegraph poles, no engine noise, no walls where they might smash their tiny skulls. Since the return of the good weather she'd been hearing the twittering of hundreds of invisible birds, hiding in tree branches that quivered with the echo of their songs. The farm's isolation, which had once so terrified her and sent her into the depths of depression, now captivated her in these gorgeous spring days.

One afternoon Amine came to join them. He lay down next to his son with a nonchalance that surprised Aïcha. 'I've met some amusing people,' he said to his wife. 'I think you'd like them.' He told her about Dragan's visit to their property, his fanciful plans, and explained all the benefits that they might gain from this partnership. Mathilde frowned. She hadn't forgotten how Bouchaib had taken advantage of her husband's naivety and she feared that he was once again being lured into trouble by false promises.

'And why did he ask *you*? Roger Mariani has whole fields full of orange trees, and he's better known around here.'

Amine, hurt by his wife's suspicions, stood up abruptly.

'Well, you can ask him yourself. He and his wife have invited us to lunch on Sunday.'

On Sunday morning Mathilde kept complaining that she had nothing to wear. In the end she put on her blue dress, which was so old-fashioned, and she blamed Amine for his failure to understand her. She dreamed of Dior's New Look collection, which was all the rage with the European women in the new town.

'I wore this dress during the war, you know. It's completely unfashionable now. What will they think when they see me in this?'

'Just wear the haik. That way you don't have to worry about fashion.'

Amine laughed and Mathilde hated him. She had woken up in a bad mood and this lunch, which should have excited her, now felt like a chore.

'But what sort of lunch is it? Will it just be the four of us or will there be other guests? Are we supposed to dress up or not?'

Amine shrugged. 'How should I know?'

The Palosis lived in the new town, near the Transatlantic Hotel, and their house had a wonderful view over the city and its minarets. The couple were waiting for them on the front steps, shaded from the burning sun by a little orange-and-white awning. As Amine and Mathilde got out of the car and walked towards the front door, the doctor held his large arms open wide, like a father greeting his children. Dragan Palosi wore an elegant sea-blue suit and a wide tie. His polished shoes shone as brightly as his thick but neatly trimmed moustache.

He had fat cheeks and fleshy lips and his entire being seemed to exude a sort of round-bellied appetite for life and pleasure. He waved his hands then placed them on Mathilde's cheeks, as if she were a little girl. His hands were enormous and covered in dark hairs, the hands of a butcher or a murderer, and Mathilde couldn't help imagining Dragan Palosi using those massive hands to pull a baby from a woman's vagina. She felt the cold touch of a gold signet ring against her cheek. He wore it on his ring finger, the tip of which was white because the ring was so tight.

Beside him stood a blonde woman. Mathilde found it hard to look at her face or admire her legs because her gaze was irresistibly drawn to the woman's enormous, breathtaking, shockingly oversized breasts. The hostess gave Mathilde a lazy smile and held out a limp hand. She had the latest hairstyle and wore a dress that looked like it had come straight from a magazine, and yet her every atom oozed vulgarity, a total lack of elegance. There was the way she'd applied her orange lipstick, the way she put her hand on her hip, and, above all, the way she clicked her tongue at the end of every sentence. She seemed eager to form an idiotic complicity with Mathilde based solely on their shared gender and nationality. Corinne was French, 'from Dunkirk', she repeated, rolling her Rs. Mathilde felt ridiculous handing Corinne two dishes containing a kouglof and a fig tart. The hostess held the dishes with the wary awkwardness of someone holding a baby for the first time. Amine was ashamed of his wife and Mathilde sensed this. Corinne was not the kind of woman to concern herself with desserts, to waste her time, her youth and her beauty in an overheated kitchen, among servants and wailing children. Dragan perhaps noticed her unease because he thanked Mathilde with a warmth and kindness that moved her. He lifted up the cloth, leaned down with his wide nose an inch or two from the cakes and took a deep, long breath. 'Mmm, how wonderful!' he exclaimed, and Mathilde blushed.

And while Corinne led Mathilde into the living room, pointing out a chair and offering her something to drink, while she sat facing her and told her about her life, Mathilde kept thinking: She's a whore. She paid no attention to what the young woman was saying because she felt certain that it was all lies and she refused to be duped. If people came here, to this lost city, it was so they could lie, reinvent themselves. She was obliged to listen to the story of how Corinne had met the rich Hungarian gynaecologist, but she didn't believe for a second that it had been love at first sight, as Corinne claimed. Over aperitifs, while Mathilde drank several glasses of an excellent port, she thought only of one thing. She watched the Moroccan butler come and go, she observed her husband's radiant smile, she stared at the signet ring that was strangling the gynaecologist's ring finger and she thought: She's a whore. Those words echoed inside her skull like machine gun fire. She imagined Corinne in a brothel in Dunkirk, a poor girl numb with shame and cold, a plump and half-naked figure in a nylon slip and ankle socks. No doubt Dragan had helped her out of the gutter; perhaps what he'd felt for her was genuine passion, or at least a noble desire to be her knight in shining armour, but that didn't change anything. This woman bothered Mathilde, she disgusted and fascinated her. She wanted to stay and watch her, and at the same time she wanted to run far away from her.

Several times during the aperitifs, when the conversation sank into an embarrassing silence, Dragan would talk about those magnificent cakes that he couldn't wait to eat and he would beam a complicit smile at Mathilde. He had always got along better with women. As a child he'd hated the all-boys' school where his parents had sent him, felt oppressed by its unrelieved masculinity. He loved women not as a seducer but as a friend, a brother. In his adult life, which had been marked by exile and restlessness, women had always been his allies. They understood the melancholy that suffocated him sometimes, they knew what it was to be reduced to the arbitrariness of their gender just as he'd been reduced to the absurdity of his religion. From women he'd learned a mix of resignation and pugnacity, he'd realised that joy was a form of vengeance against those who sought to deny you.

Amine and Mathilde were surprised by the refinement of the Palosis' home. Seeing them as a couple, it was hard to imagine such delicacy, such meticulousness, in the furnishings, in the choice of wall coverings, the blend of colours. They were sitting in a charming salon with a large bay window that opened on to a beautifully kept garden. Bougainvilleas grew on the back wall and the wisteria was in flower. Beneath a jacaranda Corinne had set a table and chairs. 'But it's too hot to eat outside, don't you think?'

Every time she spoke or laughed, her breasts would rise up as if they were about to pop out of her dress, as if the nipples might suddenly appear before their eyes like buds blossoming in spring. Amine couldn't take his eyes off them and he smiled hungrily, more handsome than ever. After all these years living outdoors, his face had been sculpted by the wind and the sun, his eyes were filled with sky and his skin gave off the most wonderful smell. Mathilde was well aware of the effect he had on women. She wondered then if it was really for her sake that he had accepted this invitation, as he'd claimed, or if he'd been lured here by this woman's lascivious curves.

'Your wife is very elegant,' Amine had remarked as they first arrived, languidly kissing Corinne's hand. 'Oh, but these cakes smell so delicious,' Dragan had replied. 'Your wife is a cordon bleu chef!' When he kept talking about the cakes during the meal, Mathilde wanted to disappear. She put her hands to her temples to adjust her hairstyle, which was collapsing. Sweat trickled down her forehead and her blue dress had stains under the armpits and between her breasts. Mathilde had spent the morning working in the kitchen, then she'd had to quickly feed the children and give Tamo her instructions. The car had stalled six miles from the farm and she'd had to get out and push it because Amine claimed she couldn't steer it properly. As she lifted a too-dense liver mousse to her mouth, she thought that her husband was a liar: he'd only made her push the car because he hadn't wanted to mess up his best jacket. It was his fault that she'd arrived at the Palosis' house in this state, sweating and exhausted, her dress rumpled, her legs covered in insect bites. She complimented Corinne on her delicious starter and slid her hand under the table to scratch her itching calves.

She wanted to ask: 'What did you do during the war?', because it seemed like the only way of getting to know people. But Amine, his tongue loosened by the white wine, started talking about Moroccan politics with Dragan and the women smiled silently at each other. Corinne let ash fall from her cigarette and it burned the fringe of the rug. Wearily, her eyes glazed from the alcohol, she asked Mathilde to accompany her into the garden. Mathilde reluctantly agreed. Let her do the talking, she told herself, feeling bloody-minded. Corinne took a pack of cigarettes from a little pedestal table and offered one to Mathilde. 'You must bring your children next time. I made some sweets and there are a few old toys in the room at the back. The previous owners left them here,' she explained in a voice tense with repressed melancholy. Corinne sat on one of the steps leading down to the garden. 'When did you arrive in Morocco?' she asked. Mathilde recounted her story, and as she slowly put the past into words she realised that this was the first time anyone had listened to her like this, with such kindly interest. Corinne had landed in Casablanca just after the start of the war. Dragan – who'd had to flee Hungary, then Germany, then France – had been told by a Russian friend that Morocco was the ideal place to make a new start. In the white town on the Atlantic coast he'd found employment as a doctor in a well-known clinic. He'd earned plenty of money, but the director's reputation and the nature of the operations he was performing had ended up making him quit. They'd decided to move to Meknes, with its easy-going atmosphere and its orchards.

'What sort of operations were they?' asked Mathilde, intrigued by Corinne's conspiratorial tone.

Corinne looked behind her, inched closer to Mathilde and whispered: 'Rather extraordinary operations, if you want my opinion. Did you know that people come from all over Europe for that? The doctor is either a genius or a madman, but apparently he's capable of transforming a man into a woman!'

At the end of the school term the nuns asked to see Aïcha's parents. Amine and Mathilde turned up outside the gate a quarter of an hour early and Sister Marie-Solange led them through to the Mother Superior's office. As they walked down the long gravel path and past the chapel, Amine turned to look at it. What did that god of theirs have in mind for him? Sister Marie-Solange invited them to sit down in front of the long cedar desk with files stacked on top of it. There was a crucifix hanging above the fireplace. When the Mother Superior entered her office, they stood up and Amine prepared himself for an onslaught. He and his wife had spent all night discussing the possible reasons for this meeting: their continual lateness, Aïcha's clothes, her mystical ravings. They'd argued. 'Stop telling her stories that scare her,' Amine had hissed. 'Buy us a car,' Mathilde had replied. But faced with the headmistress, they were on the same side. Whatever she said, they would defend their child.

The nun gestured for them to sit down. She noticed the height difference between Amine and his wife and this seemed to amuse her. She was probably thinking that only a very modest man or a man who was deeply in love could accept a wife who was a head taller than him. She sat in her chair and tried to open the desk drawer, but she couldn't find the key.

'Anyway, Sister Marie-Solange and I wanted to tell you how pleased we are with Aïcha.'

Mathilde's legs started to shake. She'd been expecting the worst. 'She is a shy and somewhat wild little girl and it wasn't easy to tame her. But her marks are exceptional.'

She pushed towards them a small notebook that she'd finally managed to extract from the drawer. Her bony finger pointed at the figures and they noticed her white, neatly trimmed nails, as thin as a child's.

'Aïcha's results are well above average in every subject. The reason we wished to see you is that we believe your daughter should skip a year. How would you feel about that?'

The two nuns watched them, both smiling radiantly. They seemed disappointed by the lack of enthusiasm in the parents' response. Amine and Mathilde didn't move. They stared at the notebook and seemed to be having a silent conversation, brows furrowed and lips pursed. Amine had not taken the baccalauréat and his memories of school mostly consisted of being caned by the teacher as a warning not to misbehave. As for Mathilde, her main memory was of the cold; it had been so freezing in her school that she hadn't been able to hold a pen. It was Mathilde who spoke first:

'If you think it will be good for her.' She almost added: 'You know her better than we do.'

When they saw Aïcha again, waiting patiently for them outside on the street, they looked at her oddly, as if seeing her for the first time. This child, they thought, was a stranger, an unsolvable riddle. It shocked them that this frail little girl with her knock knees and her frowning face, this little girl with her big hair, could be so intelligent. At home she didn't speak much. She spent her evenings playing with the fringe of the large blue rug and she was always having sneezing fits because of the dust. She never told them what she'd been doing at school; she kept her miseries, her joys and friendships to herself. When strangers came to the house she ran away as quickly as a mouse in the presence of a cat; she disappeared into her room or out into the fields. And wherever she was, she was always running, her long thin legs seeming to separate from the rest of her body. Her feet were so far ahead of her sweating torso, her swinging arms, her crimson face, that it looked as if she were merely trying to catch up with them. She didn't appear to know anything and yet she never asked for help with her homework, and when Mathilde bent over her exercise books she could only admire her daughter's neat handwriting, her poise, her tenacity.

Aïcha asked no questions about the meeting. They told her that they were proud of her and that they were going to celebrate by eating lunch at a café in the new town. She took the hand that Mathilde offered her and followed them. The only thing that seemed to make her happy was the pile of books that her mother gave her. 'I think you deserve a reward.' They sat on the terrace, beneath a large, dusty, red awning. Amine poured a few drops of beer into Aïcha's glass. He told her that this was a special day and that she could have a drink with them. Aïcha stuck her nose into her glass. The beer had no smell so she raised the glass to her lips and swallowed the bitter liquid. Her mother wiped the foam from her cheek with a gloved hand. Aïcha liked it a lot, the ice-cold liquid that slid down her throat and cooled her stomach. She didn't ask for more, she just pushed her glass closer to the middle of the table and without really thinking about it her father poured some more beer into it. He was still a little shaken. His daughter looked like a street urchin, yet she could speak Latin and she was better than all the French girls at mathematics. 'Exceptionally talented,' the teacher had said.

Amine and Mathilde started to get slightly drunk. They ordered some fried food. They laughed and ate with their fingers. Aïcha didn't say much. Her mind was fogged over. She had the impression that her body was lighter than before and she could hardly feel her arms at all. There was a sort of strange disconnect between her thoughts and her feelings, like a melody no longer anchored to its rhythm, and this perturbed her. She felt a sudden burst of love for her parents and then, within a few seconds, that feeling became alien to her; it was like a poem she'd learned whose last verse she couldn't remember. She found it hard to concentrate and she didn't laugh when a group of boys stopped outside the café and performed acrobatics to amuse the customers. She felt terribly sleepy and she could hardly keep her eyes open. Her parents stood up to wave to a couple of Armenian shopkeepers to whom they sold fruit and almonds. Aïcha heard them say her name. Her father was speaking louder than usual and he put his hand on his daughter's bony shoulder. She smiled with her mouth open. She looked at her father's black hand and pressed her cheek against it. The grown-ups asked her: 'How old are you?' 'Do you like school?' She didn't reply. There was something she'd forgotten but she knew it was something happy and it was this last thought that stayed with her as she fell asleep with her head on the table.

She woke, her cheeks wet from her mother's kisses. They walked towards the Avenue de la République and the Empire cinema with its facade in the style of a Greek theatre. Her parents bought her an ice cream, which she ate on the street, slowly and in a way that her father thought so obscene that he grabbed the cornet from her hands and threw it in a bin. 'You'll stain your dress,' he said, to justify this sudden attack. They went to see *High Noon*. Groups of teenagers laughed while men in suits argued loudly about the news. A young woman was selling chocolates and cigarettes. Aïcha was so small that she had to sit on her father's lap to see the screen. The lights went out and the old Moroccan usherette who'd led them to their seats shouted at a group of teenagers to shut up: 'Sed foumouk!' Aïcha leaned against Amine, as if dazed by the warm feel of his skin. She buried her face in her father's neck, indifferent to the images on the screen or to the torch that the usherette was waving at a young man who'd lit a cigarette. During the film Mathilde dug her fingers into her daughter's hair and gently tugged at each strand, sending shivers from the back of Aïcha's neck to the soles of her feet. When they emerged from the cinema her hair was even more puffed up and frizzy than usual and she felt ashamed at being seen like that in the street.

In the car on the way home the atmosphere curdled. It wasn't only because of the dark, stormy sky or the dust clouds raised by little tornadoes. Amine had forgotten the nuns' good news and was now brooding over the money that they'd wasted. Mathilde, forehead touching the window, talked and talked. Aïcha wondered how her mother could find so much to say about the film. She listened to Mathilde's high-pitched voice and nodded when her mother turned around and said: 'Grace Kelly is so beautiful, don't you think?' Mathilde loved the cinema, so passionately that it was painful. She watched films almost without breathing, her whole body straining towards the Technicolor faces. When she left the cinema after two hours in darkness, the clamour of the streets was like a slap in the face. It was the town that was false, incongruous, and reality seemed to her nothing more than an insignificant fiction, a lie. She was happy to have lived elsewhere for a while, to have been touched, however fleetingly, by the sublime, but at the same time she felt a sort of bitter rage at not being able to climb into the screen and experience those feelings with the same density as the characters did.

During the summer of 1954, Mathilde wrote her sister many letters but received no replies. She put this down to the political troubles in Morocco and didn't worry about Irène's silence. Francis Lacoste, the new Resident-General, had taken over from General Guillaume in May 1954, and on his arrival in Morocco he promised to crush the wave of riots and murders that was terrorising the French population. He threatened the nationalists with terrible reprisals. Omar, Amine's brother, was savage in his hatred for this man. One day he was so angry that he insulted Mathilde. He'd just heard about the death in prison of the resistance fighter Muhammad Zarqtuni, and he was foaming at the mouth with rage. 'Violence is the only way we'll liberate this country. Wait till they see what the nationalists do to them!' Mathilde tried to calm him down. 'Not all Europeans are like that – you know they're not.' She mentioned examples of French people who had declared themselves supporters of independence, some of whom had even been arrested for providing the rebels with logistical aid. But Omar just shrugged and spat on the floor.

In the middle of August, as the first anniversary of the sultan's dethronement approached, they went to spend the day at Mouilala's house. Amine's mother welcomed him with a thousand prayers, thanking God for the protection He'd given her son. They went into a room to talk about business and money, and Mathilde sat in the parlour and began braiding Aïcha's hair. Selim sprinted around the house and almost fell down the stone stairs. Omar, who adored his nephew, lifted him on to his shoulders. 'I'm going to take him to the park so he can run around,' he said before leaving, paying no attention to the advice Mathilde gave him. At five o'clock Omar still hadn't come home and Mathilde, feeling anxious, went to tell her husband. Amine leaned out of the window. He called out to his brother and a wave of shouted insults crashed over him. Some protesters were out in the streets, demanding that their fellow Muslims show their pride and stand up to the invaders. 'We have to find Selim,' shouted Amine. 'Go downstairs!' They barely even said goodbye to Mouilala, whose head was shaking as she placed a hand on her son's forehead to bless him. Amine shouted at his wife: 'Are you mad? Why on earth did you let him go out? Don't you know there are protests every day at the moment?'

They had to get out of the old town as quickly as possible. Those narrow streets were a trap and Amine was afraid that his family would be ambushed by protesters. Noises came closer, voices bouncing off the walls of the medina. They saw men running fast behind and ahead of them. They were surrounded by an ever-denser crowd and Amine, who was carrying his daughter in his arms, started sprinting towards the gate of the medina.

They reached the car and dived inside. Aïcha started crying. She wanted her mother to hug her. She asked if her brother was going to die and Amine and Mathilde simultaneously yelled at her to shut up. The crowd of protesters had closed around them and Amine couldn't reverse the car. Strangers' faces pressed against the windscreen. One man's chin left a smear of grease on the glass. Unknown eyes stared at this odd family, at this child who might be friend or enemy. One boy started shouting, his arm raised skyward, and the crowd was galvanised. The boy couldn't have been more than fifteen; he had a soft, patchy beard and gentle eyes, but his voice was deep and filled with hate. Aïcha looked at him and she knew that his face would be engraved permanently on her memory. The boy frightened her, yet she thought him handsome in his flannel trousers and his jacket like an American airman's. 'Long live the king!' he yelled, and the crowd chanted 'Long live Mohammed Ben Youssef!' so loudly that Aïcha had the impression that it was their voices that were making the car pitch from side to side. Some boys started banging on the roof with sticks, lending a beat to the almost melodic noise. They began smashing everything they could find – car windows, streetlamps – and the streets were soon paved with broken glass. The protesters walked on the shards in their cheap shoes, unaware of the blood oozing from their feet.

'Lie down!' Amine shouted, and Aïcha pressed her cheek against the floor of the car. Mathilde protected her face with her hands and started intoning: 'It's okay, it's okay, it's okay.' She thought about the war, about that day when she'd thrown herself into a ditch to avoid being shot by a plane. She'd dug her fingernails into the earth, she'd stopped breathing for a few moments, and then she'd squeezed her thighs together, so strongly that she almost came. Right now she wished she could share that memory with Amine or simply press her lips against his, dissolve her fear in desire. Then suddenly the crowd dispersed, as if a grenade had exploded at its centre, propelling bodies in all directions. The car pitched and Mathilde saw the eyes of a woman tapping on the window with her fingernails. The woman pointed at little trembling Aïcha and, without knowing why, Mathilde trusted her. She opened the window and the woman tossed two large pieces of onion inside before running away. 'Gas!' Amine shouted. Within a few seconds the car was filled with a sharp, sour odour and they were all coughing.

Amine started the engine and drove very slowly through the cloud of smoke. He came to the gates of a park and jumped out of the car, leaving the door open behind him. In the distance he could see his brother playing with his son, as if the riot that had occurred less than a hundred feet from them had actually happened in a different country. The Jardin des Sultanes was calm and peaceful. A man was sitting on a bench with a large rusty cage at his feet. Amine went over and saw a thin grey-furred monkey inside it, the animal's feet covered in its own shit. He squatted down to get a better look at the monkey, which turned to face him and opened its mouth wide, showing its teeth. The animal whistled and spat, and Amine wasn't sure if it was laughing or threatening him.

Amine called his son, who came running into his arms. He didn't want to talk to his brother – he had no time for explanations or reprimands – and he led Selim back to the car, leaving Omar alone in the middle of the grass.

On the way back to the farm there was a police roadblock. Aïcha noticed a long spiked chain strung across the street and she imagined the noise that the tyres would make if they burst. One of the policemen signalled to Amine to stop the car. He slowly approached the vehicle and took off his sunglasses to examine the faces of the people inside. Aïcha stared at the policeman with a curiosity that made him uneasy. He seemed baffled by this family that was calmly looking back at him in silence. Mathilde wondered what story he was imagining for them. Did he think Amine was the chauffeur? Did he see Mathilde as the rich wife of a colonist who had sent this servant to accompany her? But the policeman seemed indifferent to the adults; instead he stared at the children. He observed Aïcha's hands, which were wrapped around her brother's chest, as if to protect him. Mathilde slowly lowered her window and smiled at the young man.

'They're going to declare a curfew. Go home. Go on!' The policeman slapped the car's bonnet and Amine set off.

For the Bastille Day dance Corinne wore a red dress and braided leather pumps. In the garden, which was lit by coloured paper lanterns, she danced only with her husband, politely refusing the invitations of the other guests. She thought that, by doing this, she would be able to avoid making the other wives jealous, to be friends with them, but instead those women considered her contemptuous and vulgar. So our husbands aren't good enough for her? they all thought. In such circumstances, Corinne was always careful. She distrusted alcohol and enthusiasm because she knew that these things made the mornings after painful. She dreaded the feeling of having degraded herself, having talked too much, having tried too hard to be liked. Before midnight someone came to fetch Dragan, who was leaning on the bar, having a drink. A woman was giving birth; it was her third child, he had to come quickly. Corinne refused to stay on without him. 'If you're not here I won't dance.' He took her home before going to the hospital.

When she woke the next morning her husband still wasn't back. She lay in the room with the shutters closed, listening to the whirr of the fan blades, her nightdress soaked with sweat. In the end she got out of bed and walked to the balcony. Outside in the street, where the heat was already brutal, she saw a man sweeping the pavement with a palm leaf. Across the road the neighbours' children were sitting on the front steps of their house while their mother rushed from one room to another, closing the shutters and scolding the maids who had not yet finished packing the suitcases. The father – who was sitting in the car with the door open, smoking a cigarette – looked like he was already exhausted by this long journey. They were going back to France. Soon, Corinne knew, the new town would be deserted. A few days before this her piano teacher had told her that she was going to the Basque Country. 'I can't wait to escape this heat and this hate for a few weeks.'

Corinne left the balcony. She had nowhere to go, she thought. No home to return to, no childhood house filled with memories. She shivered with disgust as she remembered the dark streets of Dunkirk, the neighbour women spying on her. She saw them again, standing outside their hovels, gripping the shawls that covered their shoulders, their dirty hair tied in ponytails. They had been suspicious of Corinne, whose body, at fifteen, had suddenly ripened. Her little-girl shoulders had to hold up her enormous breasts, her fragile feet had to bear the weight of her spectacular hips. Her body was a lure, a trap in which she herself was imprisoned. At the table, her father no longer dared even look at her. Her mother just said things like: 'Look how she's dressed!' Soldiers ogled her, women judged her. 'A body like that would make a pervert of any-one!' They imagined she was sex-crazed. A woman like that, they thought, is only built for pleasure. Men threw them-selves at her; they undressed her the way children unwrap a present, rough and frantic. Then, dazzled, they contemplated her extraordinary breasts, which – freed from the constraints of a bra – spread out like a cloud of cream. They slavered over them, bit them, as if driven mad by the thought that this treat would go on forever, that they'd never reach the end of these glorious wonders.

Corinne closed the shutters and spent the morning in darkness, lying on the bed, smoking cigarettes until the filter burned her lips. Like Dragan's childhood, there was nothing left of hers but a pile of stones, buildings destroyed by bombs, bodies buried in empty cemeteries. The pair of them washed up here, and when she'd arrived in Meknes she'd thought that perhaps she'd be able to build a new life. She'd imagined that the sun, the fresh air, the tranquillity of life in this place would have a redeeming effect on her body and she would finally be able to give Dragan a child. But months passed, then years. In the house the only sound was the sad thrum of the fan, never a baby's laughter.

When her husband came home, just before lunch, she tortured him with a thousand cruel questions. 'How much did it weigh?' 'Did it cry?' 'Tell me, darling, was it a beautiful baby?' Dragan, with his drowned man's eyes, answered her gently, holding his beloved's body in his arms.

He'd planned to go to the Belhaj farm that afternoon, and Corinne suggested she go with him. She liked young Mathilde, with her nervous, clumsy ways. She'd been moved by Mathilde's account of her own life. Mathilde had said: 'I have no choice but to be alone. In my position, how could we possibly have a social life? You can't imagine what it's like being married to a native, in a town like this.' Corinne had almost replied that it wasn't always easy being married to a Jew, an immigrant, a man without a country, or being a childless woman. But Mathilde was young and Corinne didn't think she would understand.

When Corinne arrived at the farm she found Mathilde lying under the willow with her children asleep beside her. She approached in silence, so as not to wake the little ones, and Mathilde gestured for her to sit on the sheet that was spread out over the grass. In the shade, amid the sweet sound of the children's breathing, she observed the trees growing down below, with fruits of different colours on their branches.

That summer, Corinne came to the hill almost every day. She liked to play with Selim, whose beauty fascinated her, and to softly bite his cheeks and thighs. Sometimes Mathilde would turn on the radio and leave the front door open. They could hear the music from the garden and Corinne and Mathilde would each hold a child's hand and dance together. Several times Mathilde invited her to stay for dinner and at nightfall the men would join them to eat in the garden under a pergola that Amine had built, where wisteria was starting to grow.

News from the city came to them distorted by rumour. Mathilde didn't want to know about the outside world. It was like an ill wind, bringing noxious air. But when Corinne arrived one day looking haggard and carrying a newspaper, Mathilde didn't have the courage to tell her not to speak. The newspaper's headline read: 'Tragedy strikes Morocco'. Corinne whispered so that the children wouldn't hear about the horrors that had taken place in Petitjean on 2 August. 'They killed six Jews,' she said, before giving the grisly details like a diligent student answering a teacher's question. A father of eleven with his chest ripped open. Houses looted and burned. She described the savaged corpses brought to Meknes to be buried and she quoted the words of rabbis, spoken in all the synagogues. 'God will not forget. Our deaths will be avenged.'

V

In September, Aïcha went back to school. And now her constant lateness could be blamed on all the sick people. Ever since Rabia's accident, word of Mathilde's gifts as a healer had spread throughout the surrounding area. It was said that she knew the names of medicines and how to administer them, that she was calm and generous. From that day on, peasants would come to the door of the Belhaj farm every morning. The first few times it was Amine who answered the door and asked suspiciously:

'What are you doing here?'

'Hello, Master. I've come to see Madame.'

Every morning the line of patients grew longer. During harvest season many female labourers came to see Mathilde. Some had been bitten by ticks; others had inflamed veins or couldn't nurse their babies because the milk in their breasts had dried up. Amine disapproved of these women queuing on his front steps. He hated the idea that they were entering his home, spying on his things and his actions and going back to the village to tell everyone what they'd seen in the master's house. He warned his wife against the sorcery, slander and envy that lie dormant in the hearts of all men.

Mathilde could clean wounds, anaesthetise ticks with ether and teach a woman to clean a baby's bottle and change a nappy. She spoke to the peasant women with a certain severity. She didn't laugh with them when they made dirty jokes to explain their latest pregnancy. She rolled her eyes when they told her, over and over again, the same old stories about genies, babies sleeping in their mothers' bellies, or pregnant women whom no man had ever touched. She raged against the peasants' fatalism, which left everything in the hands of God, and she couldn't understand their limp resignation. She repeated at length her recommendations for better hygiene. 'You're filthy!' she yelled. 'Your wound's getting infected. Learn to wash yourself properly.' She even refused to see one woman who had come a long way because her bare feet were covered in dried shit and Mathilde suspected that she had nits. Every morning now the house echoed with the wails of neighbouring children. Often it was hunger that made them cry, since the women would wean their children too abruptly, whether because they had to return to the fields or because they were pregnant again. The babies would go from their mothers' milk to bread soaked in tea and they would grow thinner with every passing day. Mathilde cradled these children with their sunken eyes and gaunt cheeks, and sometimes tears would well in her own eyes when she couldn't console them.

Soon Mathilde was overwhelmed, and she felt ridiculous trying to treat all these patients in her improvised clinic with nothing more than alcohol, antiseptic and clean towels. One day a woman arrived with a child in her arms. The little girl was wrapped in a dirty blanket and when Mathilde moved closer she immediately saw that the skin of her cheeks was black and peeling off like the skin of a grilled pepper. In the peasants' houses the women cooked on the ground and sometimes their children would get scalded by hot tea or have their mouth or ear bitten by a rat.

'We can't just do nothing,' **Mathilde** kept telling Amine, and in the end she decided to stock up on supplies for the clinic. 'I won't ask you for money,' she promised him. 'I'll manage.'

Amine raised his eyebrows and began to laugh.

'Charity,' he said, 'is a duty for a Muslim.'

'For a Christian too,' said Mathilde.

'Then we're agreed. There's nothing else to say.'

* * *

Aïcha got into the habit of doing her homework in the clinic, with its smell of camphor and soap. She would look up from her books and see peasants holding rabbits by the ears – thank-you gifts for the healer. 'I don't want them to give me their food but I also don't want to hurt their feelings by refusing it,' Mathilde explained to her daughter. Aïcha smiled at children who coughed like old men, whose eyes were covered in flies. She was impressed by her mother, whose command of Berber was improving every day and who scolded Tamo for crying at the sight of blood. Sometimes Mathilde would laugh and sit in the grass, her bare feet touching the women's feet. She kissed the bony cheeks of an old woman, she gave sugar to a pleading boy. She asked the women to tell her old tales and they did, clicking their tongues against their toothless gums and covering their mouths with a hand whenever they laughed. They forgot that Mathilde was their mistress and a foreigner, and in Berber they shared with her their most intimate memories.

'People in peacetime should not have to live like this,' repeated Mathilde, who was revolted by poverty. She and her husband shared the same aspirations for the progress of mankind: less hunger, less pain. They were both passionate about modernity and had a wild hope that machines would provide better harvests, that new medicines would put an end to disease. Amine, however, often tried to discourage his wife's new mission. He feared for her health and he worried that these strangers' germs might spread to his family, endangering his children. One evening a woman arrived with a little boy who'd had a fever for several days. Mathilde told the woman to undress the child and let him sleep naked, covered in cool towels. The next day, at dawn, the woman came back. The child was burning hot and he'd had convulsions during the night. Mathilde ushered the woman into her car and put the child in the back seat next to Aïcha. 'I'm going to take my daughter to school and then we'll go to the hospital, okay?'

They had to wait a long time in the native hospital before a red-haired doctor finally examined the child. When Mathilde returned to pick up Aïcha at the end of the day she was pale and her jaw was trembling. Aïcha thought that something had happened. 'Did the little boy die?' she asked. Mathilde held her daughter, she pinched her arms and her legs. She began to weep and her tears wet Aïcha's face. 'My sweet angel, how do you feel? Look at me, darling. Are you all right?' That night Mathilde couldn't sleep. For once, she prayed. She believed she was being punished for her vanity. She'd thought of herself as a healer when in truth she knew nothing. All she'd done was risk her child's life and maybe tomorrow she would find Aïcha with a high fever and the doctor would tell her, as he had that morning: 'It's polio, madame. Take care, it's highly contagious.'

The clinic also caused some dissent among the men in the neighbourhood. The labourers went to Amine to complain that his wife was advising their wives not to do their conjugal duty, that she was putting strange ideas in their heads. This Christian woman, this foreigner, shouldn't be meddling in such things, sowing the seeds of discord in other families. One day Roger Mariani came to the Belhaj farm. It was the first time their wealthy neighbour had crossed the road that separated the two properties. Usually Mathilde saw him on horseback, surveying his land with a hat brim shading his face. He went into the room where the women were sitting on the floor, their children in their arms. When they saw him, some of the women ran off without saying goodbye to Mathilde, who was conscientiously applying a tulle gras dressing to a burn. Hands behind his back, Mariani walked across the room and stood behind her. He was chewing a stalk of wheat and the sound of his tongue annoyed Mathilde, made it hard for her to concentrate. When she turned around to face him he smiled at her. 'Continue, please.' He sat on a chair and waited until Mathilde had finished treating the boy with the burn. She told the boy to stay in the shade and get some rest.

When they were alone Mariani stood up again. He was slightly unnerved by Mathilde's height and by the lack of fear in her green eyes. All his life women had been scared of him, jumping at the sound of his booming voice, trying to run away when he grabbed them by the waist or the hair, weeping softly when he took them by force in a barn or behind a bush. 'Your love of the darkies is going to blow up in your face one day,' he warned Mathilde. He casually grabbed a bottle of alcohol and banged the sharp end of a pair of scissors against the table. 'What do you think's going to happen? You think they'll turn you into a saint? Build a temple for you? Those women,' he hissed, gesturing at the women working in the fields outside, 'they're hardened to pain. The last thing they need is someone teaching them to feel sorry for themselves. You understand me?'

* * *

But nothing could deter Mathilde. One Saturday in early September she went to see Dr Palosi at his third-floor office in an ugly building on Rue de Rennes. Four European women were sitting in the waiting room and one of them, who was pregnant, put her hand on her belly when she saw Mathilde, as if to protect her unborn baby. They waited a long time in the room's stifling heat, its heavy silence. One of the women fell asleep, her face leaning on her right hand. Mathilde tried to read the novel she'd brought with her, but the air was so hot that she couldn't think straight; her mind kept flitting from one idea to another, too distracted to dwell on anything for long.

At last Dragan Palosi came out of his office and when Mathilde saw him she stood up and gave a sigh of relief. He looked handsome in his white coat, with his black hair slicked back. He was very different from the jovial man she'd first met and she thought she could detect a hint of sadness in his dark-ringed eyes. His face, like any good doctor's, bore the marks of fatigue. Their patients' pain is always visible in their features; their shoulders sag under the weight of all the secrets they've been told, and they walk and speak slowly because they are exhausted by their own powerlessness.

The doctor went over to Mathilde and hesitated for a second before kissing her on both cheeks. He noticed her blush and, to ease her embarrassment, examined the cover of the book she was holding. *'The Death of Ivan Ilyich,'* he read quietly. He had a deep voice, a voice full of promises, and she sensed that his body and his heart were full of extraordinary stories. 'You like Tolstoy?'

Mathilde nodded and while he escorted her into his spacious office he told her an anecdote. 'When I arrived in Morocco, in 1939, I moved to Rabat and stayed with a Russian friend who was fleeing the revolution. One evening he invited some people to dinner. We drank, we played cards, and one of the guests, whose name was Michel Lvovich, fell asleep on the living room sofa. He snored so loudly that we started laughing, and my host said: 'And to think that he's the son of the great Tolstoy!'

Mathilde's eyes widened and Dragan went on.

'Not a word of a lie – it was the son of that great genius!' he exclaimed, pointing Mathilde to a black leather chair. 'He died at the end of the war. I never saw him again.'

A silence fell and Dragan was gripped by the incongruity of the situation. Mathilde turned her face to the sea-green screen behind which patients undressed.

'To be completely honest,' she began, 'I didn't come for a consultation. I need your help.'

Dragan perched his chin on his joined hands. How many times had he been through this situation? 'A gynaecologist must be ready for anything,' one of his professors at the university in Budapest had told him. For women prepared to submit to the most awful experiments in order to have a child. For women who have discovered, from shameful symptoms, that their husbands have cheated on them. And lastly, for women who have realised too late that their arms have grown fatter and there is a pain in their lower abdomen. 'But you must have suffered terribly,' he said to these women. 'Why didn't you come to me before?'

Dragan looked at Mathilde's beautiful face; her complexion was not made for these latitudes and her skin was covered in pink blotches. What did she expect from him? Was she going to ask for money? Had she come on her husband's behalf?

'Please go on.'

Mathilde spoke increasingly quickly, and with a passion that took the gynaecologist by surprise. She spoke about Rabia, who had strange spots on her belly and thighs and who'd been vomiting. She mentioned Jmia, whose eighteen-month-old child could not stand up. She admitted that she felt out of her depth, that she had learned to recognise the symptoms of diphtheria, whooping cough and conjunctivitis, but had no idea how to treat them. Dragan looked at her, his eyes wide and his mouth open. Impressed by the seriousness with which she described each pathology, he picked up a notepad and a biro and started writing down what she said. Occasionally he would interrupt her to ask a question: 'And these spots, are they oozing or are they dry?' 'Did you disinfect the wound?' He was moved by this woman's passion for medicine, by the desire she showed to understand the extraordinary machine of the human body.

'I normally don't give advice or medicine unless I've examined the patients myself. But those women would never let a man examine them, particularly not a foreign man.' He told her how a very rich shopkeeper in Fez had once come to see him about his wife, who was bleeding profusely. A doorman in rags had led him into the man's house and Dragan had been forced to question the patient through a thick curtain. The woman bled out and died the next morning.

Dragan stood up and pulled two thick books from his shelf. 'The anatomical plates are in Hungarian, I'm afraid. I'll try to find you some in French, but in the meantime you can familiarise yourself with the mechanism.' The other book concerned colonial medicine and it was illustrated with black-and-white photographs. On the way home Aïcha leafed through this book and she stopped at an image captioned: 'Containing a typhus epidemic, Morocco, 1944'. Men in djellabas, all standing in a line, were surrounded by a cloud of black powder and the photographer had managed to capture the mixture of fear and wonder on their faces.

Mathilde parked the car outside the post office. She opened the car door and stretched out her legs, touching her feet to the pavement. She'd never known a September as hot as this one. She took a sheet of paper and a pen from her bag and tried to finish writing the letter she'd begun that morning. In the first paragraph she'd written that they shouldn't believe everything they read in the newspapers. That of course what happened in Petitjean was terrible, but the situation was more complicated.

'My dear Irène, have you left for your holidays? I imagine – though perhaps I am wrong – that you are in the Vosges, near one of those lakes we used to swim in when we were young. I can still taste the blueberry pie served by that tall lady with warts all over her face. The taste has never left my memory and I think about it whenever I'm sad, to console myself.'

She put her shoes back on and climbed the stairs that led to the post office. A smiling woman greeted her at the counter. 'Mulhouse, France,' Mathilde explained. Next she headed to the main room, where the hundreds of post office boxes were located. Little brass doors, each one with a number on it, covered the high walls. She stopped next to box number 25: the same number as her year of birth, she'd said to Amine, who was always indifferent to this kind of remark. She took the little key out of her pocket and inserted it into the lock, but it didn't turn. She took it out and put it in again but still nothing happened and the box wouldn't open. Mathilde repeated the same actions with increasing impatience, and her annoyance was soon making people stare. Was this woman stealing letters sent to her husband by another woman? Or was she trying to take revenge on her lover by opening his post office box? An employee walked up to her slowly, like a zookeeper who had to return an animal to its cage. He was a very young man with red hair and a protruding jawline. Mathilde thought him ridiculous and ugly with his enormous feet and the pompous look on his face. He was still a child, she thought, and yet his expression was severe.

'Is there a problem, madame? May I help you?' She yanked out the key so quickly that she almost elbowed the young man in the eye. He was much shorter than her. 'It won't open,' she said angrily.

The employee took the key from Mathilde but he had to stand on tiptoe to reach the lock. His slowness exasperated her. Finally the key broke in the lock and she had to wait while he called his manager. She was going to be late for work; she'd promised Amine that she would make progress on the labourers' payslips and her husband would be furious if she wasn't home in time to serve him lunch. The employee reappeared, armed with a stepladder and a screwdriver, and with great solemnity he proceeded to unscrew the hinges of the box. In a disheartened tone he said that he'd never had to deal with 'a situation like this' before and Mathilde wanted to pull the stepladder from under his feet. At last the door gave way and the boy handed the key to Mathilde. 'How do I know this was the right key? Because if it wasn't, you'll have to pay for the box to be repaired.' Mathilde pushed him out of the way, grabbed the pile of letters and – without even saying goodbye – headed towards the exit.

Just at the moment when the heat struck her, when she felt the sun's burning touch on the top of her head, she discovered that her father was dead. A telegram, drily dictated by Irène, had been sent to her the previous day. She turned the paper over, reread the address on the envelope, stared at the letters of the telegram as if it must be some kind of joke. Was it possible that, at that very instant, thousands of miles from here, in her country turned golden by autumn, her father was being buried? While the red-haired boy was explaining the unfortunate episode with box 25 to his bosses, men were carrying Georges's coffin into the Mulhouse cemetery. As she drove, agitated and incredulous, towards the farm, Mathilde wondered how long it would take the parasites in the earth to munch through her father's huge paunch, to plug that giant's nostrils, to envelop that corpse and devour it.

* * *

When Amine found out about his father-in-law's death, he said: 'You know I really liked him', and he wasn't lying. He had felt an instant friendship for the open-hearted, joyful man who had welcomed him into his family without prejudice or condescension. Amine and Mathilde had married in the church of the Alsace village where Georges had been born. Nobody in Meknes knew about this and Amine had made his wife promise to keep it secret. 'It's a serious crime. They wouldn't understand.' Nobody had seen the photographs taken after the ceremony. The photographer had asked Mathilde to stand two steps down from her husband so that their heads were at the same height. 'It'll look a bit silly if you don't,' he'd explained. When it came to organising the party, Georges had given his daughter everything she wanted. Sometimes he would slip some cash into her hand, a secret they'd kept from Irène, who was easily upset by pointless spending. Georges had understood that it was necessary to have fun, to feel beautiful. He hadn't judged his daughter for her frivolity.

Never in his life had Amine seen men as drunk as they were that night. Georges didn't walk, he swayed; he clung to women's shoulders, danced to mask his inebriation. Around midnight he wrapped his son-in-law in a loving headlock. Georges didn't know his own strength and Amine worried that he might be killed, that Georges might break his neck through an excess of affection. He dragged Amine to the back of the overheated hall, where a few couples were dancing under the garlands of paper lanterns. They sat at the bar and Georges ordered two beers, ignoring Amine's frantic gestures of refusal. He already felt too drunk, and he'd had to run outside a few minutes before this to vomit behind the barn. Georges made him drink to see how well he could take his alcohol. He made him drink so he would talk. He made him drink because it was the only way he knew to deepen a friendship, to create a bond of trust. Like children who nick their wrists with a knife and seal an oath with blood, Georges wanted to drown his affection for his son-in-law in endless pints of beer. Amine kept retching and burping. He looked around for Mathilde, but she seemed to have disappeared. Georges grabbed him by the shoulders and drew him into a drunk conversation. In his strong Alsatian accent he slurred: 'God knows I have nothing against Africans and nothing against your race's beliefs. Actually, to be honest, I don't know shit about Africa.' The men around them, brain cells deadened by alcohol, wet mouths hanging open, sniggered at this. The name of that continent continued to echo inside their skulls, summoning daydreams of bare-breasted women, men in loincloths, endless rows of farms surrounded by tropical vegetation. They heard 'Africa' and imagined a place where they might be masters of the world if only they could survive the foul air and the epidemics. 'Africa' provoked a burst of images that said more about their fantasies than about the continent itself. 'I don't know how they treat women where you come from,' said Georges, 'but that kid of mine . . . she's not easy, is she?' He elbowed the old man slumped beside him, as if seeking a witness to Mathilde's insolence. The man turned his glassy eyes to Amine and said nothing. 'I was too lax with her,' Georges went on, although his tongue seemed to have swelled inside his mouth because he was becoming harder and harder to understand. 'The kid lost her mother – what can you do? I felt sorry for her, got too soft. I used to let her run along the banks of the Rhine and I'd get in trouble because she'd steal cherries or go skinny-dipping in the river.' Georges didn't notice Amine blush or the look of impatience on his face. 'You see, I was never brave enough to give her a good hiding. Irène kept telling me to, but I couldn't. But you shouldn't let her ride roughshod over you. Mathilde needs to know who wears the trousers, eh, lad?' Georges kept talking and in the end he forgot he was addressing his son-in-law. A crude, manly camaraderie developed between the two of them and he felt free to go on about women's breasts and bottoms, those fleshy mounds that had consoled him in all his moments of disillusionment. He banged his fist on the table and in a bawdy voice suggested that they visit the local brothel. The other men laughed and then he remembered that it was Amine's wedding night, that tonight it would be his daughter's breasts and bottom that consoled his son-in-law.

Georges was a womaniser and a drunkard, an infidel and a wily old fox. But Amine loved that giant who, on his first nights as a soldier posted in the village, had sat quietly in the living room, smoking his pipe in an armchair. In silence, Georges had observed the budding romance between his daughter and this African and he'd remembered how, when she was a little girl, he'd taught her not to believe the nonsense she read in story-books. 'It's not true that negroes eat naughty children, you know . . .'

* * *

In the days that followed, Mathilde was inconsolable. Aïcha had never seen her mother like this before. She would start sobbing in the middle of a meal or fly into a rage at Irène, who hadn't told her about their father's state of health. 'He was ill for months and I never knew. If she'd just told me, I could have taken care of him, I could have been there to say goodbye.' Mouilala came to offer her condolences. 'He is free now. You must move on, because you are still alive.'

After a few days Amine lost patience and reproached his wife for neglecting the farm and her children. 'Here people don't mope about for days. We say farewell to the dead and we continue to live.' One morning, while Aïcha was drinking her hot sweet milk, Mathilde declared: 'I have to leave or I'll go mad. I need to visit my father's grave, and when I come back everything will be better.'

A few days before his wife's departure – to which he'd agreed and for which he was paying – Amine spoke to her about the problem that was tormenting him. 'I thought about it again when Georges died. Our wedding, at the church, has no legal value here. The country will soon be independent and if I die I don't want you to find yourself with no rights over the children or the farm. When you get back, we need to deal with that.'

Two weeks later, in mid-September 1954, Amine woke in a good mood and offered to accompany Aïcha on her walk through the fields. He told her: 'For a peasant there's no such thing as Sunday.' He was surprised by his daughter's resistance to this proposal, by the way she ran ahead of him, losing herself among the rows of almond trees. She seemed to know each tree and her little feet were astonishingly agile as they avoided nettle bushes and the muddy puddles formed by the rain that had finally fallen the previous night. Sometimes Aïcha would turn around, as if tired of waiting for him, and she'd stare at him with her round, surprised eyes. For a second, a minute, he was seized by a crazy idea, before changing his mind. A woman, he thought, can't run a farm like this. He had other ambitions for Aïcha: he saw her as a city person, a civilised woman, perhaps even a doctor or a lawyer. They walked alongside a field and when the peasants saw the child they started to shout and wave their arms. They were afraid that the combine harvester would swallow her up – it had happened before and they couldn't risk it with the master's daughter. Her father went to see the labourers and they had a discussion that seemed, to Aïcha, to last forever. She lay down on the damp earth and saw a strange formation of birds in the cloudy sky. She wondered if they were messengers, coming from Alsace to announce her mother's return.

Achour, who had worked for her father since his first day on the farm, arrived on a grey-coloured horse with a muddy tail. Amine beckoned his daughter. They turned off the engine of the combine harvester and Aïcha walked fearfully towards the group of men. Amine had climbed on to the horse's back and he was smiling. 'Come on!' Aïcha refused in her thin little voice, making the excuse that she liked to run, promising that she'd keep up with him, but her father wasn't listening. He thought she wanted to play, the way he used to play when he was a child: violent games, war games, where they set traps for their friends and said the opposite of what they were thinking. He dug his heels into the horse's rump and leaned forward, his cheek against the animal's neck. The horse's nostrils dilated and it began to run in circles around the child, raising dust and blocking out the sun. He was playing the sultan, the tribal chieftain, a Saracen warrior, and soon, victorious, he would pick up this child who was no bigger than a goat. With a single, steady hand, he grabbed Aïcha and lifted her up like Mathilde picking up one of the cats by the scruff of its neck. He sat her in front of him on the saddle and whooped like a cowboy or an Indian; he thought he was being funny, but the sound frightened his daughter. She started to weep and her frail little body shook with sobs. Amine pressed her firmly against him. He put his hand on her head and said: 'Don't be afraid. Calm down!' But the girl gripped tightly on to the horse's mane; she looked down and was suddenly overcome with vertigo. It was then that Amine felt a warm liquid running along his thigh. Aïcha was still sobbing as he roughly lifted up her body and saw the wet patch on his trousers. 'I don't believe this!' he yelled, holding her at arm's length as if she disgusted him, as if he was bothered not only by the dampness and the smell but by his daughter's cowardice. He pulled on the bit and the horse came to a stop. He jumped down and put Aïcha on the ground in front of him. Father and daughter kept their eyes lowered. The horse scratched the earth with its hoof and Aïcha, terrified, threw herself at her father's leg. 'It's not good to be scared like that.' He grabbed hold of her arm and watched the urine trickle down the saddle.

As they walked back to the house, several feet apart, Amine thought that Aïcha didn't belong here, that he didn't know how to handle her. Since Mathilde had gone to Europe he'd tried to spend time with his daughter, to be a good and loving father. But he was clumsy, nervous; this seven-year-old girl made him ill at ease. His daughter needed a woman in her life, someone who understood her, and not just the tenderness offered by Tamo, who was stupid and dirty. One day he'd found the maid in the kitchen, holding the teapot above her mouth and drinking straight from the spout, and he'd wanted to slap her. He had to remove his daughter from these harmful influences and yet, on his own, he could no longer keep driving her back and forth between the farm and the school.

That evening, he went into Aïcha's bedroom and sat on the bed. He watched her as she sat at her desk.

'What are you drawing?' he asked, without moving from the edge of the bed. Aïcha didn't look up at him, she just said: 'A drawing for Mama.' Amine smiled and several times he tried to speak but gave up. He stood and walked over to the chest of drawers where Mathilde kept their daughter's clothes. He took out a pair of those woollen knickers that his wife had knitted;

they looked awfully small. He piled up a few items of clothing and stuffed them into a large brown bag. 'You're going to stay with your grandmother in Berrima for a few days. I think it'll be better for you and easier for going to school.' Aïcha folded her drawing in two, slowly, and picked up her doll from the bed. She followed her father into the hallway and went to kiss her little brother's forehead as he slept on Tamo's belly.

It was the first time the two of them had been alone together in the middle of the night and they were both nervous. In the car Amine kept turning to smile reassuringly at his daughter. Aïcha smiled back, then – emboldened by the quietness of the night – she said: 'Tell me about the war.' She sounded like an adult when she said that, her voice deeper and more assured than usual. Amine was surprised. Staring at the road ahead, he asked: 'Have you ever noticed this scar?' He placed his finger behind his right ear and ran it along his skin down to his shoulder. It was too dark to see the raised brown scar, but Aïcha knew it by heart anyway. She nodded, filled with excitement at the idea that this mystery was finally about to be solved. 'During the war, just before I met Mama . . .' – Aïcha laughed softly at this – 'I spent a few months as a prisoner in a German camp. There were lots of other soldiers like me, Moroccans from the colonial army. We were treated pretty well, for prisoners. The food was bad and there wasn't much of it, and I lost a lot of weight. But they didn't beat us or force us to work. In fact the worst thing was the boredom. One day a German officer summoned all the prisoners. He asked if any of us were barbers and, without thinking – I still don't know why – I quickly pushed my way through the crowd, stood in front of the officer and said: "I was the barber in my village, sir." The other men, who knew me, started to laugh. "You're screwed now," they said. But the officer believed me and he had a small table and a chair brought to the middle of the camp. They gave me some old clippers, a pair of scissors and this sticky stuff that the Germans like to put on their hair.' Amine put his hand to his hair, mimicking the actions of the German officers. 'My first customer sat down, and that, my sweet, is when my troubles began. I had no idea how to use those clippers and when I put them on the back of the German's neck, they jumped out of my hand. A big bald patch appeared in the soldier's hair. I was sweating and I decided the best thing to do was just shave off all his hair. But would you believe it, I couldn't get those damn clippers to do what I wanted. After a while the man started fidgeting. He put his hand to his hair and he seemed upset. He was speaking German and I couldn't understand what he was saying. Finally he got up, shoved me out of the way and grabbed a small mirror from the table. When he saw his reflection he started shouting, and although I still couldn't understand him I knew he was insulting me. He brought over the officer who'd given me the job, and he asked me to explain myself. And do you know what I said? I lifted my arms in the air, smiled and said: 'African haircut, sir!'

Amine started laughing – he even banged his hand against the steering wheel to show his enthusiasm – but Aïcha didn't laugh. She hadn't understood the story's punchline. 'But what about your scar?' I can't tell her the truth, thought Amine. She was a little girl, not a barracks buddy. How could he tell her about the escape, the barbed wire digging into his neck, the flesh that stuck to it, the fact that he didn't even feel it being torn away because the fear was stronger than the physical pain? He should keep that story for later, he decided. 'Well, all right, then,' he said, in a gentle voice that Aïcha had never heard before. The lights of the town were visible now and she could make out her father's face and the swelling on his neck. 'When I left the camp I spent a long time walking through the Black Forest. It was cold and I hadn't seen a single living soul. One night, while I was sleeping, I heard a noise, like a roar, the roar of a fierce animal. When I opened my eyes a Bengal tiger was standing in front of me. He leaped on me and his sharp claw tore at my neck.' Aïcha cried out excitedly. 'Thankfully I still had my rifle and I managed to win our duel.' Aïcha smiled and felt a desire to reach out and touch the long gash that ran from the roots of his hair to his collarbone.

She'd almost forgotten the reason for this nocturnal journey and she was surprised when her father parked the car a few feet from Mouilala's house. With one hand Amine carried the brown bag and with the other he held Aïcha's wrist. Inside the house the little girl started screaming and she begged her father not to leave her there. The women pushed Amine out the door and cuddled the child. Then Mouilala grew tired of the spectacle of Aïcha rolling around on the floor, throwing cushions and angrily shoving away the plate of cake that they handed to her. 'The little French girl has a nasty temper,' she concluded.

They put the child in the room next to Selma's, and for that first night Yasmine agreed to sleep on the floor, at the foot of her bed. Despite the presence of the maid, the sound of whose breathing should have reassured her, Aïcha found it hard to fall asleep. She had the impression that this house was like the first little pig's house in the tale of the big bad wolf: made of straw and liable to be blown away by a single breath.

In class the next day, while Sister Marie-Solange was writing figures on the blackboard, Aïcha thought: Where is my mother and when will she be home? She wondered if everyone was lying to her, if her mother's journey was the kind that you don't return from, like the one taken by the Mercier widow's husband.

Monette, who shared a desk with her, whispered something in her ear, and the teacher smacked the edge of the table with a stick. Monette was a lively, talkative child and the tallest girl in the class. She seemed to have taken a liking to Aïcha that Aïcha herself couldn't explain. Monette talked constantly, on the benches in chapel and in the schoolyard during break time, in the cafeteria and even when they were being quizzed by the teacher in the classroom. She got on the adults' nerves, and one day the Mother Superior shouted, 'For God's sake!', and her wrinkled cheeks blushed with shame. Aïcha couldn't tell how much of what Monette told her was true and how much simply made up. Did Monette really have a sister in France who was an actress? Had she really been to America, seen zebras at the zoo in Paris, kissed one of her male cousins on the mouth? Was it true that her father, Emile Barte, was an aviator? Monette described him with such passion and in such detail that Aïcha ended up believing in the existence of this prodigy of the Meknes Flying Club. Monette explained to her the differences between T-33s, Piper Cubs and Vampires; she described the most dangerous stunts that her father could pull off. She said: 'I'll take you there one day, you'll see.' This promise became an obsession for Aïcha. There were only two thoughts in her head: an afternoon at the flying club and the return of her mother. She imagined that her friend's father could go and fetch Mathilde in one of his aeroplanes. If she asked him nicely, if she begged, he would probably agree to do her this little favour.

Monette drew in her prayer book. She added thick black moustaches to the paintings of saints and angels. After initially being shocked that someone could have so little fear of authority, Aïcha started to find her friend funny. Aïcha would watch, open-mouthed with admiration, as Monette played her little tricks. Several times the nuns begged her to tell on her friend. But Aïcha never did, and she discovered that she was loyal. One day Monette led her into the school toilets. It was so cold in there that most of the girls would hold it in for hours so that they didn't have to undress, teeth chattering as they squatted above the hole. Monette looked around. 'Watch the door,' she told Aïcha, whose heart was close to bursting. Aïcha said: 'Hurry up' and 'Have you nearly finished?' and 'But what on earth are you doing?' and 'We're going to get in trouble!' Monette took a glass bottle from under her blouse. She lifted up her woollen skirt and held the hem between her teeth. She pulled down her knickers and Aïcha, horrified, caught a glimpse of her bald vulva. Monette held the little bottle under it and pissed inside. The hot liquid ran from the neck down to the glass bottom and Aïcha started shaking, with fear and excitement. Then she felt her legs give way beneath her. She took a few steps back, getting ready to flee because she was starting to worry that she'd been lured into a trap and that Monette was going to make her drink the urine. She was too naive, she knew she was, and soon Monette would call out to the other girls in the class and they would all attack Aïcha, jamming the bottle's neck against her teeth and shouting, 'Drink! Drink!' But Monette pulled up her knickers, smoothed down her skirt and grabbed Aïcha's hand. 'Follow me,' she said, and they started to run along the gravel path towards the chapel. Aïcha's job was to stand watch outside the door, but she kept looking inside to see what Monette was up to. And so it was that she saw her friend pour the bottle's contents into the holy water font. From that day on, Aïcha would always shudder when she saw anyone, young or old, stick their fingers into the stoup and cross themselves.

'How long is a month?' Aïcha asked Mouilala as the old woman hugged her. 'Mama will be back,' her grandmother promised. Aïcha didn't like the way her grandmother smelled, the long orange strands of hair that escaped her headscarf, the henna that she put on the soles of her feet. And then there were her hands, so callused, so rough that even her caresses were scratchy. Those hands with their fingernails eroded by the water she used to clean the house, with their skin covered in little scars. Here the trace of a burn; there a gash dating from the feast day when she cut herself in the scullery. Despite her revulsion Aïcha would always seek refuge in the old woman's room when she was frightened. Mouilala laughed at her granddaughter's fearful nature and attributed it to her European origins. When voices rose from the dozens of mosques in town Aïcha would start to tremble. And when the prayer was over the muezzins would blow into enormous trumpets and the cavernous sound they made would terrorise the child. In a book that one of the nuns at school had shown her, the Archangel Gabriel held a similar gold-rimmed instrument. He was waking the dead for the Last Judgement.

One evening, as she was doing her homework with Selma, Aïcha heard doors banging and Omar yelling something. The girls abandoned their schoolbooks and leaned over the balustrade to look down on to the patio. Mouilala was standing next to the banana tree and in a low voice, with a harshness that Aïcha had never heard from her mouth before, she was threatening her son with reprisals. She walked over to the front door and Omar begged her: 'I can't send them out there now! This is about the future of our country, ya moui.' He kissed his mother's shoulder, then forcibly took hold of the hand she was refusing him and thanked her.

The old woman climbed the stairs, muttering bitter insults. Her sons were going to kill her! How had she offended Allah, what crimes had she committed to deserve those two sons who lived in her house? Jalil was possessed by demons and Omar had always caused her so much anxiety. Before the war he'd gone to a school in the new town where Kadour had managed to get him a place thanks to the intervention of a European friend. But with his father dead and his brother at war, Omar had no longer been held accountable for his actions. Several times he'd returned to Berrima with his face bloodied, his lips swollen. He'd liked fighting and carried a knife in his pocket. A fatherless son is a danger to all those around him, Mouilala had thought then. For several weeks he'd hidden from his mother the fact that he'd been expelled from school, and then she'd found out from a neighbour that Omar had arrived in class with a newspaper under his arm, yelling triumphantly: 'The Germans have taken Paris! That Hitler is a great man!' At the time, Mouilala had sworn that she would tell Amine everything when he returned from the war.

Omar was as handsome as his older brother but he had a stranger appearance: an angular face, high cheekbones, thin lips and thick brown hair. Above all he was much taller and the expression on his face was always so serious, so mean, that people often believed he was older than he really was. He'd worn glasses since the age of twelve, but despite being thick the lenses were not very effective, and that myopic look gave the impression that he was lost, that he was about to reach out and ask for help. That look frightened Aïcha. It was like being close to an animal that was starving or had just been beaten.

He would never have admitted it publicly, but during the war years Omar was glad that his older brother was absent. He often dreamed of Amine's corpse, ripped to pieces by a shell, rotting at the bottom of a trench. All he knew about war was what his own father had told him. The gas, the ditches full of rats and mud. He didn't know that war wasn't like that any more. Amine survived. Worse, he returned a hero, his chest weighed down by medals, his mouth full of wonderful stories. In 1940 Amine was taken prisoner and Omar had to pretend to be worried, upset. In 1943 he came home and Omar feigned relief, then admiration when his elder brother decided to return to the front as a volunteer. How many times had Omar had to listen to the stories of his brother's heroism, the escape from the camp and through icy fields where a poor farmer pretended that Amine was his employee? How many times had he had to laugh as Amine acted out his journey in a coal wagon and described the prostitute in Paris who gave him shelter? When his brother made a spectacle of himself, Omar smiled. He patted him on the shoulder and said: 'Spoken like a true Belhaj!' But it killed him to see girls hanging on his every word, licking their lips, giggling and wishing they could be taken by a war hero.

Omar hated his brother as much as he hated France. The war had been his vengeance, his moment of grace. He'd pinned so much hope on that conflict, imagining that he would be freed twice over. His brother would be killed and France would be defeated. In 1940, after the surrender, Omar took great delight in showing his contempt towards anyone who showed the slightest obsequiousness towards French people. He took pleasure in shoving past them in lines for the shops, spitting on the ladies' shoes. In the European town, he insulted the servants, caretakers and gardeners as they lowered their eyes and handed their work certificates to the French policemen who threatened them: 'As soon as your shift is over, you get out of here, understand?' He called on them to revolt, pointing at the signs on buildings forbidding natives to use the lifts or go swimming.

Omar cursed this town, this rancid and conformist society, these colonists and soldiers, these farmers and students who were convinced that they were living in paradise. For Omar, lust for life went hand in hand with an appetite for destruction. He wanted to destroy the lies, smash the images, melt down the language and forge from it all a new order, with himself as one of the masters. In 1942, during the 'year of vouchers', Omar had to survive on meagre rations. While Amine was a prisoner of war, Omar raged at being trapped in such a trivial battle. He knew that the French were entitled to twice as much as Moroccans. He'd heard that the natives didn't receive chocolate because it wasn't part of their usual diet. He made a few contacts among the black marketeers and offered to help them sell off their goods. Mouilala asked no questions about the origin of the dead chickens that Omar proudly tossed on to the kitchen counter-top, nor about the sugar or the coffee. She shook her head and sometimes even looked annoyed. This drove her son mad. The ingratitude killed him. Was this food too good for her? Couldn't she at least say thank you, given that he was feeding her, his sister, his crazy brother and that greedy slave? No, his mother only cared about Amine and that little idiot Selma. No matter what he did for his family or for his country, Omar felt misunderstood.

By the end of the war he had many friends in the secret organisations formed to overthrow French occupation. To start with, their leaders were reluctant to give him any responsibilities. They distrusted this impulsive boy, who was too impatient to listen to speeches on women's emancipation and who barked out his demand for armed conflict. 'Now! What are we waiting for?' Omar roughly pushed away the newspapers that his leaders encouraged him to read. Once, he lost his temper with a scarred Spaniard who had fought against Franco and claimed he was a communist. The man, who'd called for a proletarian uprising, was in favour of independence for all peoples. Omar insulted him, called him an infidel, mocked him for his fine speeches and said – as he always did – that actions spoke louder than words.

His faults were compensated by an unshakeable loyalty and physical courage that ultimately won over the cell's leaders. More and more often, he would disappear from the house for a few days or even a week. Mouilala had never told him this, but she was sick with worry whenever he went away. She got out of bed as soon as she heard the creak of the front door. She would blame poor Yasmine, then end up weeping in the slave's arms despite the repulsion she felt for her black skin. She spent whole nights praying and imagining that her son was in prison or that he'd been killed over some girl or politics. But he always came back, his eyes and ideas hardened by what he'd seen.

That evening, Omar had told his mother that there would be a meeting in her house and made her swear not to tell Amine. At first Mouilala had refused; she didn't want any trouble in her home, she refused to hide weapons inside these walls built by Kadour Belhaj himself. She wasn't interested in Omar's speeches about nationalism. He almost spat on the ground and told her: 'But when your son was fighting for the French, you were happy.' But he controlled himself and begged her instead, swallowing his shame and kissing her papery hands. 'I can't lose face. We're Muslims! We're nationalists. Long live Sidna Mohammed Ben Youssef!'

Mouilala was touchingly deferential towards the sultan. Mohammed Ben Youssef had a special place in her heart, all the more so since his exile. Like the other women, she would go up to the roof terrace at night to see the sovereign's face in the moon. She had been unhappy when Mathilde laughed at her tearful reaction to Sidna Mohammed's exile to the country of Madame Gascar. It was clear that her daughter-in-law hadn't believed her when she described how, upon his arrival on that strange island full of negroes, the elephants and tigers had prostrated themselves before the sultan and his family. Mohammed had performed a miracle in the aeroplane that took him to that cursed island. He and his family had almost crashed when one of the engines failed, but the sultan had placed his handkerchief on the fuselage and the plane had reached its destination without further difficulty. When she thought about the sultan and the Prophet, Mouilala finally gave in to her son's demands. She rushed upstairs so she wouldn't see those men coming into her house. Omar followed her and when he saw Aïcha, sitting on a step, he shoved her.

'You, move! Go on, get out of here. Don't just sit there like a bag of smid! You understand Arabic, nassrania? Semolina, your mother would call it. Now don't let me catch you spying on me again, you hear me?'

He raised his arm and showed her the palm of his hand and Aïcha thought that he could crush her against a wall, like those big green flies that Selma killed with her fingernails. Aïcha hurtled upstairs and slammed her bedroom door behind her, her forehead covered with sweat.

On 3 October 1954 Mathilde had flown to Le Bourget airport in Paris, and from there, in a smaller plane, to Mulhouse. The journey seemed interminable because she was so eager to pour out her anger at Irène. How dare her sister keep her away from her dying father? She'd taken Georges hostage, hoarding Papa's love for herself and covering his forehead with hypocritical kisses. In the plane Mathilde wept as she thought about her father calling for her and Irène lying to him. She imagined the words she would use, the things she would do once she was face to face with her sister. She relived one of those childhood scenes when Irène had goaded her into a rage and then laughed and called out: 'Papa, come and see. Little Mathilde looks like she's possessed!'

But when she landed in Mulhouse and a cool wind caressed her face, all her anger evaporated. Mathilde looked around like someone in a dream, half afraid that if she made a single wrong move, said a single wrong word, the entire landscape would dissolve before her eyes. As she handed her passport to the customs officer, she longed to tell him that she was from Mulhouse, that she was coming home. His Alsatian accent was so charming that she wanted to kiss him on both cheeks. Irène was waiting for her, thin and pale in her elegant mourning dress. She gently waved her black-gloved hand and Mathilde walked towards her. Irène looked older. She was wearing big glasses now, which made her look harsh and masculine. Just below her right nostril a few thick white hairs grew from a mole. She kissed Mathilde with such tenderness that Mathilde hardly recognised her. She thought about how they were orphans now, and this thought made her cry.

Mathilde was silent during the car journey to the house. The emotion of her return was so powerful that she was afraid of expressing what she was feeling and awakening her sister's cruel irony. The country she had left behind had rebuilt itself without her; the people she'd known had moved on. Her vanity was a little hurt by the idea that her absence had not prevented the lilacs from flowering or the square from being paved. Irène parked in the little side street opposite the house where they'd grown up. Mathilde, standing on the pavement, let her eyes linger over the garden where she'd spent so many hours playing and then looked up to see the office window where she'd so often glimpsed her father's imposing profile. Her heart stopped and she turned pale; she couldn't tell if it was the familiarity of the place that seemed so overpowering or quite the opposite: a disturbing sense of strangeness. As if by coming here she hadn't moved only through space but through time as well, back into the depths of the past.

In the first few days she had many visitors. She spent her afternoons drinking tea and eating cakes and after a week she'd regained all the weight she'd lost while bedridden with malaria. Some of her former classmates had children and others were pregnant; most had been transformed into domineering wives who complained about their husbands' fondness for the bottle or for easy women. They ate cherries soaked in eau de vie and gave them to their children too, staining their little mouths red and eventually sending them to sleep on the sofa in the entrance hall. Joséphine, who'd been her best friend in school and who now drank too much schnapps, told Mathilde how she'd found her husband with a woman one afternoon when she was supposed to be visiting her parents. 'They were doing it in my bed!' Her friends came because they wanted to find out if Mathilde's life was as disappointing as theirs had turned out to be. They wished to know if she too had experienced the wretched futility of married life, with its heavy silences, its loveless sex.

One afternoon a storm broke and the young women sat closer to the fireplace. Irène was growing somewhat weary of her sister's relentless vanity parade. But Mathilde had looked so grief-stricken kneeling in front of their father's gravestone that she couldn't refuse such innocent distractions. 'Tell us about life in Africa! You lucky sod – we've never even been out of the country.'

'Well, it's not as exotic as all that, really,' Mathilde simpered. 'To start with, of course, you feel like you've landed on another planet, but soon after that you have to deal with all the mundane chores – and they're the same in Morocco as anywhere else.'

She could tell that they were hungry for more detail and she enjoyed the anticipation that she read in the eyes of these housewives who looked so much older than her. Mathilde lied. She lied about her life, about her husband's personality, she gave rambling speeches punctuated by high-pitched laughter. She kept repeating that her husband was a modern man, an agricultural genius who single-handedly ran an immense farm. She talked about 'her' patients and described the clinic where she performed miracles, concealing from them her lack of knowledge or resources.

The next day Irène ushered Mathilde into their father's office and handed her an envelope. 'This is part of your inheritance.' Mathilde didn't dare open it, but she hefted the envelope's thickness and had to force herself not to smile with joy. 'You know Papa wasn't a very prudent businessman. When I went through his account books I discovered certain aberrations. We'll go to see the notary in a few days so he can clear that up and you can go back to Morocco with peace of mind.' Mathilde had been in Alsace for almost three weeks now and Irène kept mentioning her departure with increasing frequency. She asked if Mathilde had booked her flight yet, if she'd received a letter from her husband, who she imagined was desperate to see her again. But Mathilde turned a deaf ear to her sister's insinuations and managed to insulate herself from the thought that she had a life elsewhere, that people were waiting for her return.

She left the office, envelope in hand, and told her sister that was going to town. 'I have some shopping to do before I go back.' She ran on to the high street as into the arms of a lover. She was shaking with excitement and had to take two deep breaths before entering an elegant shop run by a man named Auguste. She tried on two dresses, one black and one mauve, and it took her a long time to decide between them. She bought the mauve dress but left the boutique in a dark mood, irritated at having had to choose and already wishing she'd bought the black dress, which made her look thinner. On the way home she swung her shopping bag like a little girl returning from school and daydreaming about throwing her schoolbooks in a ditch. In the shop window of the most elegant milliner's in town she caught sight of a wide-brimmed straw hat from Italy, decorated with a red ribbon. Mathilde climbed the steps that led to the front door and a salesman opened it for her. He was elderly and rather affected; a queer, thought Mathilde, who was disappointed by the shop's sad-looking interior.

'How may I help you, madame?'

Without a word she pointed at the hat with the ribbon.

'Of course.'

The man glided along the floorboards and slowly extricated the hat from its window display. Mathilde tried it on and when she saw herself in the mirror she felt startled. She looked like a woman, a real woman, a sophisticated Parisienne, a member of the bourgeoisie. She thought about her sister, who always said that vanity was the devil's domain and that it was sinful to admire oneself in a mirror. The salesman paid her a half-hearted compliment then seemed to grow impatient because Mathilde kept adjusting the hat, moving it an inch to the right and then to the left. For a long time she stared at the price on the label, before drifting into a deep, complicated series of thoughts. A man came into the boutique and the salesman held out his hand for the hat, looking annoyed.

The man walked up to Mathilde and said: 'Beautiful.'

She blushed and took off the hat, which she then moved slowly over her chest, unaware of how sensual and flirtatious she looked.

'You, mademoiselle, are not from around here. I would bet that you're an artist. Am I right?'

'Absolutely,' she replied. 'I work at the theatre. I've just been hired for the season.'

She headed towards the counter and took the envelope of cash from her bag. While the salesman packaged up the hat with incredible slowness, Mathilde answered the young man's questions. He was wearing an elegant overcoat and a khaki felt hat that half-concealed his eyes. She dug herself deeper into the lie, with a mixture of shame and excitement. The salesman crossed the room and, standing by the glass door, handed the package to Mathilde. When the man in the overcoat asked if he could see her again, she replied: 'Unfortunately I'm very busy with rehearsals. But you must come and see me perform one night.'

When she arrived at the house she felt ashamed of all the packages she was carrying. She walked quickly through the living room and locked herself in her bedroom, her face flushed with happiness. She took a bath and moved the gramophone from her father's office to her bedside table. She'd been invited to a party that evening and as she got ready she listened to an old German song that Georges had loved.

At the party the women complimented her on her mauve dress and the men stared, smiling, at her smooth silk stockings. She drank sparkling wine so dry that, after an hour, her mouth was like a desert and she had to drink more in order to keep talking. Everyone asked about her African life and they kept getting Morocco mixed up with Algeria. 'So you speak Arabic?' asked one charming man. She downed the glass of red wine that someone had handed her and spoke a sentence in Arabic that drew thunderous applause.

She went home alone and savoured the pleasure of walking in the street without anyone chaperoning her or spying on her.

She staggered slightly as she hummed a dirty song that made her laugh. She climbed the stairs on tiptoe and lay on her bed without taking off her dress or her stockings. She was happy to be tipsy and alone, happy to be able to invent a life without fear of contradiction. She turned and buried her face in the pillow to suppress the sudden nausea that had overcome her. A sob rose through her body. A sob born of her joy. She cried because she was so happy without them. Eyes closed, nose pressed against the pillow, she let herself think a secret little thought, a shameful thought that had been nesting in her brain for days now. A thought that Irène must have guessed at, and which explained her anxious looks. That night, as she listened to the wind in the leaves of the poplars, Mathilde thought: I'm staying here. Yes, it occurred to her that she could not go back to Morocco, that she could – even if the words were impossible to speak aloud – abandon her children. The violence of this idea made her want to cry out and she had to bite the sheet. But the idea wouldn't leave her. On the contrary, it grew clearer and more concrete in her mind. A new life seemed possible and she began to think about all its advantages. Of course, there was Aïcha, there was Selim. There was Amine's skin and the infinitely blue sky of her new country. But with time and distance the pain would ease. Her children would hate her, they would suffer, but eventually, perhaps, they would manage to forget her and they would be as happy on their side of the sea as she was on hers. Perhaps there would even come a day when they felt as if they'd never met, like perfect strangers whose destinies had always been separate. There is no tragedy that cannot be overcome, thought Mathilde. Even after a disaster you can still rebuild your life on the ruins of the old one.

People would judge her, of course. All those speeches she'd made about the beauty of her life in Morocco would be thrown back in her face. 'So why don't you go back if you're so happy there?' In fact she could already sense her neighbours' impatience; it was time for her to return to her life, time to get back to her dreary, peaceful routine. Furious with herself, with fate, with the whole world, Mathilde wondered if she might go somewhere else instead, to Strasbourg or Paris, where nobody knew her. She could go to university, become a doctor, even a surgeon. She devised impossible scenarios that made her guts twist. She had the right to put herself first, didn't she? She sat up in the middle of the bed, nauseous, head spinning. Her pulse was beating hard in her temples, making it impossible to think. Was she going crazy? Was she one of those women with no maternal instincts? She closed her eyes and lay down again. Vague images travelled with her as she slowly fell asleep. That night she dreamed of Meknes and the fields that stretched out around the farm. She saw the cows with their sad eyes and jutting ribs and the beautiful white birds that flew down to eat the parasites from their backs. Her dream mutated into a nightmare, filled with distressed lowing. Peasants as thin as their animals brought their sticks down on the cows' necks as they chewed the toxic grass. They squatted down and tied the cows' hind legs together with rope to stop them running away.

The next morning she woke in her dress, with her stockings around her ankles. Her head ached so badly that she found it hard to keep her eyes open during breakfast. Irène drank her tea slowly, bit into a slice of bread covered in jam and took care not to stain her newspaper. Ever since her sister had left France all those years ago, Irène had eagerly devoured news of the colonies. When Mathilde came into the dining room, she was cutting out an article about clashes in the countryside and negotiations between the sultan and the Resident-General. Mathilde shrugged. 'Maybe . . . I don't know.' She wasn't in the mood to make conversation. Little surges of bile kept burning her throat and she had to take deep breaths to stop herself throwing up.

She had not had an argument with Irène since she'd come back to France. During the first few days she'd felt like she was treading on eggshells: one word out of place, she thought, and everything would be ruined, the old disagreements would resurface. But a new complicity had developed between the two sisters. As children they'd competed with each other for their parents' love, so no sibling tenderness had been possible. But now they were alone in the world, the sole memory-keepers of the dead. Distance and age had pared things back to their essential core, erased all pettiness.

Mathilde lay on the living room sofa and dozed through the rest of the day. Irène stayed with her, covering her bare feet and turning away all visitors. When she woke it was dark outside. A fire was burning in the hearth and Irène was knitting. Mathilde felt sad and groggy. She thought back to her ridiculous behaviour at the party the night before and embarrassment washed over her. Irène must think her childish. Mathilde sat up and turned her feet towards the fire. She felt a need to talk. This place was her refuge; here she would find consolation. In this living room, against the quiet background of the clicking needles and the crackling fire, she told Irène about her husband. His outbursts. She didn't go into too many details, nothing that would sound like a lie or an exaggeration. She said just enough and she felt certain that Irène understood. She talked about the farm's isolation, the fear that tormented her in the dark night when the silence was broken only by the howling of jackals. She tried to make her sister understand what it was like to live in a world where she had no place, a world governed by unfair, repulsive rules, where men never had to justify themselves, where she was not allowed to cry if her feelings were hurt. She started sobbing as she described the long days and the vast solitude, the yearning she felt for home and childhood. She had never guessed how lonely exile was. She folded her legs under her and turned to face her sister, who was staring into the flames. Mathilde wasn't afraid, because she believed her sincerity would overcome her sister's qualms. She wasn't ashamed of her tear-stained cheeks, her rambling words. She didn't care about playing a role any more; she was content to let Irène see her for what she was: a woman prematurely aged by failure and disillusionment, a woman without pride. She had told her sister everything and now that she'd finished she looked at Irène, who sat motionless.

'You made a choice. Now you have to live with it. Life is hard for everyone, you know.'

Mathilde hung her head. How stupid she had been to hope for a shred of compassion! How ashamed she felt now at having believed, even for an instant, that she might be afforded some understanding, some consolation. Mathilde didn't know how to react to such cold indifference. She would have preferred it if her sister had mocked her, lost her temper, said 'I told you so!' It would have seemed natural for Irène to blame

Arabs, Muslims, men for Mathilde's unhappiness. But this coldness left her shrivelled and silent. She was convinced that her sister had been preparing her reply for a long time, that she'd been chewing over it, waiting for the right moment to throw it in her face. It wouldn't have taken much to persuade Mathilde not to leave France again, to give up on this crazy idea of being a foreigner, living abroad, suffering in solitude. Irène stood up without glancing at her sister. She did not open her arms. She was going to let Mathilde drown. At the foot of the stairs Irène called out: 'You should go to bed now. We have an appointment with the notary in the morning.'

* * *

They left after breakfast. When Irène got in the car, she still had a few breadcrumbs stuck to her lips. They arrived early at the notary's office, on the first floor of an opulent-looking building. A young woman opened the door and showed them into a cold waiting room. They kept their coats on and their mouths shut. They were strangers once again. When the door opened, they turned towards it and Mathilde let out a small cry. Standing in front of her was the young man from the boutique. The man who'd admired her hat. She gave him her clammy hand and looked at him imploringly. Irène, oblivious to all this, walked into the office.

'Hello, Maître.' He let them go through and gestured to two chairs facing his solid wooden desk. The young man had taken over from the old notary, who'd drunk himself to death. He smiled like a blackmailer at a powerless victim.

'So, madame, how is life in Morocco?'

'Very good, thank you.'

'Your sister explained to me that you live in Meknes.'

She nodded, looking away from the notary, who leaned over his desk like a cat ready to pounce on its prey. He looked through a file, took out a document and turned back to Mathilde: 'Tell me, are there any theatres in Meknes?'

'Absolutely,' she replied in an ice-cold voice. 'But my husband and I are very busy with work. I have better things to do than having fun.'

VI

Mathilde flew back on 2 November. Aïcha was allowed to miss school that day and she waited for her mother by the road, sitting on a wooden crate. When she saw her father's car arrive she stood up and waved. The flowers that she'd collected that morning had all wilted so she decided not to give them to her mother. Amine braked a few feet from the gate and Mathilde got out. She was wearing a new dress, some elegant brown leather shoes and a straw summer hat, incongruous in the November cold. Aïcha stared at her, her heart overflowing with love. Her mother was a soldier back from the front, a wounded but victorious soldier, hiding her secrets under her medals. She held her daughter close and buried her nose in the child's neck, her fingers in her curly hair. Aïcha looked so slight, so fragile, that Mathilde was afraid she might crack one of her ribs if she hugged her too tightly.

They walked hand in hand to the house and Selim appeared, in Tamo's arms. He'd changed a great deal in the past month and Mathilde thought he'd got fatter because the food that the maid cooked for him was too greasy. But that day nothing could vex or anger her. She was calm and serene because she had resigned herself to her fate and decided to embrace it, to make the most of it. As she entered the house, as she walked through the living room filled with winter sunlight, as she had her suitcase carried up to her bedroom, she thought that it was doubt that was the problem, it was choice that created pain, that gnawed away at the soul. Now she'd made her decision, now she knew that there was no escaping this life, she felt strong. The strength that comes from not being free. She thought about the pathetic liar she'd been, the actress in an imaginary theatre, and she recalled a line from Racine's *Andromaque* that she'd learned at school: 'Blindly I follow now the fate that claims me.'

All day long the children wouldn't let her out of their sight. They clung to her legs and she made it a game, trying to walk forward with those weights on her calves. She opened her suitcase with solemnity, as if it were a treasure chest, and took out cuddly toys, children's books, strawberry bonbons covered with icing sugar. In Alsace she had put away her own childhood; she'd tied it up, silenced it and shoved it to the back of a drawer. She would no longer think about her own naive dreams, her childish whims. She drew her children to her chest, lifted them up, one in each arm, and rolled on the bed with them. She kissed them passionately and in the kisses that she planted on their cheeks there was not only the strength of her love but the burning intensity of her regrets. She loved them all the more because of all the things she'd given up for them: happiness, passion, freedom. She thought: I hate myself for being chained like this; I hate myself not preferring anything to you. She placed Aïcha in her lap and read her stories. 'Again!' the child begged, and Mathilde obeyed. She had brought a whole suitcase of books, and Aïcha caressed the cover of each one with a religious fervour before opening it. She was intrigued and frightened by Struwwelpeter, with his tangled hair and his claw-like nails. Selim said: 'He looks like you', and that made her cry.

* * *

On 16 November 1954 Aïcha turned seven, and Mathilde decided to organise a birthday party at the farm. She made the beautiful invitations herself, with a little slip of paper on which the parents could indicate whether their children would attend or not. Every evening she would ask Aïcha if her classmates had responded yet. 'Geneviève isn't coming. Her parents won't let her. They say she'd catch fleas and diarrhoea because we live in the back of beyond.' Mathilde shrugged. 'Geneviève is an idiot and her parents are morons. Don't worry, we'll be better off without them.'

For a week the party was all Mathilde talked about. In the mornings, in the car, she would describe the cake she was going to order from the best patisserie in town, the garlands that she would make from crêpe paper, the games from her childhood that she would teach them and that they would love so much. She looked so happy and enthusiastic that Aïcha didn't have the heart to tell her the truth. Her classmates taunted her constantly. She was the youngest girl in her year and the other girls were forever pulling her hair and pushing her on the stairs. They hated her even more because she was top of the class and won all the prizes for Latin, mathematics and spelling. 'It's a good thing you're clever. You're so ugly that no one will ever want to marry you.' In chapel, kneeling next to Monette, Aïcha sullied herself with evil thoughts and hateful prayers. She prayed that the other girls would die. She dreamed that they would suffocate, catch incurable diseases, fall from trees and break their legs. *'Forgive us our trespasses, as we forgive those that trespass against us.'* But she never actually did anything stupid, never carried out any of her fantasies of vengeance. She suppressed her jealousy towards Selim and balled her fists tightly when the urge came over her to pinch the little boy whom her mother stared at with such hurtful tenderness. Since Mathilde's return, Aïcha had heard her father complain several times about the constant shuttling between home and school. 'It's ruining our health,' he'd said. 'It's wearing out the children.' Aïcha made herself as quiet and invisible as possible after that because she lived in terror that her parents would force her to board at school and she'd see her mother only on weekends, like most of the other girls.

* * *

The day of her birthday party arrived. It was a wet, gloomy Sunday. When she woke, Aïcha stood on her bed and looked through the window at the branches of the almond trees shivering in the wind. The sky was sad and crumpled, like a bedsheet after a night of bad dreams. A man in a brown homespun djellaba walked past, the hood over his head, and the child heard the sound of mud squelching under his shoes. At noon the wind died down and the rain ceased, but the sky was still obscured by grey clouds and there was the hint of a storm in the air. It's so unfair, thought Mathilde: the sky here is always so blue, and today of all days the sun disappears.

Amine had to go to the patisserie to pick up the cake, then to the school where three girls – who did not get to go home on weekends – had accepted Aïcha's invitation. Amine was running late. Twice he had to park by the side of the road and wait for the rain to stop because his windscreen wipers didn't work properly and he couldn't see where he was going. He had to wait at the patisserie. There'd been some mix-up and his daughter's cake had been given to someone else. 'There aren't any strawberries left,' the woman explained. Amine shrugged. 'Never mind, I just need a cake.'

At the farm Mathilde paced impatiently. She'd decorated the living room and set the dining room table with plates that had paintings of scenes from life in Alsace. She walked around the house, nervous and irritated, the most terrible scenarios running through her head. Aïcha didn't move. With her nose pressed to the bay window, she stared at the sky as if trying to move away the clouds and make the sun appear with only the power of her thoughts. What could they do in this dusty house? What games could they play indoors? She wanted to take them running through the countryside, show them her hiding places in the trees, the donkey in the stable that was too old to work, and the horde of cats that Mathilde had tamed. *'Lord, give me strength, You who love everyone.'*

At last Amine arrived, his clothes soaked, holding a cake box covered with cream stains. Behind him were Monette and three scared-looking girls.

'Aïcha, go and say hello to your friends,' Mathilde said, pushing her daughter's back.

Aïcha wished she could vanish. She'd have given anything for those girls to be taken back to their homes, for her to be left in solitude, out of danger. But Mathilde started singing, like a woman possessed, and Selim clapped his hands. The girls tried to sing along; they got the words mixed up and dissolved into laughter. Mathilde blindfolded Aïcha and spun her around.

Blindly she advanced, hands groping forward, guided by her classmates' stifled giggles. At five o'clock the daylight faded. Mathilde shouted: 'I think it's time!' and she went into the kitchen, leaving behind the little girls who had nothing to say to each other. When she opened the box she almost wept. It wasn't the cake she'd ordered. Hands shaking with rage, she put it on a plate and Aïcha heard her mother's voice singing: 'Happy birthday to you . . . Happy birthday to you . . .' Kneeling on her chair, Aïcha leaned in close to the candles, and just as she was about to blow them out her mother stopped her. 'You should make a wish first. But keep it secret.'

They turned on the lamps. Ginette, whose nose wouldn't stop running, started to whine. She was scared here and she wanted to go home. Mathilde put her face close to the girl's and reassured her, but what she wanted to do was shake the little brat and tell her to stop being so selfish. Couldn't she see that today wasn't about her? But the expressions on the faces of the other girls, with the exception of Monette, suddenly changed.

'We want to go home too. Ask your chauffeur to take us back.'

'Our chauffeur?' Mathilde thought about Amine's sullen face, the brutal way he'd slammed the cake box on the kitchen table. So those children had thought he was the chauffeur and he hadn't contradicted them . . .

Mathilde started to laugh. She was about to clear this matter up when Aïcha exclaimed: 'Mama, can the chauffeur take them home?'

Aïcha stared at her mother with the same dark gaze as when she'd been punished and she seemed to hate the entire world. Mathilde's heart contracted and she slowly nodded. The little girls followed her like ducklings to the office, where Amine had locked himself in. He'd spent the afternoon there, trying to calm himself down by smoking cigarettes and cutting articles from a magazine. The schoolgirls mumbled their goodbyes to Aïcha and got in the back of the car.

It had started raining again, so Amine drove slowly. The three girls fell asleep, heads on each other's shoulders, and Ginette snored. They're only children, Amine reminded himself. You have to forgive them.

* * *

The following Thursday, Mathilde took her children to a photography studio on Rue Lafayette. The photographer sat them on a stool in front of a backdrop representing Notre-Dame Cathedral. Selim refused to keep still and Mathilde lost her temper. She fixed Aïcha's hair and adjusted the collar of her white dress. 'Good . . . Now, whatever you do, don't move!' On the back of the picture Mathilde wrote down the date and the place. She put it in an envelope and wrote to Irène: 'Aïcha is top of her class and Selim is learning very quickly. Yesterday was Aïcha's seventh birthday. They're my pride and joy. They're my vengeance on all those who humiliate us.'

One evening, as they were finishing dinner, a man knocked at the door. In the darkness of the entrance hall Amine didn't at first recognise his former army comrade. Mourad was soaked from the rain and shivering in his wet clothes. With one hand he kept his coat closed; with the other he shook water from his cap. Mourad had lost his teeth and he spoke like an old man, chewing the insides of his cheeks. Amine pulled him inside and hugged him so tightly that he could feel all his ribs. He started laughing. He didn't care about getting his clothes wet. 'Mathilde! Mathilde!' he yelled, dragging Mourad into the living room. Mathilde let out a cry. She remembered her husband's orderly, a shy, delicate man for whom she'd felt an affectionate friendship that she'd never been able to express. 'He needs to change – he's soaked to the bone. Mathilde, go and get him some clothes.' But Mourad was not having this. He waved his hands frantically in front of his face. No, he would not take his commander's shirt, he would not borrow a pair of shoes from him and certainly not a vest. Never could he do such a thing; it would be indecent. 'Don't be ridiculous!' said Amine. 'The war is over.' These words were like a slap in the face for Mourad. They made him uncomfortable, creating a sort of whistling in his head, and he felt that Amine had said them only to wound him.

In the bathroom, the walls covered in blue earthenware tiles, Mourad undressed. He avoided glancing at his skeletal reflection in the large mirror. What was the point of examining this body devastated by war, childhood poverty and years spent wandering foreign roads? On the edge of the sink Mathilde had left him a clean towel and a bar of soap in the shape of a seashell. He washed his armpits, his neck, his hands and forearms. He took off his shoes and put his feet in a bowl filled with cold water. Then, reluctantly, he put on his commander's clothes.

He left the bathroom and walked down the hallway of this unknown house, guided by voices. He heard the child's voice asking: 'Who is that man?' and 'Tell me about the war again!' He heard Mathilde's voice, begging for the window to be opened because the cooker was smoking. And, at last, he heard Amine's voice, impatient: 'Where on earth's he got to? Do you think I should go and make sure he's all right?' Before entering the kitchen where they were all gathered, Mourad stopped and observed them through the half-open door. His body was slowly warming up again. He closed his eyes and breathed in the smell of coffee. A feeling of sweetness came over him and made his head spin. It was like a sob impossible to stifle. He cleared his throat and widened his eyes to rid himself of the taste of salt that had filled his mouth. Amine was sitting opposite his messy-haired daughter. It felt like centuries since Mourad had seen all this. A woman busy in the kitchen, a child smiling, gestures of tenderness. Mourad thought that he had, perhaps, finally reached his destination. That he had come to a good place where his nightmares would no longer pursue him.

He went in and the adults said, 'Ah!' while the little girl stared at him. All four of them sat around the table, which Mathilde set with a tablecloth she'd embroidered herself.

Mourad drank his coffee, sip by sip, his hands gripping the enamel cup tightly. Amine didn't ask him where he'd come from or what he was doing there. He smiled and put his hand on Mourad's shoulder and kept repeating: 'What a wonderful surprise!' and 'I'm so happy to see you!' All evening long they shared memories as the little girl listened, fascinated, and begged them not to send her to bed. They talked about the boat trip that had taken them towards civilised, warlike men in September 1944. At the port of La Ciotat they'd sung together to give themselves courage. 'Are you a good singer, Papa? What did you sing?'

Amine had made fun of his aide-de-camp, Private Mourad, who was amazed by everything and kept tugging on his sleeve to whisper questions. 'Do they have poor people here?' he'd asked. In the fields of southern France he'd been surprised to see white women, women who looked just like the ones in his country, who never spoke to him unless they were forced to. Mourad liked to say that he had enrolled to defend France, this country he knew nothing about but which – he didn't know why – governed his destiny. 'France is my mother, France is my father.' The truth was: he'd had no choice. When the French had arrived in his village, fifty miles from Meknes, they'd gathered all the men who were not too old or too young or too sick and pointed at the back of a van. 'Go to war or go to prison,' they'd said. So Mourad had gone to war. Not once had it crossed his mind that a prison cell might have been more comfortable or safer than the battlefields of that snow-covered land. Anyway, it wasn't their blackmail that had convinced him. It wasn't the fear of shame or incarceration. Nor was it the bonus he was given for joining the army or the wages that he could send home to his family, for which his mother was so grateful. Later, when he joined the Spahi Regiment where Amine was a lance corporal, he realised that he'd been right. That something great had happened to him. That he'd given his life – his poor, ordinary peasant's life – an unexpected grandeur, a nobility of which he wasn't even worthy. Sometimes he had no longer been sure if it was for France or for Amine that he felt ready to die.

When he thought back to the war, Mourad was struck by the memory of silence. The noise of bombs, rifles and shouting had faded away and all that remained in his mind was the memory of things unspoken, of those men of few words. Amine had told him to keep his head down and not do anything that would get him noticed. They had to fight, win, and then go home. Don't make a scene. Don't ask questions. From La Ciotat they'd travelled east and been greeted as liberators. Men had opened the best bottles of wine in their honour and women waved little flags. 'Vive la France! Vive la France!' One day a child had pointed at Amine and said, 'Negro.'

Mourad had been there when Amine saw Mathilde for the first time, during the autumn of 1944. Their regiment was stationed in a small village a few miles from Mulhouse. She invited them to dinner at her house that evening. She apologised in advance: 'Rationing,' she said, and the soldiers nodded. They were shown into the living room and it was full of people. Villagers, other soldiers, old gentlemen already struggling to walk straight. They gathered around a long wooden table and Mathilde sat facing Amine, watching him greedily. To her, this officer seemed heaven-sent. What upset her at that time was not the war but the absence of adventures.

She'd been walled up for four years with no new clothes to wear, no new books to read, and Amine was like the answer to all her prayers. She was nineteen and hungry for life, and the war had taken it from her.

Mathilde's father entered the living room singing a dirty song and everyone joined in. Amine and Mourad remained silent. They stared at this giant with his huge belly and his black moustache without a single grey hair. They all sat down for the meal. Mourad was pushed ever closer to Amine. A man sat at the piano and the guests linked arms and sang together. They called for food. The women, their cheeks covered in rosacea, put large plates of cold meat and cabbage on the table. They served tankards of beer and Mathilde's father yelled for schnapps. Mathilde pushed the plate to Amine. They were the soldiers of the Liberation, after all, so they should be served first. Amine stabbed a sausage with his fork. He said, 'Thank you', and ate.

Beside him Mourad trembled. He was as pale as a ghost and sweat was pouring down the back of his neck. All this noise, these women, the indecent songs . . . It all made him uneasy and reminded him of the Bousbir in Casablanca, the red-light district where some French soldiers had once taken him. He'd been haunted ever since by those men's laughter, by the brutal way they'd acted. They'd stuck fingers in the vagina of a girl his sister's age. They'd pulled the prostitutes' hair and sucked their breasts, not with sensuality but as if they were purging an animal's teats. The girls' bodies had been covered in purple love bites and red scratches.

Mourad pressed close to his commander. He tugged on his sleeve and Amine grew annoyed. 'What's the matter?' he asked in Arabic. 'Can't you see I'm talking to someone?' But Mourad insisted. He looked at Amine with panic-stricken eyes. Pointing at the plates on the table, he said: 'That's pork, isn't it? And that . . .' – here he gestured with his eyebrows at the glasses – '. . . that's alcohol, isn't it?' Amine stared at him and said coldly: 'Shut up and eat.'

'What's the big deal?' he asked later, while they were walking through the dark village streets to their barracks. 'What are you scared of? Going to hell? We've already been, remember, and we got out alive.'

Hadn't they dreamed of a warm room, a full plate, a young woman's smile when they were marching behind the SS, who'd taken them prisoner after the battle of La Horgne in May 1940? They'd walked for hours, days, and Mourad had insisted on carrying Amine's kit. What did any of this have to do with them? All they'd wanted was a small farm, on a hill far from this land. They had no enemies they could name and, faced with giant men who spoke an unknown language, they'd thrown down their weapons and stood in line. One night when they'd stopped beside a field, they'd scratched at the icy ground in total darkness. Silently they'd dug up tiny potatoes and eaten them, taking care not to make any noise as they chewed. That night all the men had vomited and some had soiled themselves. When day broke and they were told to start marching again, they'd taken one last look at the field. It was criss-crossed with thin, ragged furrows, as if small creatures with sharp claws had been tearing at the earth. Then they had taken a train to a POW camp near Dortmund. 'Tell me about the camp!' Aïcha asked now, fighting against her heavy eyelids. 'We'll save the camp stories for later,' Amine promised. He was exhausted by these reminiscences.

Amine guided Mourad to the end of the hallway and opened a door into a small bedroom with floral-print wallpaper. Mourad didn't dare go inside. He was embarrassed by the room's delicate femininity. On the bedside table was a carafe of water with a bouquet of violets painted on its side. Mathilde had made frilly curtains for the windows and the bed was covered with a pile of colourful cushions. Mourad, who'd been expecting to sleep on a bench or even the kitchen floor, was dumbstruck. 'Stay with us as long as you like,' Amine told him reassuringly. 'I'm glad you came.'

Mourad undressed and slipped between the fresh sheets. The house was perfectly quiet but he couldn't sleep. He opened the window, threw the sheets on the floor, but nothing could calm his anxiety. He was in such a panic that he felt like getting out of bed, putting on his drenched jacket and vanishing into the night. This sweetness, this brightness, this human warmth . . . It was not for the likes of him. He had no right, he thought, to bring his sins here, to stain these people's lives with his secrets. In his bed Mourad felt ashamed of not having told Amine everything. When he discovers the truth, Mourad thought, he'll kick me out, insult me, accuse me of taking advantage of his generosity.

Mourad wished he could put his hand on Amine's and let his head rest on his commander's shoulder, breathe in his scent. He wished that their embrace, on the doorstep, could have lasted forever. He'd pretended, like the hypocrite he was, to be delighted to see Mathilde and the children, but in fact he'd have preferred it if they weren't there, if there'd been nobody in this house but him and the commander. Earlier he'd worn Amine's vest and shirt and felt a dizzying lust that he repented now. How shameful this was! Tears rose to his eyes as he felt his cock harden, his guts twist with desire. He tried to rid his mind of the images. He bit his hand. He had to stop thinking about this, just like he had to stop thinking about the corpses, the torn bodies rotting in muddy pools, the terrible monsoon that drove his comrades mad in Indochina, the dark oozing blood of those who'd decided to kill themselves rather than go back into battle. He had to stop thinking about the war and he had to stop thinking about the crazy, overpowering need he felt to seek tenderness in the arms of Amine.

He had come to this place and now it was impossible for him to make the decision to leave. The truth was that he had deserted with only one thought in mind, only one objective. All those nights that he'd spent walking, that he'd hidden in cattle wagons, in barns and cellars, all those days when, dazed with fatigue, he'd fallen asleep in train stations, forgetting even his fear, it had been Amine's face that led him onward. He thought about his commander's smile, that lopsided smile that showed only half of his white teeth. He'd have crossed another continent for that smile. And while the other soldiers held photographs of bare-legged dolls to their hearts, while they wanked over memories of some whore's milk-engorged breasts or some vague fiancée, Mourad had sworn to find his commander again.

The next morning Amine was waiting for him in the kitchen. Mathilde was sitting with Aïcha on her lap, the two of them deep in contemplation of an anatomical drawing of the kidneys. Selim, who smelled of urine, was playing on the floor with some empty saucepans. 'Ah, there you are!' said Amine.

'I was thinking about this all night, and I have a proposal for you. Come on, let's talk while we walk.' Mathilde handed Mourad a cup of coffee, which he downed in a single mouthful. Amine picked up his jacket and sunglasses, kissed his wife on the shoulder and gently stroked her bottom with his fingertips. 'Go on, get out of here,' she said with a laugh.

They walked towards the stables. 'I wanted to show you everything I've done here in only five years. A few months ago I hired a foreman, a young Frenchman recommended by my neighbour, the Mercier widow. He was a good boy, honest and hard-working, but he went back to France not long ago. There's a lot of work here and a lot of potential. I'd like you to help me. If you can stay, I'll make you my new foreman.' Mourad walked in silence, in step with his commander. He knew nothing about agriculture, but he'd grown up in the countryside and no mission seemed impossible to him if Amine was the one giving him orders. Amine showed him the plantations of fruit trees that now covered a large part of the property. He talked about his passion for the olive tree, a noble tree on which he was attempting several experiments. 'I'd like to build a greenhouse to grow my own plants and increase productivity. We'd need to create a nursery and install a heating and humidification system. And I need time to devote to my studies and to the development of new varieties.' Face red with excitement, Amine squeezed Mourad's hand. 'I have a meeting with the Chamber of Agriculture today. We can talk more about this when I return, if that's all right?'

That evening Mourad accepted the offer and moved into the storeroom near the giant palm tree, ten feet from the house. At night he could hear the sound of rats climbing the creeper that wound around the huge trunk. He had few needs: a camp bed, a blanket that he folded every morning with irritating care, a mess tin and a large pitcher of water to give himself a cursory wash. He would not have been shocked or put off had they told him to shit in the fields, but he was allowed to use the outside toilets, which had been set up in the kitchen courtyard for Tamo, the maid (who was not allowed to piss in the same place that Mathilde pissed). Mourad treated the labourers with military strictness, and in less than three weeks the whole village hated him. 'The secret of all victorious armies is discipline,' he repeated. He was even worse than certain Frenchmen, the ones who locked shirkers in a box room or whipped them. This man, the fellahs complained, was worse than a foreigner. He was a traitor, a sell-out, and he belonged to the race of slave traffickers who built empires on the backs of their own people.

One day, while Mourad and Achour were walking past Mariani's farm, the labourer noisily cleared his throat and spat on the ground. 'A curse on you!' he yelled, staring at the property's fence. 'Those colonists took our best land, our water and our trees.' Mourad told him to shut up, then asked, in a serious voice: 'What do you think there was here, before he came? They're the ones who drilled for water, they're the ones who planted the trees. They lived in poverty when they first came here, didn't they? In mud huts with corrugated-iron roofs? Huh? So shut your mouth! We're not here to talk politics, we're here to work.' Mourad decided to take a roll call every morning and he blamed Amine for never having formalised the labourers' working hours. 'Without authority there's only anarchy. How do you expect your farm to flourish if you let them do whatever they want?'

Mourad would be out with his machines from dawn until dusk and he didn't even leave the fields to eat lunch. The labourers didn't want to eat with him, so he sat alone in the shade of a tree, chewing his bread and staring at the ground so he wouldn't see the taunting eyes of his men.

In the days after he started working at the farm, Mourad set about solving the water problem. With an old Pontiac engine he created a pump house. He hired a few men to drill for water. When it started spurting out of the earth the workers yelled with joy. They held their callused hands under the jet, splashed the cool water over their wind-burned faces and thanked God for His generosity. But Mourad was not as magnanimous as Allah. At night he organised 'water guards' to protect the well. Two trusted workers took it in turns to stand in front of the hole with rifles on their shoulders. They'd light a fire to keep the dogs and jackals away and fight to stay awake until the changing of the guard.

Mourad wanted Amine to be happy and proud of him. He didn't care if the labourers hated him; his only obsession was satisfying his commander. Every day, Amine delegated more and more tasks to Mourad, devoting himself to his experiments and numerous meetings with the bank. He was often absent, leaving Mourad in despair. When he'd accepted this job, Mourad had imagined being as close to Amine as he'd been during the war, the two of them enjoying the country air, walking for hours, confronting danger together and laughing, as men do, at stupid jokes. He'd thought that their old complicity would return and that – despite the permanently hierarchical nature of their relationship – they would be the best of friends again, a friendship that would exclude Mathilde, the labourers, and even Amine's children.

He felt a surge of joy when, in the middle of December, Amine offered to help him repair the combine harvester. They spent three afternoons in the hangar together. Amine was surprised by Mourad's enthusiasm, the way he whistled cheerfully as he hoisted himself up on to the enormous machine. Mourad had always been the one to repair tanks during the war. One evening, his face smeared with grease, his hands shaking with fatigue and frustration, Amine threw a tool at the wall, furious at having wasted his time and money on this machine. He was missing certain parts and no mechanic in the region could supply him with them. 'Let's just forget it. I'm going home.' But Mourad stopped him and, in a loud, comical voice, encouraged Amine to be brave and optimistic. He was convinced that he could manufacture the missing parts himself, and he said that if it would genuinely help make the harvester work again he would gladly cut off one of his legs or arms. This made Amine laugh, and back then Amine didn't laugh very often.

Amine was delighted by his foreman's efficiency but he worried about the oppressive atmosphere created by his military methods. The labourers would often come to him to complain. Mourad was always insulting the nationalists and the men had seen him walking on the main road, his little finger entwined with the little finger of the moqaddem, the local government's chief of intelligence. The foreman boasted about being an agent of order and prosperity. When Amine became concerned about the fighting that was breaking out more and more often on the farm, when he expressed regret at seeing the sad, angry expressions on the peasants' faces, Mourad reassured him: 'This is not the moment to be weak. All over the country young people are creating disorder. We have to be firm with them.'

'I can't stand it any more,' Mathilde admitted one day. She felt oppressed by Mourad's presence during family meals, including – Amine insisted – on Sundays. She thought he looked like a vulture with his wide, sloping shoulders, his beak-like nose and his scavenger's solitude, and Amine, for once, didn't contradict her. Mourad talked in metaphors of war and often Amine had to reprimand him. 'Don't say that kind of thing in front of the children. Can't you see that you're scaring them?' For the foreman, everything was a question of honour and duty, and all the stories he told were about battles. Amine felt bad for his aide-de-camp, trapped in the past like an insect in amber, held in a state of eternal suspension. Behind Mourad's arrogance he could detect his awkwardness, and one evening, as they were returning from the fields together, he said: 'I want you to eat Christmas dinner with us. It's an important day for Mathilde.' He wanted to add 'No talking about France or the war', but he didn't dare.

* * *

Mathilde invited the Palosis to spend Christmas with them, and Corinne joyfully accepted. 'Christmas without children is so sad, don't you think?' she said to Dragan, who felt his heart contract. Corinne didn't think he could understand how it felt not to be a mother. She imagined that her grief was inaccessible to him and, more generally, that men knew nothing of such private sufferings. Corinne was wrong. One day, when he was still a child living in Budapest, little Dragan had put on one of his sister Tamara's dresses. The little girl had laughed until she almost peed herself, crying out, 'You're so pretty! You're so pretty!' When he found out about this, Dragan's father had grown angry and punished his son. He'd warned him not to play such perverted games, arguing that they were the start of a slippery slope and that he should stay well away from them. Thinking about this later, Dragan believed that it was at this moment that his fascination for women was formed. He'd never wanted to possess them, or even be like them; what overwhelmed him was that magic power of theirs, the belly that swelled like his mother's had. He didn't tell his father this, though. In fact he didn't even tell his professor of medicine when the man balefully asked him why he wished to be a gynaecologist. Instead he replied simply: 'Because women will always have babies.'

Dragan loved children and they felt the same way towards him. Aïcha adored the doctor, who would wink as he slipped mints or liquorices into her palm. She was grateful less for the sweets than for the shared secret, because she had the impression that she was important to him. He intrigued her too, with his strange accent and his frequent references to an 'iron curtain' behind which he wanted to send oranges and – one day, perhaps – apricots. Mathilde had said that at Christmas he'd be bringing his sister, Tamara, who lived behind that iron curtain, and Aïcha imagined this woman standing behind a big metal shutter, like the one that the grocer Soussi would close every evening to protect his shop. How strange, Aïcha thought. Why would anyone want to live like that?

The Palosis were the last guests to arrive on Christmas Eve, and Aïcha watched them from behind her mother's legs. Tamara appeared: her complexion was yellowish and the little hair she had was pulled into a sort of bun on the side, a hairstyle that had been fashionable in the 1930s. Her face was dominated by a pair of bulging eyes, softened by long white lashes, which gave the impression that she was staring deeply into the past, magnetised by sad memories. She was like a child trapped on a merry-go-round. Selim was so scared of her that he didn't want to let her kiss his cheek. She wore an old-fashioned dress whose sleeves and collar had been darned many times. But her neck and her earlobes were decorated with beautiful jewellery that immediately drew Mathilde's gaze. The necklace and earrings were heirlooms from a distant time, a lost world, and Mathilde was so impressed by them that she treated Tamara as a special guest.

As soon as they arrived the house filled with laughter and exclamations of surprise. Everyone complimented Corinne on her outfit, a flared dress that revealed her ankles and showed so much décolletage that the men were hypnotised. Even the Mercier widow, who had twisted her ankle and was sitting under the living room window, told Corinne how elegant she looked. Dragan played Father Christmas that evening. He asked Tamo and Amine to help him empty the boot of his car and when they entered the living room, their arms filled with packages, Mathilde rushed over to them. Aïcha watched her mother throw herself to the floor and thought: Mama is a child too. 'Thank you, thank you!' Mathilde kept saying as she unwrapped the bottles of Hungarian Tokay that Dragan had managed to unearth. He opened one of the bottles there and then. 'It'll bring back memories of late grape harvests in Alsace,' he promised her, pouring the golden liquid into a glass that he sniffed ceremoniously. 'Now open this box!' Mathilde tore off the string and inside the box she found a panoply of medicines, medical equipment and medical books. She picked up one of the books and held it to her chest. 'That one's in French!' Dragan exclaimed, raising his glass and toasting the children's health and the joy of being together.

Before dinner Tamara agreed to sing for her hosts. In her youth she had enjoyed fleeting fame as a singer and had performed in Prague, Vienna and in Germany, next to a lake whose name she'd forgotten. She stood in front of the large window, placed one hand on her belly and pointed the other towards the horizon. From her skinny torso emerged a powerful voice, and the precious stones around her neck seemed to vibrate. Her song was desperately sad, like the lament of a siren or some strange animal exiled on earth that was calling out to its lost loved ones. Tamo, who had never heard anything like it before, ran into the living room. Mathilde had again forced her to wear a black-and-white maid's uniform and a small pleated headdress. She smelled of sweat and her frilly apron was stained where she'd wiped her fingers, despite Mathilde's constant reminder that it was not a tea towel. The maid stared, dumbstruck, at the singer, and Mathilde hurried her back into the kitchen before she had time to start laughing or to say something stupid. Aïcha clung to her father. There was beauty in that song, perhaps even a certain magic, but all Amine's emotions were strangled by a terrible feeling of embarrassment. The spectacle of this old lady singing filled him with shame and he had no idea why.

After dinner the men went out on to the front steps to smoke. It was a clear night and they could make out the obscene shape of the cypresses against the purple sky. Amine was a little drunk and he felt happy, standing there on the steps, outside his house filled with guests. I'm a man, he thought, I'm a father, I possess things. He let his mind drift into a strange, floating reverie. Through the window he could see the living room mirror reflecting the figures of his wife and children. He turned towards the garden and felt a sense of friendship towards the men around him that was so deep, so vivid, that he had a sudden idiotic urge to hug them. Dragan, who was expecting his first orange harvest that spring, told them that he'd probably found a distributor, that they were close to signing a contract. The effects of the alcohol made it difficult for Amine to concentrate; his ideas flew away from him like dandelion seeds. He didn't notice that Mourad was drunk too and that he was struggling to stay upright. The foreman grabbed Omar's arm and spoke to him in Arabic. 'He's a pussy,' he said, gesturing at Dragan, and when he laughed, saliva squirted between his missing teeth. He was envious of the Hungarian's elegance, jealous of Amine's attentiveness towards him, and he felt ridiculous in his frayed shirt and the jacket that Mathilde had given him, less out of generosity than fear of being shamed by him in front of all these foreign guests.

Omar was repulsed by the former soldier. He wiped the saliva from his neck and rolled his eyes as Mourad began one of his interminable stories about the war. All the men lowered their heads. Neither the Jew nor the Muslim nor any of those who had been through those years of shame and betrayal wished to see the evening ruined by such stories.

Mourad, his gaze wavering, started talking about his years in Indochina and the Battle of Dien Bien Phu. 'Communist bastards!' he yelled, and Dragan looked back inside the house, seeking a woman's eyes. Abruptly, Omar freed himself from Mourad's grip and the foreman lost his balance and collapsed on to the ground.

'Dien Bien Phu! Dien Bien Phu!' Omar repeated, hopping about, his mouth contracted with rage. He bent down, grabbed Mourad by the collar and spat in his face. 'You filthy sell-out! You stupid soldier – you were exploited by the French. You're a traitor to Islam, a traitor to your country.' Mourad had cut his head when he fell, and Dragan crouched down to examine the wound. Amine, suddenly sober, went over to his brother and – even before trying to reason with him – was paralysed by Omar's myopic glare. 'I'm out of here. I don't know what I'm doing in this house of degenerates, celebrating a god that isn't even mine. You should be ashamed of yourself, in front of your children and your workers. You should be ashamed of the contempt you show your people. You ought to watch yourself. Traitors will get what's coming to them when we take over the country.' Omar turned his back and walked away into the night, his slender figure gradually disappearing as if being absorbed by the landscape.

The women had heard the shouting and become alarmed when they saw Mourad lying on the ground. Corinne ran towards them and – despite his anger, despite his pain – Amine couldn't help laughing when he saw her. Her breasts were so huge that she ran in a funny way, back straight and chin out, skipping like a mountain goat. Dragan patted his host on the shoulder and said something to him in Hungarian that meant: 'Don't let this spoil the party. Let's drink!'

VII

Omar did not reappear. A week passed, then a month, and there was still no sign of him.

One morning Yasmine found two baskets full of food outside the hobnailed door. They were so heavy that she had to drag them along the floor to the kitchen, where she yelled for Mouilala to come and see. 'Two chickens, some eggs and broad beans. Look at those tomatoes, and that sachet of saffron!' Mouilala angrily hit the old slave. 'Put it all away! You hear me? Put it away!' Her withered face was wet with tears and she was shaking. Mouilala knew that the nationalists gave baskets of food and sometimes even money to the families of martyrs and prisoners. 'Idiot! Imbecile! Don't you understand? This means something has happened to my son!'

When Amine came to visit, the old woman was sitting on the patio, and for the first time he saw her hair, long, coarse and grey, falling down her back. She stood up in a fury and stared at him with hate.

'Where is he? He hasn't been home for a month! May the Prophet protect him! Don't keep things from me, Amine. If you know anything, if anything's happened to my son, tell me, I beg you!' Mouilala had not slept for days. Her face was drawn and she'd lost weight.

'I'm not hiding anything. Why are you accusing me? Omar's been hanging around with a gang of rebels for months.

He's the one putting our family's safety at risk. Why blame me for it?'

Mouilala started to weep. This was the first time she'd ever had a row with Amine.

'Find him, ya ouldi. Find your brother. Bring him home.' Amine kissed his mother's forehead, he rubbed her hands and he promised.

'Don't worry. I'll bring him to you. I'm sure there's a rational explanation.'

In truth Amine had been tortured by Omar's absence. For weeks he'd knocked at the houses of neighbours, family friends, his few contacts in the army. He'd gone to the cafés where his brother was often seen, he'd spent whole afternoons sitting outside the bus station, watching buses leave for Tangier and Casablanca. Sometimes he would see a man whose silhouette or gait reminded him of his brother and he'd jump up and run after him, pat him on the shoulder, and when the stranger turned to face him he'd say: 'I beg your pardon, monsieur. I thought you were someone else.'

He remembered Omar often talking about Otmane, a former schoolmate from Fez, so he decided to pay him a visit. It was early afternoon when he reached the heights of the holy city and entered the damp backstreets of the medina. A sad, cold February day, its murky light spread over the green fields and splendid mosques of the imperial city. Amine kept asking the way from passers-by; they were all shivering, all in a rush, but each one gave him different directions and after two hours of turning in circles he started to panic. He kept having to press his body to the walls to let a donkey or a cart go past. 'Balak,

balak!' men would yell – 'Get out of the way!' – and Amine would jump, his shirt soaked with sweat despite the coolness of the air. At last an old man with discoloured patches on his face came up to him and, in a gentle voice, rolling his Rs, offered to escort him to the house. They walked in silence, Amine following in the footsteps of this distinguished man who was greeted by everyone they passed. 'It's here,' the stranger said, gesturing to a door then vanishing into an alleyway before Amine could thank him.

A young maid opened the door and escorted him to a ground-floor courtyard. He waited for a long time in this empty, silent riad. Several times he stood up and cautiously walked around the central patio. He peeked through half-open doors, stamping his feet on the zellige and hoping that the inhabitants – who were perhaps asleep at this mid-afternoon hour – would be woken by the noise. The riad was vast and decorated with exquisite taste. Across from the fountain was a large room with a mahogany desk and two sofas upholstered with precious fabrics. Fragrant jasmine grew on the patio, as well as a wisteria that climbed up to the first-floor balustrades. To the right of the entrance the walls of the Moroccan living room were decorated with plaster sculptures and the cedar ceiling covered in coloured patterns.

Amine was about to leave when the door opened and a man came in. He wore a striped djellaba and a fez. His beard was neatly trimmed and under his arm he held a red leather folder containing a stack of files. The man frowned with surprise at the sight of this stranger in his house.

'Hello, Sidi! I'm sorry to disturb you. Your maid let me in.'

The house's owner remained silent.

'My name is Amine Belhaj. Once again, I apologise for bothering you at home. I've come in search of my brother, Omar Belhaj. I know that your son and he are friends and I thought perhaps that I might find him here. I've looked everywhere for him and my mother is sick with worry.'

'Omar . . . Yes, of course, I see the resemblance now. You fought on the front in 1940, didn't you? I'm sorry, but your brother isn't here. My son, Otmane, was expelled from school and is now studying in Azrou. It's been a long time since he saw your brother, you know.'

Amine couldn't hide his disappointment. He dug his hands into his pockets and said nothing. 'Please, sit down,' said the man, and at that moment the young maid returned and placed a teapot on the copper table.

Hadj Karim was a wealthy businessman. He ran a firm that advised clients on property purchases and investments. He had one employee and a typewriter, and his judgement was trusted in his neighbourhood and beyond. In Fez and throughout the surrounding region people sought out the protection of this influential man, who was close to the nationalist parties but also had many European friends. Every other year he would go to Châtel-Guyon to be treated for his asthma and eczema. He loved wine, listened to German music and had decorated his riad with nineteenth-century furniture bought from a former British ambassador. He was an elusive man, suspected by some of being an intelligence officer for the French authorities and by others of being a high-ranking accomplice of the Moroccan nationalists.

'I worked for the French in the 1930s,' he told Amine. 'I wrote contracts, did some legal translation. I was an honest employee and they had no reason to reproach me, thanks be to God. And then, in 1944, I supported the independence manifesto and took part in the uprisings. The French fired me and that was when I opened my own office as a certified defence lawyer specialising in Moroccan law. Who says we need them, eh?' Hadj Karim's expression darkened. 'Others weren't as lucky as me. Some of my friends were exiled to Tafilalt, others were tortured by sadists who stubbed out cigarettes on their backs, tried to drive them insane. What could I do? I did my best to help my friends. I organised fundraisers to pay for the defence of political prisoners. One day I went to court, hoping to help a young man who'd been accused of a crime or just to offer support to a father devastated by the cruelty of a verdict. Outside the building I saw a man sitting on the ground and shouting out a word that I didn't understand. I went over to him and saw, carefully laid out on a cloth, three or four ties. The vendor thought he'd spotted a customer and he tried to sell me one, but I told him I wasn't interested and went on towards the court. There was a crowd of people gathered around the entrance. Men praying, women scratching at their faces and invoking the name of the Prophet. Believe me, Si Belhaj, I can remember the face of each and every one of them. Fathers, humiliated by their own powerlessness, handing me documents that they couldn't read. They looked at me imploringly and told the women to move out of the way and shut up, but a tearful mother doesn't listen to anyone. When I finally made it to the entrance I introduced myself and presented my credentials as a lawyer, but the doorman was categorical: I couldn't go in if I wasn't wearing a tie. I found this hard to believe. Hurt and embarrassed, I went back to the vendor sitting cross-legged on the ground and picked up a blue tie. I paid for it without uttering a word and tied it over my djellaba. I would have felt ridiculous had I not seen, on the steps leading up to the courtroom, several anxious fathers, the hoods of their djellabas lifted up, each one with a tie around his neck.' The man sipped his tea. Amine slowly nodded. 'I am like all those fathers, Si Belhaj. I'm proud to have a nationalist son. I'm proud of all those sons who rise up against the occupiers, who punish traitors, who struggle to end an unjust occupation. But how many murders will it take? How many men must go before the firing squad before our cause triumphs? Otmane is in Azrou, far from all of that. He must study so he is ready to lead this country when it becomes independent. Find your brother. Search everywhere for him. If he's in Rabat, or Casablanca, take him home. I admire all those people who sincerely accept the martyrdom of their loved ones. But I understand even better those who will do anything to save them.'

Night was falling now and the servants lit candelabras in the patio. Amine noticed a beautiful wooden clock on a shelf; it was French-made and the gilt face shone in the gloom. Hadj Karim insisted on walking Amine to the gates of the medina, where his car was parked. Before leaving him Hadj Karim promised to ask around and to let him know as soon as he heard anything. 'I have friends. Don't worry, someone will talk.'

On the way home Amine couldn't stop thinking about what the lawyer had told him. It occurred to him that perhaps he lived too far from everything, that his isolation had made him guilty in some way, had blinded him. Like the coward that he was, he'd hidden away in the hope that nobody would find him. Amine had been born among these men, he belonged to this people, but he had never felt any pride in that fact. On the contrary, he'd often wanted to reassure the Europeans he met. He'd tried to convince them that he was different, that he wasn't a liar or a superstitious fool or a lazy bastard, as the colonists liked to describe their Moroccan workers. He lived his life in accordance with the image, engraved deep in his heart, that French people had of him. As a teenager he'd got into the habit of walking slowly, head lowered. He knew that his dark skin, his stocky physique, his broad shoulders made him suspicious in the eyes of white people, so he shoved his hands into his armpits like a man who has sworn not to fight. Now it seemed to him that he lived in a world populated entirely by enemies.

He envied his brother's fanaticism, his ability to belong. He wished that he didn't believe in moderation, didn't fear death. In moments of danger he always thought of his wife and his mother and he felt obliged to survive. In Germany, in the POW camp, his fellow prisoners had offered to let him in on their escape plans. They'd studied the options open to them in great detail. They'd stolen scissors to cut the barbed wire; they'd gathered a few provisions. For weeks Amine kept finding excuses not to put the plan into action. 'It's too dark,' he told them. 'Let's wait for a full moon.' 'It's too cold, we'll never survive in those freezing forests. Let's wait until the weather improves.' The men trusted him, or perhaps they heard, in these cautious words, the echo of their own fears. Two seasons passed, two seasons of delays and a guilty conscience, two seasons spent pretending to be eager to escape. Of course, he was obsessed by the idea of freedom – it infiltrated all his dreams – but he couldn't resolve himself to the possibility of being shot in the back, of getting snagged on barbed wire and dying like a dog.

For Selma, Omar's disappearance marked the beginning of a time of happiness and freedom. Now there was nobody watching her, worrying about her absences, her lies. All through adolescence she'd taken a sort of mean pride in her bruised calves, her swollen cheeks, her black eyes. To her friends, who refused to follow her in her wild excursions, she always said: 'Why not enjoy life? You'll get beaten anyway.' To go to the cinema she wrapped herself in a haik, out of fear that someone would recognise her, and once inside the darkened room she let men caress her bare legs and told herself: This is so much happiness that they can't take away from me. Omar would often be waiting for her on the patio and, watched by Mouilala, he would beat her until she bled. One evening, when she was still only fourteen, Selma had come home late from school and, when she'd knocked at the door of the house in Berrima, Omar had refused to open it. It was winter, so night had fallen early. She'd sworn that she'd been kept behind for private study, that she'd done nothing wrong. She'd invoked Allah and His mercy. Behind the hobnailed door she'd heard Yasmine begging Omar to forgive his sister. But Omar had held firm and Selma had spent the night in the garden next door, shivering with cold and fear as she lay in the wet grass.

She hated that brother of hers, who wouldn't let her do anything, who called her a whore and had on several occasions spat in her face. A thousand times she had wished him dead and cursed Allah for making her live under the reign of such a brutal man. He laughed at his sister's desires for freedom. 'My friends, my friends,' he mimicked her in a bitter voice whenever she asked permission to visit another girl. 'All you care about is having fun!' Then he would pick her up by the collar, press his face against hers, savour the fear in her eyes, the trembling of her limbs, and smash her head against a wall or throw her down the stairs.

With Omar gone and Amine too busy on the farm to visit very often, Selma was free. She lived like a tightrope walker, aware that her liberty would not last long and that soon, like most girls her age in Berrima, she wouldn't even be able to go up on the roof terrace any more, because of her swollen belly and her jealous husband. At the hammam the other women would stare at her body and some would caress her hips. Once, the masseuse put her hand between Selma's thighs with a certain brutality and said: 'He'll be a lucky guy, your husband.' The touch of that oily hand, those black fingers strong from kneading other bodies, was overpowering. Selma realised that there was something unquenched inside her, something insatiable, a chasm waiting to be filled, and alone in her bedroom she did to herself what that woman had done to her, feeling no shame but no satisfaction either. Men came to ask for her hand in marriage. They sat in the living room while she crouched on the stairs, anxiously watching those middle-aged, pot-bellied suitors slurp their tea and pretend to hawk up phlegm to scare off the prowling cats. Mouilala let each one in excitedly, and listened to his questions, and when she realised that he had not come about her son, that he knew nothing of what had happened to Omar, she stood up and left, and the man would remain where he was for a few minutes, in a daze, before leaving this madhouse without a backward glance. Selma thought that they'd forgotten her then, that nobody in this family remembered her existence, and she was happy.

She started playing truant, hanging around in the streets. She threw away her schoolbooks, she shortened her skirts, and – with the help of a Spanish friend – she plucked her eyebrows and had her hair cut in the latest fashion. From the drawers of her mother's bedside table she stole enough money to buy cigarettes and bottles of Coca-Cola. And when Yasmine threatened to tell on her she took the old slave in her arms and said: 'Oh no, Yasmine, you won't do that.' Yasmine, who had lived her whole life in other people's homes, under other people's command, now took control of the household. Hanging from her belt was a heavy bunch of keys and the jangling it made could be heard in the corridor and out on the patio. She was in charge of the stores of flour and lentils that Mouilala, traumatised by years of war and scarcity, continued to build up. She alone could open the locks on all the doors, the cedar chests decorated with palmettes and the large cupboards where Mouilala's trousseau had been left to gather mould. At night, when Selma disappeared while her mother slept, the old servant sat on the patio and waited for her. In the darkness all that could be seen of her was the incandescent end of the filterless cigarettes she smoked, dimly and flickeringly illuminating her black-skinned, battered old face. In a vague way she understood the young woman's desire for freedom. Selma's escapes awoke ancient, long-extinguished desires in the former slave's heart.

* * *

In the cold months of early 1955, Selma spent her mornings at the cinema and her afternoons at her friends' houses or in the back of a café where the owner demanded that all drinks be paid for in advance. There the girls talked about love and travel, beautiful cars and the best way to escape their parents' prying eyes. Their parents were at the centre of all their conversations. Those old people who understood nothing, who couldn't see that the world had changed, who scolded the young for their obsession with dancing and sunbathing. As for the boys, they played table football and – intoxicated by their idle days – loudly proclaimed that they didn't care what their parents said. They were sick of hearing about Verdun and Monte Cassino, about Senegalese Tirailleurs and Spanish soldiers. They were sick of their parents' memories of famine, dead babies, land lost in battles. All these boys cared about was rock 'n' roll, American films, beautiful cars and dates with girls who weren't afraid to sneak out at night. Selma was their favourite. Not because she was the most beautiful or the most brazen, but because she made them laugh and she had a lust for life so intense that it seemed nothing could hold her back. She was irresistible when she imitated Vivien Leigh in *Gone With the Wind*, shaking her head and saying, 'Fiddle-dee-dee! War, war, war!' in a girly, high-pitched voice. Other times she would make fun of Amine, and all her friends would be bent double with laughter as she stood there frowning and puffing out her chest like an old soldier proud of his medals. 'Think yourself lucky that you've never gone hungry!' she said in a deep voice, pointing her finger accusingly. 'You're just a silly little girl who's never been through a war.' Selma wasn't afraid. It never crossed her mind that someone might recognise her, denounce her. Or even that she was doing anything wrong. She believed in her lucky star and she dreamed of finding love. Every day, to her fear and excitement, the world seemed a little vaster, the possibilities open to her ever more infinite. Meknes grew so small, like a dress she'd outworn, a dress so tight that she found it hard to breathe, a dress that might rip open at the slightest movement. Sometimes that smallness made her angry and she would run screaming from a friend's room or smash glasses full of hot tea from a café tabletop. 'You're going round in circles, can't you see?' she would yell at them. 'Always the same conversations. Always!' Her friends seemed so ordinary then, and she guessed that, behind their rebellious adolescent poses, they were really just obedient conformists. Some of the girls started to avoid her company. They didn't want to risk their reputations by being seen with her.

In the afternoons Selma would sometimes take refuge with her neighbour, Mademoiselle Fabre. This Frenchwoman had lived in the medina since the late 1920s, in a dilapidated old riad. The place was a mess: the living room filled with dirty benches, open chests, books stained with tea or food. The hangings had been nibbled by mice and the air smelled of unwashed cunt and rotten eggs. All the medina's undesirables gathered in Mademoiselle Fabre's riad, and Selma would often see orphans and poor young widows sleeping there, on the ground or in a corner of the living room. In winter the roof leaked, and the sound of the raindrops crashing against iron cisterns was mingled with the cries of children, the creaking of cartwheels out in the street, the clatter of weaving machines upstairs. Mademoiselle Fabre was an ugly woman. Her nose, with its dilated pores, was large and misshapen, her eyebrows were grey and sparse, and in the past few years she'd developed a tremble in her jaw that made it difficult to understand what she was saying. Under the baggy gandouras that she wore, Selma could see her paunchy belly and her thick legs covered in varicose veins. Around her neck she wore an ivory cross that she would stroke constantly like a charm or an amulet. She'd brought it from Central Africa, where she'd grown up, although she didn't like to talk about that. Nobody knew anything about her childhood or about the years that had preceded her arrival in Morocco. The people in the medina said that she used to be a nun, that she was the daughter of a rich industrialist, that she'd been dragged here by a man she was madly in love with and then abandoned.

Mademoiselle Fabre had lived among the Moroccans for more than thirty years, speaking their language, learning their customs. She was invited to weddings and religious ceremonies and had gradually become indistinguishable from the native women, drinking her hot tea in silence, blessing children and calling for God's mercy on a house. When women gathered she was let in on their secrets. She gave advice, wrote letters for those who couldn't read, worried about shameful diseases and the marks of beatings. One day a woman told her: 'If the pigeon had kept silent, the wolf wouldn't have eaten it.' Mademoiselle was always extremely discreet. She refused to rock the foundations of this world where she was only a foreigner, but that didn't stop her raging at the poverty and injustice she found here. Once, and only once, she had dared knock at the door of a man whose daughter showed exceptional gifts. She'd begged the girl's strict father to support his child in her studies and offered to send her to a university in France.

The man had not got angry. He hadn't thrown her out of the house or accused her of spreading debauchery and disorder. He had just laughed. The old man had roared with hilarity and raised his arms in the air. 'University!' After wiping his eyes, he'd accompanied Mademoiselle Fabre to the door, almost tenderly, and thanked her.

Everyone forgave Mademoiselle Fabre her eccentricity because she was old and unattractive. Because they knew her to be good-hearted and generous. During the war she'd fed poor families and given clothes to children in rags. She'd chosen her camp and never lost an opportunity to show it. In September 1954 a Parisian journalist had come to write a feature on Meknes. He'd been advised to meet this Frenchwoman who'd organised a weaving workshop in her house and who was so helpful towards the town's poor. The young man went there one afternoon and almost fainted in that hot, airless house. On the floor children were sorting bits of wool into different colours and then putting them in straw baskets. Upstairs young women were sitting in front of large vertical looms, weaving and chatting. In the kitchen two old black women were dunking their bread in chestnut puree. The reporter asked for a glass of water and Mademoiselle Fabre tapped his forehead and said: 'Poor boy. Don't get worked up. Don't try to fight it.' They spoke about her good works, about life in the medina, about the moral and hygienic conditions of the young women who worked there. Then the journalist asked her if she was afraid of terrorists, if – like the rest of the French community – she was nervous about her safety. Mademoiselle Fabre looked up at the white, late-summer sky above her and balled her fists, as if to compose herself.

'It's not so long ago that we called people terrorists in France when they were resisting the Germans. Then they became Resistance heroes. After more than forty years of the protectorate, how can anyone expect the Moroccans not to demand freedom? They helped us fight for it, and we gave them a taste for it and taught them the value of it. They deserve it.' The journalist, who was pouring with sweat, responded that independence would eventually be granted, but that it should be a gradual process, and that it was wrong to attack those French people who'd sacrificed their lives for this country. What would become of Morocco once the French had left? Who would run the country? Who would work the earth? Mademoiselle Fabre cut him short. 'I don't care what the French think, to be perfectly honest. They seem to think that they're the ones who've been invaded by the Moroccans, who are growing and asserting themselves. The French need to understand the reality here: they're the foreigners.' And she told the journalist to leave, without offering to accompany him to his hotel in the new town.

Every Thursday afternoon a group of girls from good families would go to see the Frenchwoman. Their parents thought she was teaching them to knit, cross-stitch and play the piano. They trusted her because they knew Mademoiselle Fabre would never dare try to convert their children. And it was true that she never mentioned Jesus or His love spreading all over the world, but all the same she did convert them. None of those girls learned to play more than two notes or darn a sock, but they would spend hours on the patio or in the Moroccan parlour, lying on mattresses and stuffing themselves with honey cakes. The old lady would play a record and teach them to dance, she would read out poems that would make them blush, and some of the girls would even run away, crying, 'Ouili, ouili, oh là là!' She lent them copies of *Paris Match* and afterwards torn-out pages would be seen flying on the wind from terrace to terrace and portraits of Princess Margaret would be found lying in the gutter.

One afternoon in March 1955, while she was carrying over a tray of tea for her students, Mademoiselle Fabre overheard them deep in conversation. For the past week the students at the local secondary school had been on strike because one of the teachers had humiliated a young female student. He'd accused her of writing a subversive composition on Joan of Arc's battle against the English and of using it to demonstrate her nationalist sympathies. From upstairs they could hear the workers laugh as they repaired the roof and the girls craned their necks, trying to catch a glimpse of them. Mademoiselle Fabre ceremoniously poured mint tea into chipped glasses, then she whispered to Selma: 'Come with me, mademoiselle. I need to speak with you.'

Selma followed her into the kitchen. She wondered what this could be about. She almost said that she didn't care about politics, that her sister-in-law was French, that she didn't want to take sides, but Mademoiselle Fabre just smiled at her and invited her to sit at a little wooden table where a basket of fruit sat, midges hovering. For a few minutes, which seemed interminable to Selma, the old woman stared out at the bougainvillea that stretched out over the back wall of the garden. She picked up a wormy peach. Beneath the skin its flesh was black and soft.

'I heard today that you're not going to school any more.'

Selma shrugged. 'What's the point? I didn't understand any of it.'

'You're an idiot. Without education you'll never make anything of your life.'

Selma was surprised. She'd never heard Mademoiselle Fabre sound this strict before.

'This is about a boy, isn't it?'

Selma blushed. She wished she could just run out of that house and never return. Her legs started to shake and the old woman put a hand on her knee.

'You think I don't understand? You probably imagine I've never been in love . . .'

Make her shut up, thought Selma, make her let me go. But the old woman went on, fingering her ivory cross, which had been smoothed to a shine.

'Right now you're in love and it's wonderful. You believe everything the boys tell you. You imagine that it will last and that they'll always love you as much as they do now. Next to that, your studies seem unimportant. But you don't know anything about life! One day you'll have sacrificed everything for them, you'll have nothing left and you'll be completely dependent on them. At the mercy of their good moods, their affection, their brutality. Believe me when I tell you that you must think about your future. You must study. Times have changed. You are not doomed to the same fate as your mother. You could become someone, a lawyer, a teacher, a nurse. Or even a pilot! Haven't you heard about that girl, Touria Chaoui, who passed her flying exam at sixteen? You can be whatever you want to be, if you work for it. And you will never ever have to ask a man for money.'

Selma listened, hands tightly gripping her glass of tea. She listened so attentively that Mademoiselle Fabre thought she'd managed to convince her. 'Go back to school. Revise for your exams. I'll help you if you need help. Mademoiselle, promise me you won't give up.' Selma thanked her, kissed her wrinkled cheeks, and said: 'I promise.'

But as she walked back home Selma thought about the old woman's face, her skin as white as chalk, her lips so thin that she looked like she'd eaten her own mouth. Alone in the narrow streets, she laughed and thought: What does that old nun know about men? What does she know about love? She felt a vast contempt for the Frenchwoman's fat, sad body, for her solitary existence, for those ideals of hers which were nothing more, in truth, than a way of masking the lack of tenderness in her life. The previous day, Selma had kissed a boy. And ever since, she'd found herself constantly wondering how it was possible that men – who bullied and oppressed her – could also be the ones she was so desperate to be with. Yes, a boy had kissed her and she remembered with super-human accuracy the precise path that his kisses had taken on her skin. She kept closing her eyes and reliving that delicious moment, her excitement unfading. She saw again the boy's pale-blue eyes, she heard his voice, the words he spoke – 'Are you trembling?' – and a shiver ran through her body. She was a prisoner of that memory, she dwelled on it constantly and touched her fingertips to her mouth, to her neck, as if trying to find the trace of a wound, a mark that the boy's mouth had left on her. Each time he'd put his lips on her skin she'd felt as though he was liberating her from fear, from the cowardice in which she'd been raised.

Was that what men were for? Was that why everyone talked about love all the time? Yes, they mined the courage that lay deep in your heart, they brought it out into the daylight and forced it to bloom. At the thought of a kiss, a new kiss, she felt an immense strength fill her. How right they are, she thought, walking up the stairs to her bedroom, how right they are to suspect us and to warn us, because what we're hiding, under our veils and our skirts, is so fiery and glorious that we might betray anything for it.

At the end of March a cold snap hit Meknes and the water in the patio well froze. Mouilala fell ill and was bedridden for days, her thin face barely visible above the thick layer of blankets that Yasmine spread over her. Mathilde often came to see her and tried to make her better in spite of her resistance, her refusal to swallow the medicines. Mathilde had to treat her like a scared and wilful child. Mouilala did recover, but when she finally got out of bed and went to the kitchen, in a dressing gown that Mathilde had given her, she realised that something was wrong. At first she didn't know what it was that was making her panic like this, giving her the feeling of being a stranger in her own home. She walked through the corridor, shaking off Yasmine, and went up and down the stairs despite the pain in her legs. She leaned out of the window and looked at the street, which seemed to her oddly dull, as if something had been stolen from it. Was it possible that the world had changed so much during the few weeks that she'd been ill? She thought she was going crazy, that demons had taken possession of her just as they had her son Jalil. She remembered stories she'd heard about her ancestors, who would parade half-naked in the streets and talk to ghosts. So now she'd been struck by the family curse and she was slowly losing her mind . . . She was frightened. To calm herself she did what she always did. She sat in the kitchen, grabbed a bunch of coriander and began mincing it. Then she raised her hands, their fingers twisted and covered with finely chopped herbs, to her mouth, to her nose, coating her face with the minced coriander until she started to cry. She stuck her fingers in her nose, rubbed her eyes like a madwoman. Still she couldn't smell anything. With some witchcraft that she didn't understand, the illness had robbed her of her sense of smell.

So it was that she didn't notice when her daughter came home smelling of stale tobacco and dust from building sites. Mouilala was unaware of the cheap perfume that Selma had bought in the medina with stolen money and which clung to the fabric of her blouses. Above all the old woman couldn't tell that the sugary perfume was mingled with the fresh citrus odour of a man's cologne. Selma would come home every evening, her cheeks red, her hair tangled, her breath smelling of another's mouth. She would sing on the patio, talk to her mother with shining eyes and hug her sweetly. 'I love you so much, Mama!' she would say.

One evening Mathilde was waiting for Amine when he came home. 'I was in town today,' she told him. 'I saw your mother.' Mouilala had behaved strangely towards Aïcha. When the child had put her mouth close to her grandmother's hand, the old woman had started yelling. 'She accused Aïcha of trying to bite her. She was sobbing and holding her hand to her chest. She was really frightened, Amine, you understand?' Yes, he understood. He'd already noticed his mother's thinness, her vacant gaze, her absences. She'd stopped dyeing her hair with henna and she sometimes left her bedroom without first tying her headscarf over her grey hair. When Mathilde had gone to see her, she could have sworn that Mouilala hadn't recognised her. The old woman had stared at her for a few seconds, glassy-eyed and open-mouthed, and then she'd looked relieved. She hadn't pronounced her daughter-in-law's name – she never did – but she'd smiled and put her hand on the young woman's arm. Mouilala would spend hours sitting at the kitchen table, staring limply at baskets of vegetables. When her mind recovered some of its old strength she would stand up and start cooking, but her meals didn't taste the way they used to. She would forget ingredients or fall asleep on her wooden chair and let the bottom of the tajine burn. This woman who had always been so silent and austere now spent her days humming childish songs that made her burst out laughing. She walked in circles and lifted up her kaftan while sticking her tongue out at Yasmine.

'We can't just leave her like that,' said Mathilde. Amine took off his boots, hung his jacket on the chair in the entrance hall and said nothing. 'She should come and live with us. Selma too.' His wife stood with her hands on her hips, watching him tenderly. When Amine glanced at her he saw the passion in his eyes. Surprised, she touched her hair flirtatiously and untied the string of the apron she was wearing. At that moment he regretted his inarticulacy. He wished he was one of those men who find the time to think deeply and show tenderness, the time to express all that they carry in their hearts. He observed her for a long time, thinking that she'd become a woman of this country, that she suffered just like he did, that she worked just as hard, and that he was incapable of thanking her.

'Yes, you're right. Anyway, I didn't like them being alone there, in the medina, with no man to protect them.' He walked over to Mathilde, stood on tiptoe and slowly kissed her cheek, which she'd leaned down towards him.

At the start of spring Amine helped his mother move. Jalil was sent to stay with an uncle, a holy man who lived near Ifrane and who assured them that altitude would be good for his nephew's weak mind. Yasmine, who had never seen snow, offered to go with him. Mouilala was given the brightest room, near the entrance of the house. Selma had to share a bedroom with Aïcha and Selim, but Mourad had managed to get hold of some bricks and mortar and he'd begun building a new wing to the house.

Mouilala rarely left her room. Often Mathilde would find her sitting by the window, staring at the red-tiled floor. Wrapped up in white, she would gently nod her head, revisiting a life of silence, a mute existence where grief was forbidden. Her dark, wrinkled hands stood out against the white fabric. Those hands seemed to contain this woman's entire life, like a book without words. Selim spent a lot of time with her. He would sit on the floor, his head resting in his grandmother's lap, and he'd close his eyes while she stroked his back and nape. He refused to eat anywhere except in the old woman's bedroom, and they had to accept the bad habits he formed there: eating with his fingers and burping noisily. Mouilala, who had for as long as Mathilde had known her been very thin and only ever eaten other people's leftovers, was now a terrible glutton, as many old people are in their last years, finding in these frivolous pleasures one last particle of meaning.

All day long Mathilde rushed about: from school to home, from the kitchen to the laundry room. She washed the old woman's thighs and her son's thighs too. She made meals for everyone and ate standing up, because she didn't have time to sit. In the morning, when she was back from the school, she healed the sick then washed and ironed clothes. In the afternoon she went to the suppliers and brought chemical products or spare parts. She lived in a state of permanent anxiety: for their finances, for Mouilala's health, for her children. She worried about Amine's dark moods. The day that Selma arrived at the farm, her husband had warned Mathilde: 'I don't want her going near the men. I don't want her hanging around. It's school and home and that's all, you understand?' Mathilde had nodded, her heart torn with anguish. When her brother wasn't there – which was most of the time – Selma was insolent and cruel. Mathilde gave her orders, but Selma just ignored them. 'You're not my mother,' she said.

Mathilde feared the violent rains of March, the hail that the labourers had been predicting because of the yellow late-afternoon skies. She jumped when the telephone rang and prayed, hand on the receiver, that it wasn't the bank or either of the schools. Often Corinne would call her mid-afternoon and invite her to come for tea. 'You're allowed to have fun, you know!'

The letters that Mathilde wrote to Irène now were dry and formal, with no secrets or feelings. She asked her sister to send her recipes for meals from their childhood. She would have liked to be a perfect housewife, like the ones who appeared in the magazines that Corinne lent her. The ones who knew how to run a household, who kept the peace, the ones who held everything together through a combination of love and fear. But as Aïcha told her one day in her reedy little voice: 'Anyway, everything goes wrong in the end.' Mathilde didn't contradict her. She would peel vegetables while reading a book. She would hide novels in the pockets of her aprons and sometimes she would sit on a pile of laundry that needed ironing to read novels by Henri Troyat or Anaïs Nin that she'd borrowed from the Mercier widow. She cooked dishes that Amine hated. Potato salads covered with onions and stinking of vinegar, platefuls of cabbage that she boiled for so long that the house reeked of it for days, meat loaves so dry that Aïcha spat them out and hid the remains in the pocket of her jacket. Amine complained. With his fork he pushed away escalopes drenched in cream, which were not suited to this climate. He missed his mother's cooking and convinced himself that Mathilde was just provoking him by claiming that she didn't like couscous and lentils with smoked meat. At mealtimes she would encourage the children to talk, asking them lots of questions, and she'd laugh when they banged their spoons on the table and demanded dessert. Then Amine would grow angry with these disrespectful, noisy children, he would curse this house where he could no longer find the peace that a working man had a right to expect. Mathilde would pick up Selim, take a dirty handkerchief from her sleeve and cry. One evening, watched by his astounded daughter, Amine started singing a Maurice Chevalier song: 'She cried like a baby, she cried and cried and cried . . . She cried like a fountain, all the tears she had inside . . .' He pursued Mathilde into the corridor and shouted: 'Oh là là, what a tragedy! What a tragedy!' And Mathilde, wild with rage, screamed insults in Alsatian. When they asked her, later, what those words had meant, she would always refuse to explain.

Mathilde put on weight and a few white hairs appeared at her temples. During the daytime she wore a wide raffia hat, like the ones the peasants wore, and black rubber sandals. The skin on her cheeks and neck was scattered with little brown patches and fine lines started to form. Sometimes, at the ends of those interminable days, she sank into a profound melancholy. On the way to school, her face caressed by the wind, she thought about how she'd first come to this land ten years earlier, and what had she accomplished during all that time? What would she leave behind? Hundreds of meals eaten and vanished, fleeting moments of happiness of which no trace remained, songs whispered at a child's bedside, afternoons spent consoling people for long-forgotten sadnesses. Sleeves resewn, solitary anxieties that she never shared with anyone out of a fear of being mocked. Whatever she did – and however great and sincere the gratitude of her children and her patients – it seemed to Mathilde that her life was constantly being swallowed up. Everything she achieved was doomed to disappear, to be erased. That was the fate of all small, domestic lives, she thought, where endless repetition of the same tasks ended up eating away the soul. She looked through the window at the plantations of almond trees, the acres of vines, the young shrubs reaching maturity that would – in a year or two – start bearing fruit. She envied Amine this domain he'd built, stone by stone, and which, that year – 1955 – was providing him with his first feelings of satisfaction.

The peach harvest had been good and he'd sold his almonds for a handsome profit. To the extreme annoyance of Mathilde, who needed money for school supplies and new clothes, Amine had decided to invest all his profits in the development of the property. 'A woman from here would never dare stick her nose into that kind of thing,' he told her. He was going to build a second greenhouse, hire a dozen extra workers for the harvests and pay a French engineer to draw up plans for the construction of a reservoir. Amine had long been passionate about growing olive trees. He'd read everything he could find on the subject and had grown some densely packed experimental plantations. He was convinced that he alone could create new varieties, more resistant to the heat and the lack of water in this region. At the Meknes Fair in the spring of 1955 he gave a confused speech on his findings, reading from the notes in his sweating hands as he tried to explain his theory to a sceptical audience. 'All innovations are mocked at first, aren't they?' he said to his friend Dragan. 'If things go as planned those trees will have a yield up to six times higher than the varieties I'm growing at the moment. And their need for water is so reduced that I could go back to traditional irrigation methods.'

During all those years of labour Amine had grown used to working alone, not relying on anyone else's help. His farm was encircled by those of colonists whose wealth and power had always made him feel inferior. At the end of the war the colonists in Meknes had still held considerable sway. It had been said that they could make or break a Resident-General, that all they had to do was lift a finger and the politicians in Paris would do their bidding. Nowadays, Amine's neighbours were more agreeable towards him. At the Chamber of Agriculture, where he requested subsidies, he was received with deference and – even if they refused to grant him the money he asked for – he was congratulated for his creativity and determination. When he told Dragan about this meeting, the doctor smiled.

'They're scared of you, simple as that. They can feel the wind turning, they know that the natives will soon be in charge here. They're just covering their backsides by treating you as an equal.'

'An equal? They say they want to support me, that they believe in my vision for the future, but they refuse to give me credit. And when I fail they'll say I was lazy, that Arabs are all the same, that without the French and their work ethic we would never make anything of ourselves.'

In May, Roger Mariani's farm burned down. The pigs were killed and in the days that followed the air all around was filled with the smell of charred flesh. The labourers, who didn't try particularly hard to put out the fire, covered their faces with cloths and some of them threw up. 'It's haram,' they said, 'to breathe this cursed air.' The night of the fire, Roger Mariani came up the hill and Mathilde took him to the living room, where he drank an entire bottle of Tokay on his own. This man who had once been so powerful, who'd threatened General Noguès at his office in Rabat and got what he wanted, now sat in the old velvet armchair and cried like a child. 'Sometimes I feel like my heart is breaking. I can't think any more, it's like my brain is lost in thick fog. I don't know what the future holds for us now. Where is the justice if I have to pay for crimes that I will always deny having committed? I believed in this country, the way a saint believes in God: unthinkingly, unquestioningly. And now I hear that they want to kill me, that my peasants have hidden weapons in secret caches so they can shoot me, or that they're going to hang me. So, all this time, they'd just pretended to stop being savages . . .'

The relationship between Amine and Mourad had been stretched thin during the Christmas holidays, and for weeks afterwards Amine consciously avoided his former aide-de-camp. Every time Mourad appeared on the dirt path that led from the farm to the douar, every time he saw that gaunt face, those yellow eyes, Amine felt sick. He looked at the ground when he gave orders, and when Mourad approached him to discuss a problem or celebrate a coming harvest Amine couldn't keep still: he would stamp his feet and often he had to ball his fists and grit his teeth to prevent himself simply running away.

During Ramadan, which fell in April that year, Mourad refused to let the fellahs work at night or set their own hours based on the heat and their fatigue levels. 'Watering and harvesting have to take place in the daytime! I can't change that and neither can God!' he yelled at a peasant, who put his hand in front of his mouth and recited a prayer. He would let them take a nap in the afternoon, but afterwards he would insult them, harass them, accuse them of playing on their master's generosity. One day he attacked a man he'd found in the garden, a few feet from the house. He grabbed the man's hair and punched him repeatedly, accusing him of spying on the Belhaj family, of following young Selma, of trying to sneak a look at the Frenchwoman through the mosquito nets in the living room. Mourad spied on the maid, whom he accused of imaginary thefts. He interrogated Mathilde's patients, whom he suspected of taking advantage of her.

One day Amine summoned Mourad to his office and, as he used to during the war, spoke to him in simple, martial terms, giving him orders without any explanation. 'From now on, if a peasant from the region comes to ask for water, we will give him water. Nobody will be refused the right to use our well. If a sick person comes here to be healed, you will make sure that they are. Nobody will be beaten on my property and everyone will be allowed to rest.'

All day long Amine stayed on the farm, but in the evenings he felt compelled to flee his squawking children, his nagging wife, the angry glare of his sister who couldn't stand living on this remote hill any longer, and he went to the village to play cards in smoke-filled cafés. He drank cheap alcohol in windowless bars with other men as drunk and ashamed as him. He would often bump into former army friends, silent soldiers who he knew would not try to engage him in conversation.

One evening Mourad followed him there. The next day Amine couldn't remember how his foreman had convinced him to let him tag along. But that evening, Mourad got in the car and the two of them went together to a bar north of the main road. Together they sat and drank, but Amine ignored his friend. Let him get drunk, he thought. Let him get so drunk that he ends up unconscious in a ditch. In the sordid place where they'd washed up, an accordionist was playing and Amine felt like dancing. He wanted to be someone else, someone with no one else depending on him, someone with a carefree, easy life, a sinner's life. A man grabbed him by the shoulder and they swayed from side to side. His companion started laughing hysterically. The laughter spread through the room, contaminating all the other customers like some sort of enchantment. Their mouths opened wide, exposing rotten teeth. Some clapped their hands or stamped their feet in time with the music. A tall, underfed man whistled and everyone turned towards him. 'Let's go,' he said, and they all knew where they were going.

They walked around the edge of the medina to El Mers, the red-light district. Amine was so drunk he could barely walk or see where he was going. Strangers took it in turns to help him stay on his feet. One of the men relieved himself against a wall and suddenly all the others felt an urge to piss. Amine stared, wild-eyed, at the long stream of urine that ran from the town walls to the cobbled street. Mourad went over to him and tried to persuade him not to go any further along this wide street lined with brothels run by cantankerous madams. The street turned into a dark, narrow path, then came to a sort of dead end where criminals lay in wait for men rendered care-less by the relief of fucking. Amine shoved him away, glaring at the hand that Mourad had placed on his shoulder, and they stopped outside a door. One of the men knocked. They heard a clicking noise, the shuffle of oriental slippers on the floor, bracelets jangling. The door opened and half-naked women rushed outside, swarming around the men like locusts around crops. Mourad didn't see Amine disappear. He wanted to reject the brunette who took him by the hand, but instead he let her lead him into a tiny room containing nothing but a bed and a leaking bidet. The alcohol had slowed his reactions and he found it impossible to stay focused on his objective of saving Amine. Already the anger was rising inside him. The girl, who was very young, wore a turban on her head and her skin smelled of cloves. She pulled down Mourad's trousers with a dexterity that horrified him. He saw her unfastening her slip. There were fresh scarifications on her legs, forming some kind of symbol, the meaning unknown to him. He wanted to poke his fingers into the prostitute's eyes then, to punish her. The girl, perhaps recognising that look on his face, hesitated for a moment. She turned towards the door before – clearly in a stupor herself, whether from alcohol or hashish – shrugging and stretching out on the mattress. 'Hurry up. It's hot.'

Later, he wasn't sure if it was this phrase or the sweat that ran between the girl's breasts, if it was the creaking noises coming from other rooms or the vague feeling that he'd heard Amine's voice. But suddenly, staring at this girl with her dilated pupils, images of the war in Indochina flashed into his head, images of those military whorehouses that the Native Affairs Bureau organised for the soldiers. Into his mind came the sounds of that place, the humidity of the air, the dishevelled landscape, which he'd once tried to describe to Amine, who couldn't grasp the nightmarish darkness of that jungle. Mourad ran his hands down his bare arms and felt a chill. He had the impression that a swarm of mosquitoes had filled the room, that his belly and the back of his neck were once again covered by those itchy red blotches that had kept him awake for nights on end. Behind him he heard the yelling of French officers and he thought that he'd seen them, the guts of those white men, that he'd seen Christians dying from diarrhoea, driven crazy by the pointless wars. No, it wasn't killing that was the hardest part. And as he thought this, the click of the trigger echoed in his head and he slapped his own temples as if to empty his mind of these dark ideas.

While the madam kept yelling that they had to hurry up because there were other customers waiting, the prostitute wearily got to her feet. Naked, she walked towards Mourad. 'Are you sick?' she asked, and when the man started sobbing and banging his head against the stone wall, she called out for help. They were all thrown out and the madam spat in the face of the delirious aide-de-camp. The prostitutes made gestures and yelled insults at him. 'A curse on you. A curse on all of you!' Mourad and Amine wandered aimlessly. It was just the two of them now – all the others had fled – and Amine couldn't remember where he'd left the car. He stopped by the side of the street and lit a cigarette, but as soon as he took a puff he felt like he was going to vomit.

The next day he told the labourers that the foreman was ill, and he couldn't help feeling sad when he saw the relief and joy on their faces. When Mathilde offered to look after Mourad, give him some medicine, her husband replied coldly that he only needed rest. 'I think we should find him a wife,' Amine added. 'It's not good to be so alone.'

VIII

Mehki had spent twenty years working as a photographer on Avenue de la République. Whenever he had time – which was pretty often – he would walk along the Avenue, camera hanging from a strap over his shoulder, and offer to take pictures of the people he saw. In his early years he'd struggled with the competition, particularly from one young Armenian man who knew everyone from the shoeshine boy to the bar manager, and took all the customers for himself. In the end Mehki realised that he couldn't rely on chance to find models. That it wasn't enough to keep asking or to lower his prices or talk up his talents. No, what he needed to do was spot the people who wanted a souvenir of that precise moment in their lives. The ones who thought they looked beautiful, who were afraid of growing old or who kept looking at their children getting taller and repeating, 'Time goes by so fast!' There was no point wasting his charm on old people or businessmen or harassed housewives. Children were always the best bet. He pulled faces at them, explained how the camera worked, and the parents could never resist the temptation to immortalise their toddler's angelic face on a rectangle of thick, glossy paper. Mehki had never taken a photograph of his own family. His mother thought his camera was the devil's work, that it would steal the soul of anyone vain enough to pose for it. At the start of his career he'd worked as a photographer for the local authorities and many grooms had refused to let their brides be photographed. Certain high-ranking Moroccans had even written threatening letters to the Resident-General, explaining that they were fiercely opposed to the idea that the women of their town should reveal their faces to strangers. The French had given in, and after that there were numerous leaders and pashas who merely gave brief descriptions of their wives to be appended to their identity papers.

But young lovers were his favourite prey. And on this particular spring day Mehki happened upon the most beautiful couple he'd ever seen. The air was sweet and full of promises. A creamy light flooded the centre of town, caressing the buildings' white facades, bringing out the vivid reds of geraniums and hibiscus flowers. He spotted the couple amid the crowd and ran towards them, finger on the button of his camera, and he was sincere when he said: 'You're so beautiful that I could take your picture for free!' He said this in Arabic and the young man, who was European, raised his hands to show that he hadn't understood. From his pocket he took a banknote and handed it to Mehki. Young lovers are generous, Mehki thought. They want to impress their girlfriends. That generosity never lasts long, but in the meantime it's good for Mehki!

Such were the photographer's thoughts and he was so happy and enthusiastic that he didn't notice how nervous the young woman was, the way she kept looking around as if she were a fugitive. She started when the young man, who was wearing an American-style jacket, stroked her shoulder. They were so beautiful together, so terribly beautiful, that Mehki was dazzled. Not for a second did he think they were badly matched.

He wasn't perceptive enough to understand that these two lovers were not supposed to be together.

What was she doing on the Avenue that Tuesday afternoon, this child from a good family, an honourable family that made her wear straight skirts and plain jackets? She was nothing like those floozies who paraded up and down the Avenue, who fled the vigilant eyes of fathers and brothers, who got pregnant after copulating in the back seat of a car. This girl had a freshness to her that took his breath away, and while he was setting up his camera Mehki thought that there would be something wonderful about being the one person on earth to freeze this instant for eternity. He felt swept up by a sort of grace. The moment was so fleeting, and that face had not yet been soiled by vice, or a man's hand, or the harshness of life. That is what he would capture on film: the naivety of a young woman and the spark of desire for adventure that he could already detect in her gaze. The man, too, was very handsome and the people walking past all turned to stare at his long, lean, muscular body, his solid neck bronzed by the sun. He smiled, and Mehki was a good judge of a person's smile. His teeth and lips were immaculate, not yet stained by too many cigarettes or bad coffee. Thankfully most of his models kept their mouths closed when they posed for him, but this young man was so transported by joy and felt so lucky that he couldn't stop laughing and talking.

The girl refused to pose. She wanted to leave and she whispered something into the man's ear, something that Mehki couldn't hear. But her boyfriend insisted, he held her by the wrist, turned her around and said: 'Come on, it'll only take a second. It'll be a nice souvenir.' Mehki couldn't have put it better himself. A few seconds for a memory that will last a lifetime – that was his slogan. She stood there so stiffly, her face so blank, that Mehki approached her and, in Arabic, asked her name. 'Okay then, Selma, smile and look at me.'

When he'd taken the photograph Mehki handed them a ticket and the young man put it in his jacket pocket. 'Come back tomorrow. If you don't see me on the Avenue, I'll leave your photo in the studio, just over there on the corner.' And Mehki watched as they walked away, melting into the crowd that moved along the pavement.

The next day the young man did not come back. Mehki waited for him for days; he even changed his routine in the hope of bumping into him. It was an excellent photograph, perhaps the best portrait he'd ever taken. He'd managed to capture the light of that May afternoon, and he'd framed it so that palm trees and the cinema sign were visible in the background. The two lovers were looking into each other's eyes. The shy, waif-like girl had turned to face the handsome young man, whose mouth was half-open as he smiled.

One evening Mehki went into Lucien's studio. Lucien developed his films and had let him buy a new camera on credit. They did their business, settled up, and at the end of their conversation Mehki took the photograph from his little leather knapsack. 'It's a shame they never came to get it,' he said.

Lucien, who put all his energy into hiding his desire for men, bent over the photograph and exclaimed: 'What a handsome boy! Yes, it's a shame they didn't come back.' Mehki shrugged and, as he reached out to take the photograph back, Lucien said: 'It's a very beautiful photograph, Mehki, really very beautiful. You're improving, you know? Listen, how about this? I'll

262

put the photo in my window: it'll bring in customers, which is good for me, and it'll show everyone that you're the best photographer of young lovers in all of Meknes, which is good for you. What do you think?'

Mehki hesitated. Of course he was flattered, and it was true that this photograph could bring him quite a few new customers. But he also had a strange desire to keep the image all to himself, to make this young couple his imaginary friends, his anonymous companions. He was a little fearful of throwing them to the wolves on the Avenue. But Lucien was very persuasive, and in the end Mehki agreed. That evening, just before closing up the shop, Lucien hung the photograph in his window, so everyone in Meknes could admire the pilot Alain Crozières and his young girlfriend, Selma Belhaj. Less than a week later Amine walked past the window and saw it.

Later, Selma and Mathilde would believe that fate was against them. That even chance was on the side of men, the side of power, the side of injustice. Because in that spring of 1955 Amine rarely went into the new town. The rising number of killings and kidnappings, and the increasingly violent response of the French military to the nationalists' actions, had created an oppressive atmosphere in the town and Amine preferred to stay away. But that day, he broke with his usual habits and went to Dragan Palosi's office because the doctor had decided to order some young fruit trees from Europe. 'Come to my office. We can talk business and then I'll go with you to the bank to negotiate the credit you need.' And that was what happened. Amine sat, steeped in shame, in the waiting room filled with women, at least half of whom were pregnant. He talked for nearly half an hour with the doctor, who showed him a glossy catalogue displaying varieties of peach, plum and apricot trees, and after that they walked side by side to the bank, where they were greeted by a man with scaly skin. According to Dragan this man was married to an Algerian woman and lived just outside the town, near one of those orchards rented by city dwellers so they could picnic there on Sundays. The banker asked about Amine's agricultural plans with an enthusiasm and precision that surprised him. At the end of the interview they shook hands on the deal and Amine left the bank with a feeling of great satisfaction.

He was happy, and that was why he walked slowly along the Avenue. He deserved to stroll for a while, he thought, to look at women, to stand so close to them that he could smell their scent. He didn't want to go home yet and that was why, hands in pockets, eyes dwelling on the shop windows, he kept walking, forgetting the news, forgetting his brother, forgetting Mathilde's criticism of his latest investments. He gazed at the window of a lingerie shop, at the pointed bras and satin knickers. He admired a display of chocolates and candied cherries in a patisserie window. And then, in the window of a photography studio, he saw the picture. For a few seconds he couldn't believe it. He laughed nervously and thought: How strange, that girl looks just like Selma! She must be an Italian or a Spaniard, he thought – a European girl, in any case – and she's very pretty. But then his throat tightened. He felt as if someone had punched him in the stomach and his whole body stiffened with anger. He moved closer to the window, less to observe the details of the picture than to block it from the view of passing pedestrians. He had the impression that his sister was standing naked in public and that his own body was the only thing that could preserve her modesty. It took all his self-restraint not to smash the window with his forehead, grab the photograph and run away.

He went into the shop and found Lucien playing patience behind the wooden counter.

'Can I help you?' the shop owner asked. He looked anxiously at Amine. What could this frowning, sullen-looking Arab possibly want? Just his luck: the studio was empty and now one of those nationalists – perhaps even a terrorist – had come in to attack him just because he was alone, defenceless and French. Amine took a handkerchief from his pocket and wiped his forehead.

'I would like to see the photograph in the window. The one with the young girl.'

'This one?' Lucien walked slowly to the shelves, picked up the photograph and placed it on the counter.

Amine stared at it for a long time, in silence. At last he asked: 'How much?'

'I beg your pardon?'

'How much for the photograph? I would like to buy it.'

'Oh, it's not for sale. That couple paid for the photograph and the man was supposed to come in and claim it. They haven't dropped by yet. But we mustn't give up hope,' Lucien added sourly, before starting to laugh.

Amine glared at him.

'Tell me how much you want for this photo and I'll pay it.'

'But I just told you—'

'Listen to me. That girl,' he said, pointing, 'that girl is my sister and I have no intention of leaving her for one minute longer in the window of your shop. Tell me how much I owe you and I'll be on my way.'

Lucien didn't want any trouble. He'd left France after being blackmailed, and he'd come to this new world – a world just as mean as the old one, but with better weather – with the idea of sticking to his vows to be discreet. He'd heard far too much about the Arabs' sense of honour to dare provoke them. 'Touch their women and you'll regret it,' a customer had told him just after he opened the studio. No risk of that, Lucien had thought. A few days before this, he'd read in the newspaper about a French bureaucrat, in Rabat or Port Lyautey, who'd been stabbed by an old Moroccan man. When asked why he'd done it, the Moroccan said that the Frenchman had touched the headscarf that concealed his wife's face, then laughed and said: 'But she's as blonde as a German, the fatma. And blue eyes too!' Lucien shivered and handed the picture to Amine.

'Take it,' he said. 'She's your sister, after all. You can give it to her. Or do whatever you want with it – it's no business of mine.'

Amine took the photograph and left the studio without saying goodbye. Lucien drew down the blinds and decided to close the shop early.

When Amine got back to the farm it was dark and Mathilde was darning in the living room. He stood in the doorway for a long time, watching her, while she remained unaware of his presence. He swallowed mouthfuls of his own saliva; it was sticky and salty.

At last Mathilde saw him and almost immediately looked down at the cardigan she was mending. 'You're back late,' she said, and she wasn't surprised when he didn't reply. Her husband came up to her. He stared at the cardigan with the torn sleeve, and then at his wife's middle fingertip, protected by a silver-plated thimble. He took the photograph from his jacket pocket, and when he placed it on top of the cardigan Mathilde covered her mouth with her hands. The thimble banged against her teeth. She looked like a murderer, caught in the act. She was confused, trapped.

'It's completely innocent,' she stammered. 'I'd been meaning to talk to you about it. That boy has serious intentions. He wants to come to the farm, to ask for her hand in marriage. He's a good boy, I promise you.'

Amine stared at her and Mathilde had the impression that his eyes were growing bigger, his features distorting, his mouth becoming enormous, and she jumped when he started yelling: 'Are you completely insane? My sister isn't going to marry a Frenchman!'

He grabbed Mathilde by the sleeve and pulled her out of the chair. He dragged her towards the dark hallway. 'You humiliated me!' He spat in her face and then slapped her with the back of his hand.

She thought about the children and stayed silent. She didn't throw herself at her husband or scratch his face or defend herself. Don't say a word, she told herself. Wait for his anger to fade. Pray that it gives way to shame and that the shame is enough to stop him. She let him drag her, like a dead weight. But her passivity only increased Amine's rage. He wanted a confrontation, he wanted her to defend herself. With his large dark hand he grabbed a fistful of her hair, forcing her to stand up, pulling her face close to his. 'This isn't over,' he said, punching her in the face. At the entrance of the hallway that led to the bedrooms he let go of her. She kneeled in front of him, her nose bleeding. He unbuttoned his jacket, then started to shake. He knocked over a little wooden bookshelf. It smashed and the books scattered all over the floor.

Mathilde looked up and saw Aïcha watching them from the doorway. When Amine looked in his daughter's direction his face relaxed and it seemed for a moment that he was about to burst out laughing, to claim that this was just a game he played with Mama, a game that children couldn't understand, and that she should go back to bed now. Instead he stepped furiously towards the bedroom.

Mathilde stared at the cover of a book on the floor. *The Wonderful Adventures of Nils*, which her father used to read to her when she was little. She focused all her attention on the drawing of young Nils sitting on a goose's back. She didn't raise her eyes when the sound of Selma's screams reached her.

She didn't move when her sister-in-law called for help. Then she heard Amine's voice threatening them.

'I'm going to kill you all!'

In his hand was a revolver, the barrel pointed at Selma's beautiful face. A few weeks before this he'd applied for a fire-arms licence. He'd said it was to protect his family, that the countryside was a dangerous place, that they couldn't rely on anyone but themselves. Mathilde put her hands over her eyes. It was the only thing she could do, the only idea that came to mind. She didn't want to see this, didn't want to look death in the face, didn't want to see her husband, the father of her children, become a murderer. Then she thought about her daughter, about her infant son sleeping peacefully, about Selma who was sobbing now, and she turned towards the children's bedroom.

Amine followed her gaze and saw Aïcha, her hair illuminated by a faint halo of light. She looked like a ghost. 'I'm going to kill you all!' he yelled again, waving the gun around dement-edly. He didn't know who to kill first, but once he'd made that decision he would shoot all of them, one after another, with coldness and determination. Their sobs and screams fused, Mathilde and Selma begging for his forgiveness, and then he heard his name, he heard 'Papa', and he started sweating in his suddenly too-small jacket. He'd already shot someone before. A man, a stranger. He'd already shot someone so he knew he could do it, that it would be over very quickly, that the fear would fade and be replaced by an immense feeling of relief, a sort of omni-potence. But he heard 'Papa' and it came from over there, from the doorway where his child stood in her soaked nightshirt, her feet in a puddle of urine. For an instant he thought about shooting himself. That would solve everything. There would be no need for any more words or explanations. And his best jacket would be covered in his blood. He dropped the revolver and, without looking at them, left the room.

Mathilde put her finger to her lips. She was weeping silently and she gestured for Selma to stay where she was. She crawled over to the gun. Her vision was blurred by tears, her nose was pouring with blood and she was struggling to breathe. Flashes of pain ran through her head and she had to hold her hands to her temples for several seconds to stop herself fainting. She picked up the revolver. It was very heavy and she started frantically turning it in her hands. She looked around, in search of something, a way to make the gun disappear. She stared desperately at her daughter and then, standing on tiptoe, she reached up to grab the enormous terracotta vase that sat on top of the large bookshelf. She tipped it slightly and tossed the revolver inside. Then she let go of the vase, which slowly swayed from side to side, and for those few seconds the three of them stood paralysed, terrified by the thought that the vase would smash and Amine would return, see the gun amid the shards, and kill them all.

'Listen, my darlings.' Mathilde drew Selma and her daughter towards her and held them to her heart, which was beating so hard that it scared the child. The smell of piss and blood. 'Never tell him where the gun is, you hear me? Even if he begs you or threatens you or promises something in exchange. Never tell him it's in the vase.' They nodded slowly. 'I want to hear you say, "I promise!" Say it!' Mathilde looked angry now and the girls obeyed.

Mathilde led them into the bathroom. She filled a large bowl with warm water and put Aïcha into it. She washed the stained nightshirt, then she soaked a cloth in alcohol and cold water and wiped it over both girls' faces. Her nose was burning with pain. She didn't dare touch it, but she knew that it was broken. And – despite her pain, despite her anger – she couldn't help feeling sad at the thought that she would always be ugly now. Not only had Amine stolen her dignity; he had given her a boxer's nose.

Aïcha knew about women with bruised faces. She'd often seen them: mothers with half-closed eyes, purple cheeks, split lips. At the time, in fact, she thought that was why make-up had been invented. To conceal the effects of men's fists.

All three of them slept in the same room that night, legs intertwined. Before falling asleep with her back leaning on her mother's belly, Aïcha said her prayers out loud. *'O Lord, bless the sleep that I will take to recover my strength so that I can better serve you. Holy Virgin, mother of God, and after Him my greatest hope, my good angel, my patron saint, protect me all through this night, all through my life and at the hour of my death. Amen.'*

They woke in the same position, as if they'd been frozen by the fear that he would return, somehow convinced that together the three of them formed an invincible body. In their restless sleep they had transformed into a sort of animal, a hermit crab protected by its shell. Mathilde hugged her daughter tight, wishing she could make them both disappear. Sleep, my child, all this is nothing but a bad dream.

* * *

All night long Amine walked through the countryside. In the darkness he bumped into trees and the branches scratched his face. As he walked he cursed every acre of this barren earth. Delirious, he started counting the stones and he felt certain that they were conspiring against him, multiplying in the shadows, thousands of them spreading through every field in his domain, making the soil impossible to plough, ridding it of all hope of new life. He wished he could crush all those rocks with his bare hands, with his teeth, chew them up and spit them out in an enormous dust cloud that would cover everything. The air was cold. He sat at the base of a tree, his whole body trembling. He hunched over, curled into a ball, and fell into a half-sleep, dazed by alcohol and shame.

He didn't return to the house until two days later. Mathilde didn't ask where he'd been and Amine didn't look for the revolver. For several days the house was filled with a thick, deep silence that nobody dared break. Aïcha spoke with her eyes. Selma didn't leave her room. She spent her days lying in bed, weeping into her pillow, cursing her brother and swearing vengeance. Amine had decided to take her out of school. He didn't see the point in disturbing the girl even more by filling her head with crazy ideas.

Amine spent his days outside. He couldn't bear to look at Mathilde's face, the purple rings under her eyes, her nose that had doubled in size, her cut lip. He wasn't sure, but he thought she might have lost a tooth. He left at dawn and went home when his wife was asleep. He slept in his office and used the outside toilets, to the disgust of Tamo, who didn't want to share her bathroom with a man. For days he surrendered to cowardice.

The following Saturday he was up before the sun. He

washed himself, shaved, splashed cologne on his neck. He went into the kitchen, where Mathilde was frying eggs, her back to him. She smelled his scent and she couldn't move. Standing in front of the cooker, wooden spatula in hand, she prayed that he wouldn't say anything. It was the only thing she cared about. Please don't let him be stupid enough to open his mouth, she thought. Please don't let him say something banal and act as if nothing has happened. If he says, 'I'm sorry', I will slap him. But the silence remained unbroken. Amine walked about behind Mathilde. She couldn't see him, but she could tell that he was pacing the kitchen like a wild beast, nostrils flared, breathing heavily. He leaned against a large blue cupboard and watched her. She ran her hand through her hair and tightened the string of her apron. She let the eggs burn and coughed into her fist when the smoke made her choke.

She was ashamed to admit it, but the silence between them was having a strange effect on her. She thought that if they never spoke again they might become animals once more, opening up all kinds of possibilities. They could learn new ways to love, they could roar, fight, scratch each other until they bled. There would no longer be any need for those end-less explanations and debates that never resolved anything. She had no desire for vengeance. And her body – the body that he'd damaged, that he'd broken – she wanted to surren-der it to him completely. For days they didn't say anything, they just fucked. Up against a wall, behind a door. Even out-side, once, leaning against the ladder that led to the roof. To shame him she abandoned all inhibitions, all modesty. She threw her lust, her vice, her womanly beauty in his face. She gave him orders so crude that he was shocked, and excited.

She proved to him that there was something mysterious inside her, something dirty that he had not made that way. A darkness that was hers and that he would never understand.

One evening, while Mathilde was ironing, Amine went into the kitchen and said: 'Come with me. He's here.'

Mathilde put down the iron. She left the kitchen, then retraced her steps. Watched by Aïcha, she leaned over the kitchen tap, splashed water on her face and smoothed down her hair. She took off her apron and said: 'I'll be back.' Of course, the child followed her, quiet as a mouse, and her eyes shone as she walked through the dark hallway. She sat behind the door and through a crack in the wood she glimpsed an old, stocky, badly shaved man with spots on his skin, wearing a brown djellaba. There were bags under his eyes, so swollen that she imagined the brush of a fingertip or a breath of wind would be enough to burst them and for viscous liquid to ooze from the flabby sac. He was sitting on a chair in the office, with a young man standing behind him. There was a large yellow stain on the young man's khaki jacket, as if a bird had shat on him. He handed the old man a large leatherbound notebook.

'Your name?' said the old man, looking at Mathilde.

She answered, but the adoul turned to Amine. Frowning, he repeated: 'Her name?' and Amine spelled out his wife's name.

'Her father's name?'

'Georges,' said Amine, and he leaned down over the notebook, embarrassed at having to reveal this Christian first name, so impossible to spell.

'Jourge? Jourge?' the adoul said, then began to chew his pen. Behind him the young man fidgeted.

'I'm just going to write it the way it sounds,' the man of law concluded, and his young assistant looked relieved.

The adoul stared at Mathilde for a few seconds, examining her face then her hands, which she held clasped together. Then Aïcha heard her mother reciting, in Arabic: 'I swear that there is no god but God, and that Muhammad is His prophet.'

'Very good,' said the man of law. 'And what name will you take now?'

Mathilde didn't know what to say. Amine had told her about the need to be rebaptised, to adopt a Muslim name, but she'd been so weighed down by other worries recently that she hadn't given it a thought.

'Mariam,' she said finally, and the adoul appeared very satisfied with this choice. 'Let it be so, Mariam. Welcome to the community of Islam.'

Amine came close to the door. He saw Aïcha and told her: 'I don't like the way you spy on people all the time. Go to your room.' She stood up and walked through the long hallway. Her father followed her. She lay down in bed and saw Amine grab Selma's arm, the same way the nuns grabbed girls at school when they were going to be punished and the Mother Superior wanted to see them.

Aïcha was already asleep when Selma and Mourad entered the office and – witnessed by Mathilde, Amine and two labourers who'd been summoned for the occasion – the adoul pronounced them man and wife.

276

Selma wouldn't listen. When Mathilde knocked at the door of the storeroom – where Selma now slept with her husband – her sister-in-law refused to open it. Mathilde kicked the door, she banged on it with her fists, she yelled, and then, resting her head against the wooden slats, she began speaking very quietly, as if she hoped Selma would press her face against the door too and listen to her advice, the way she always used to. In a gentle voice, without thinking, without calculating, Mathilde asked her sister-in-law to forgive her. She spoke to her about inner freedom, about the need to resign herself to her fate, about the illusory dreams of true love that lured young girls to the rocks of despair and failure. 'I was young once too, you know.' She spoke to her about the future. 'One day you'll understand. One day you'll thank us.' It was important, she told Selma, to look on the bright side. Not to let her sadness contaminate the birth of her first child. Not to brood over the loss of a young man who, although handsome, had also been cowardly and thoughtless. Selma didn't reply. She was crouched against the wall, far from the door, her hands covering her ears. She'd confided in Mathilde, she'd let her touch her aching breasts, her still-flat belly, and Mathilde had betrayed her. No, Selma wouldn't listen. She'd pour tar into her ears if she had to. Her sister-in-law had done what she'd done out of jealousy. She could have helped her run away, kill this baby, marry Alain

277

Crozières. She could have put into action all those pretty speeches she'd given about the emancipation of women and the right to choose love. Instead she'd let the law of men rise up between them. She'd denounced Selma, and her brother had immediately turned to the old ways to solve the problem. She probably can't stand the idea of me being happy, thought Selma. Happier than her and with a better marriage than hers.

When she wasn't locked in her room Selma stayed close to the children or to Mouilala, making it impossible to have a private conversation. This was torture for Mathilde, who was desperate to be forgiven. She ran up behind Selma whenever she saw her alone in the garden. Once, she grabbed the back of her blouse and almost strangled her. 'Let me explain. Please stop running away from me.' But Selma spun around and began hitting Mathilde with both hands, kicking her in the shins. Tamo heard their yells as they fought like children, but she didn't dare get involved. They'd find a way to blame me for it, she thought as she closed the curtain. Mathilde protected her face and begged Selma: 'Try to be reasonable. Your pilot disappeared anyway, as soon as he found out about the child. You should think yourself lucky that we found a way for you to avoid the shame.'

At night, while Amine snored beside her, Mathilde thought over what she'd said. Did she really believe it? Had she become that kind of woman? The kind that encourages others to be reasonable, to give up, to choose respectability over happiness? But ultimately, she thought, there was nothing she could have done. And she repeated this, over and over, not because she felt sorry for herself, but in an attempt to convince herself, to alleviate her guilt. She wondered what Mourad and Selma were doing at that moment. She imagined the aide-de-camp's naked body, his hands on the young woman's hips, his toothless mouth pressed against her lips. She envisioned them together in such detail that she had to force herself not to scream, shove her husband out of the bed and weep over the fate of that child they'd abandoned. She got out of bed and started pacing up and down the hallway to calm her nerves. In the kitchen she ate leftover Linzer Torte with jam until she felt sick. Then she leaned out of the window, convinced that she would hear a moan or a grunt. But all she heard was the rats running up the trunk of the giant palm tree. She understood then that what tormented her, what revolted her, was less the marriage itself or the morality of Amine's choice than the simple act of that unnatural copulation. And she had to admit that the real reason she kept following Selma around was not to apologise but to ask her questions about that vile, monstrous coupling. She wanted to know if the teenager had been frightened, if she'd felt a shiver of disgust when her husband's penis penetrated her. If she'd shut her eyes and thought about her young pilot to blot out the reality of that ugly old man.

* * *

One morning a pick-up truck parked in the courtyard and two boys unloaded a large wooden bed. The elder of the two couldn't have been more than seventeen. He wore a pair of trousers that only reached halfway down his calves and a canvas cap faded by the sun. The younger boy had a doll-like face that offered a strange contrast with his massive, muscled body. He stood back and waited for the older boy to give him orders. Mourad pointed out the storeroom but the boy in the cap just shrugged. 'It won't fit through the door.' Mourad, who'd bought the bed from one of the best artisans in town, exploded. He wasn't there to have a discussion. He ordered them to take the bed in sideways, dragging it along the ground. For more than an hour they shoved the bed, carried it, turned it over. They hurt their backs and their hands. Sweating and red-faced, the two boys laughed at Mourad's stubbornness. 'Come on, old man, be reasonable!' said the younger boy. 'If it's too big for the hole, you'll never get it in there.' The foreman was disgusted by the boy's lewd double-entendre. Exhausted, the teenager sat on the bed base and winked at his companion: 'It's his missus who'll be disappointed. This is a really nice bed for such a small house.' Mourad stared at the boys as they jumped on the bed and laughed. He felt stupid and he wanted to cry. When he'd seen this bed in the medina it had seemed perfect. He'd thought about Amine then, and how proud of him his boss would be: a man capable of buying a bed like this would be the best possible husband for his sister, Amine would think. 'I'm an idiot,' Mourad muttered, and it took a huge effort of self-control not to beat the boys and take an axe to the bed. Instead he watched the truck vanish in a cloud of dust, his heart filled with a calm despair.

For two days the bed stayed where it was and nobody asked any questions. Amine said nothing, and nor did Mathilde. They were both so embarrassed and ashamed that they pretended it was perfectly normal for a double bed to sit there, in the middle of a sandy courtyard. Then, one morning, Mourad asked for the day off and Amine said yes. The foreman picked up a mallet and smashed down the wall of the storeroom that faced the fields, then pushed the bed through the gap. After that, he got some bricks and mortar and began enlarging the room where he would live from now on with Selma. All day and long into the night he built a new wall. He intended to install a bathroom in the house for his wife, who currently had to use the outside toilets. Tamo stood on tiptoe to watch through the window as the foreman laboured. Mathilde told her to mind her own business and get back to work.

When the house was ready Mourad felt proud, but it didn't change his habits. At night he left the big bed to Selma while he slept on the floor.

To find Omar they had to follow the smell of blood. That was what Amine said, and in that summer of 1955 there was no lack of blood. It ran through the streets of Morocco's cities, where more and more people were murdered in broad daylight, where bombs exploded in the streets. The violence spread through the countryside: crops were burned, plantation owners beaten to death. These killings were a mixture of politics and personal vengeance. People were killed in the name of God and of country, to wipe out a debt, to pay back a humiliation or an adulterous wife. The white authorities responded with racist attacks and torture. The only thing the two sides had in common was fear.

Every time he heard about a killing Amine would wonder if Omar was involved. Was he dead? Was he a murderer? He thought about it when an industrialist was assassinated in Casablanca, when a French soldier died in Rabat, when an old Moroccan perished in Berkane and when a town planning officer was the target of an attack in Marrakech. He thought about Omar when – two days after the murder of the pro-independence newspaper owner Jacques Lemaigre-Dubreuil by counter-terrorists – he listened to the Resident-General Francis Lacoste give a speech on the radio. 'Violence, in all its forms, is horrifying and contemptible.' A few days later Lacoste was replaced by Gilbert Grandval, who arrived at a moment of high tension. At first Grandval sparked hopes that the terrorism could be brought to an end, that a dialogue could be re-established between the two communities. He reversed a number of convictions and distancing measures. He stood up to extremists in the French community. But on 14 July an attack in Place Mers Sultan in Casablanca destroyed all those hopes. Grieving women, their faces veiled in black, refused to shake hands with the French representative. 'We have no attachment to mainland France and now we're going to lose what we spent years building: the country where we raised our children.' Europeans rushed into the medina of the white town, grabbing all the French flags that had been put out to line the streets for Bastille Day. They pillaged shops, set fires and committed all kinds of atrocities, sometimes egged on by the police. A chasm filled with blood now gaped between the two communities.

On the night of 24 July 1955 Omar reappeared. He came to Meknes hidden in the back seat of a car driven by a Casablancan teenager. They parked below the medina, in a dead-end road that smelled of urine, and smoked cigarettes while they waited for the sun to rise. Gilbert Grandval's retinue was supposed to drive through Place El-Hedim around nine that morning, and Omar and his companions considered it their duty to welcome him. In the boot of the car, hidden inside large bags filled with rubble, were two revolvers and a few knives.

The sky lightened and the square filled with French troops in ceremonial uniform. They were going to present arms as the retinue passed and then escort the Resident-General to the Mansour Gate, where he would be given dates and milk. Women stood behind barriers. They waved cross-shaped dolls in robes made of cloth and small bouquets of flowers. In exchange for their presence they'd been given a few coins, and they were laughing among themselves. Despite their cheerfulness it was obvious that their fervour was fake, that their chants of 'Vive la France' were nothing more than a sad farce. Some amputees tried to get as close as they could to the passage of the procession in the hope that the people of France would be alerted to their fate. When the police pushed them back, they shouted: 'We fought for France and now we're living in poverty.'

At dawn special protection groups began setting up blockades in front of each gate leading to the old town. But soon they were overwhelmed by the massing crowds. A van parked on Place El-Hedim and the police, in a panic, ordered the passengers to get out and drop the Moroccan flags that they were waving. The men refused and began stamping their feet in the back of the van, making it sway. The sound of those stomping feet galvanised the crowd. Boys and old men, peasants from the mountain, bourgeois businessmen and shopkeepers all gathered in the vicinity of the square. They carried flags and photographs of the sultan and they chanted: 'Youssef! Youssef!' Some held clubs, others carving knives. Near the tribune where the Resident-General was due to give his speech, local worthies looked anxious and their white djellabas were stained with sweat.

Omar gave a signal to his companions and they leaped out of the car. They walked up to the increasingly agitated crowd and melted into it. Behind them veiled women had climbed on to trestles and were shouting: 'Independence!' Omar made a fist and started yelling along. To the men who surrounded him he gave out bags filled with rubbish. They threw rotten fruit and dried shit at the policemen's faces. Omar's deep, vibrant voice was like a flame in a forest. He stamped his foot, spat on the ground, and his rage spread around him. Young boys and old men all swelled with courage and pride. One teenage boy, wearing a white vest and a pair of trousers that revealed his hairless calves, started throwing stones at the security guards. The other protesters imitated him and soon the police were caught in a rain of stones. All other sounds were drowned out by the clatter of rocks on the cobblestones and the shouts of the policemen, calling – in French – for calm. One of them, bleeding from his eyebrow, grabbed his submachine gun. He fired into the air and then – jaw tensed, eyes filled with fear – aimed his gun at the crowd and fired again. In front of Omar, the boy from Casablanca fell to the ground. Despite the chaos of people running and women crying, his companions gathered round him and one of them started looking around frantically. 'There are ambulances coming. We have to get him out of here!'

But Omar made a commanding gesture with his hand and said: 'No.'

The young men, used to their leader's coldness, stared at him. Omar's face was totally calm. He smiled. Things were going exactly as he'd hoped. This disorder, this confusion, was the best thing that could have happened.

'If we take him to the hospital and he survives, they'll torture him. They'll threaten to send him to Darkoum or somewhere and he'll talk. No ambulance.'

Omar squatted down and with his skinny arms he picked up the wounded boy, who screamed with pain.

'Run!'

In the panic Omar lost his glasses, and later he would believe that it was this blindness that enabled him to run through the crowds, avoiding bullets and making it to the gate of the medina, where he could lose himself in the maze of backstreets. He didn't look round to see if the others were still with him; he made no attempt to console the injured boy, who was calling for his mother and praying to Allah. He also didn't see, on his way out of the square, the hundreds of abandoned slippers strewn across the ground, the blood-stained fezzes, the weeping men.

In the streets of Berrima he heard the ululations of women gathered on roof terraces. He felt as if they were encouraging him, guiding him towards his mother's house, and like a sleep-walker he found his way to the hobnailed door and knocked. An old man opened it. Omar pushed him out of the way and ran on to the patio. When the door had been closed behind him he asked: 'Who are you?'

'Tell me who you are first,' said the old man.

'This is my mother's house. Where are they?'

'They left. Weeks ago. I'm looking after the house for them.' The caretaker glanced uneasily at the body slumped over Omar's shoulder and added: 'I don't want any trouble.'

Omar lay the wounded boy on a damp bench. He put his ear close to the boy's mouth. He was breathing.

'Keep an eye on him,' Omar ordered, then went upstairs, feeling his way with his hands. All he could see were vague shapes, haloes of light, disturbing movements. He smelled smoke then and realised that houses all over the city were burning, that the protesters had set fire to traitors' businesses, that the revolt was really happening. He heard the roar of an aeroplane flying over the medina and the sound of gunfire in the distance. His heart filled with joy as he thought that right now, outside, men were still fighting, and that France – in the person of Gilbert Grandval – must be trembling before this uprising. By late morning gendarmes and uniformed goumiers had surrounded the medina of the new town. Near the Poublan Camp three tanks took up position, aiming their guns at the native town.

When Omar went downstairs again the boy had fainted. The caretaker was with him, sniffing and tapping his forehead. Omar told him to shut up, and like a cat the old man walked across the patio and went to hide in Mouilala's old room. All afternoon Omar sat on the hot patio. Sometimes he massaged his temples and opened his wide, owl-like eyes as if hoping that his sight would miraculously return. He couldn't risk going out and getting arrested. The police were prowling the medina's backstreets now, knocking on doors, threatening to break in and pillage everything if the inhabitants didn't open up. Jeeps drove through the streets, picking up the few Europeans who still lived in the old town and evacuating them to the fairground or the Bordeaux Hotel, which had been requisitioned for that purpose.

After a few hours Omar fell asleep. The old man, who started at the slightest noise, began to pray. He looked at Omar and thought how cold-hearted and amoral he must be to be able to sleep in such a situation. During the night the wounded boy started twitching and groaning. The caretaker went over, held his hand and tried to hear what the boy was whispering. The boy was just a poor peasant who'd fled a life of deprivation in the mountains to try his luck in the slums of Casablanca. For months he'd looked for work on one of those building sites that people were always telling him about. But nobody had wanted him and, like thousands of other peasants, he'd gone to work the quarries, at the edge of the white town, too poor and ashamed to even think of going home. It had been there, among houses with corrugated-iron roofs, in that shanty town where fatherless children shat in the street and died from throat infections, that a recruiter had found him. The man must have looked at the hate and despair in that boy's eyes and thought: Perfect. Now, feverish and in terrible pain, the boy was begging for someone to contact his mother.

Early in the morning Omar called out to the caretaker: 'Find a doctor. If the police ask you where you're going, tell them a woman is giving birth and it's urgent. Hurry up! You find a doctor and then you come back here, understood?'

He handed him some money and the old man, relieved to be free of that cursed house, quickly left.

Two hours later Dragan arrived. He hadn't asked the old man any questions, he'd just picked up his old leather bag and followed him. He wasn't expecting to see Omar and he took a step back when the young man's tall body appeared in front of him.

'This guy's wounded.'

Dragan followed him and leaned over the boy, who was breathing weakly. Behind him Amine's brother fidgeted. Without his glasses he looked more childlike, his fine features drawn with tiredness. His hair was sticky with sweat and his neck was covered with dried blood. He stank.

Dragan rummaged around in his bag. He asked the old man to boil some water so he could clean his instruments. The doctor disinfected the wound and made a sort of bandage around the injured arm, then gave the boy a tranquilliser. While he was treating him Dragan spoke softly, stroked the boy's forehead and reassured him.

While Dragan was busy sewing up the wound, Omar's comrades had come into the house. Observing the deference with which they treated their leader the caretaker became suddenly obsequious. He ran to the kitchen and began making tea for the resistance fighters. He cursed the French, calling them infidels, and when his eyes met Dragan's the doctor just shrugged to show that he didn't care.

The doctor went over to Omar before leaving.

'You'll have to check the wound and keep it clean. I can drop by again tonight if you want. I'll bring a clean bandage and some medicine for the fever.'

'That's very kind of you, but we'll be gone by tonight,' Omar replied.

'Your brother's worried about you. He's been searching for you. The rumour was that you were in prison.'

'We're all in prison. As long as we live in a colonised country we can't call ourselves free.'

Dragan didn't know what to say to this. He shook Omar's hand and left. He walked through the deserted streets of the medina and the few faces he saw were marked with grief and sorrow. The voice of a muezzin rose into the sky. That morning four boys had been buried. The French police had set up a security cordon at dawn, and they had protected the funeral procession as it peacefully entered the mosque. When Omar had seen Dragan to the door he'd offered him money but the doctor had coldly refused. He's a cruel man, Dragan thought on his way home. Amine's brother reminded him of other men he'd met during his travels. Men full of fine words and grandiose ideals who had used up all their humanity in the speeches they gave.

Dragan let his chauffeur go for the day. He sat at the wheel of his car and drove, windows open, to the Belhaj farm. Outside, the sky was a tender blue and the heat so oppressive that he half expected the fields to burst into flame at any moment. He opened his mouth and breathed in the hot wind, the ill wind that warmed his lungs and made him cough. The air smelled of bay leaves and crushed stink bugs. As always in such moments of melancholy he thought about his trees, about the ripe, juicy oranges that would one day roll on Czech and Hungarian tables, as if he'd sent a parcel of sunlight to those nightlands.

When he reached the hill he felt almost guilty at being the bearer of sad news. He wasn't one of those people who believed in the myth of villages filled with easy-going, happy Berber peasants. All the same, he knew that there was a sort of peace and harmony in this place, which Amine and Mathilde felt responsible for maintaining. He didn't realise that they kept themselves deliberately apart from the fury of the town, that they kept the radio silent, and that newspapers were used here only for packing up fresh eggs or making little hats and aeroplanes for Selim. He parked his car. In the distance he could see Amine hurrying home. In the garden Aïcha had climbed a tree and Selma was sitting on the swing that Amine had hung from the branches of the 'lemange' tree. The hot concrete tiles had been watered and a cloud of steam was rising from the ground. Inside the foliage, birds flew and sang, and tears welled in Dragan's eyes as he contemplated the indifference of nature and the stupidity of men. We will all kill one another, he thought, and butterflies will continue to fly.

Mathilde looked so happy to see Dragan that he felt his heart contract even more. She wanted to lead him into the clinic, show him the progress she'd made in arranging her instruments and medicines. She asked about Corinne, who was staying in their cabin by the sea, and whom he missed. She said he should eat lunch with them and, as he noticed that her neck and cheeks were covered with red blotches, she apologised that all they were going to eat was coffee and toast. 'It's silly, but the children like it.' Dragan, afraid of being overheard, whispered that he'd come about something serious and that perhaps they should talk about it in the office.

He sat facing Amine and Mathilde and, in a neutral voice, told them about last night's events. Amine shifted in his chair and stared through the window, as if he had more urgent business elsewhere. His expression seemed to say: 'What does this have to do with me?' When Dragan spoke Omar's name the couple froze, suddenly attentive and united. Not once did they look at each other, but Dragan could see that they were holding hands. At that moment they were not in opposing camps. They weren't rejoicing in the other's misfortune. They weren't waiting for the other to cry or punch the air so that they could angrily insult them. No, at that moment they both belonged to a camp that didn't exist, a strange camp where forgiveness for violence and compassion for both the killers and the killed was mixed in equal measure. All the feelings that rose inside them seemed like a form of treachery, and so they preferred to stay silent. They were at once victims and murderers, companions and enemies, two hybrid beings incapable of giving a name to their loyalties. They were excommunicated; two worshippers who could no longer pray in any church and whose god was a secret god, a private god whose name they didn't even know.

IX

Eid al-Adha fell on 30 July that year. In the town, as in the village, people feared that the festival celebrating Abraham's sacrifice would turn into a massacre. The Resident-General gave very strict instructions to the soldiers stationed in Meknes and to the bureaucrats, who were angry that they wouldn't be able to return to France for the summer. Many of the colonists near the Belhaj farm were leaving their properties. Roger Mariani was going to Cabo Negro, where he owned a house.

One week before the festival Amine bought a ram. He tied the animal to the weeping willow and Mourad fed it straw. From the tall window in the living room Aïcha and her brother watched the ram, with its yellowish hair, its sad eyes, its menacing horns. Selim wanted to go outside and stroke the animal, but his sister wouldn't let him. 'Papa bought it for us,' he kept repeating, and Aïcha felt a sudden urge to be cruel. In gory detail she described exactly what would happen to the ram. The children weren't allowed to watch when the butcher came to slit the animal's throat and the blood gushed out then spread through the grass of the garden. Tamo fetched a bowl and cleaned the red grass while thanking God for His generosity.

As the women ululated, one of the labourers butchered the animal on the ground. Its skin was hung on the front gate. Tamo and her sisters made large fires in the backyard where the meat would be grilled. Through the kitchen window the children watched as embers flew and listened as hands were plunged into the animal's entrails, making a sound like sponges soaked with mucus, a slimy, sucking sound.

Mathilde put the heart, lungs and liver into a large iron vat. She summoned Aïcha and pushed the child's face towards the purplish heart. 'Look, it's exactly like it is in the book. The blood goes through there.' She stuck her finger in the aorta then pointed out the two ventricles and the atrium, concluding with the words: 'And I've forgotten what that one's called.' Next she picked up the lungs as the maids stared in horror at this sacrilegious behaviour. Mathilde placed the two grey, viscous bags under the tap and watched them fill with water. Selim clapped his hands and she kissed him on the forehead. 'Imagine it's air instead of water. You see, my love, that's how we breathe.'

Three days after the festival, men from the liberation army turned up in the douar in the middle of the night, faces hidden under black balaclavas. They ordered Ito and Ba Miloud to feed them and find them some petrol. And they left the next morning, promising that victory was close and that the years of depredation were behind them.

* * *

At the time, Mathilde thought her children were too young to understand what was happening. She didn't explain the situation to them, but that was not out of indifference or a determination to keep them in the dark. She believed that children lived in a bubble of innocence that no adult could pierce, no matter what was going on. Mathilde thought she understood her daughter better than anyone; she believed she could read her soul as easily as she could look at a beautiful landscape through a window. She treated Aïcha like a friend, an accomplice, telling her secrets that she was too young to know, then reassuring herself with the thought: What she doesn't understand can't hurt her.

And she was right: Aïcha didn't understand. To her the adult world appeared hazy, indistinct, like the countryside at dawn or in the evening twilight, those hours when the shapes of things faded and blurred. Her parents talked in front of her and she caught snatches of those conversations when they lowered their voices and used words like murder and disappearance. Aïcha would sometimes ask herself silent questions. She wondered why Selma didn't sleep with her any more. Why the female workers let themselves be dragged into the tall grass by the men, with their cracked hands and sun-reddened necks. She suspected that there was something called misfortune and that men were capable of cruelty. And she sought explanations in the nature that surrounded her.

That summer she returned to her life as a little savage, a life with no timetable or constraints. She explored the world of the hill, which was, for her, like an island in the middle of the plain. Sometimes there were other children, boys of her age carrying dirty, frightened lambs. They walked through the fields bare-chested, and their skin was browned by the sun, the hair on their forearms and the backs of their necks turned blonde. Trickles of sweat ran down their dusty chests. Aïcha felt something stir inside her when these young shepherds came towards her and offered to let her stroke the animals. She couldn't stop staring at their muscular shoulders, their thick ankles, and she saw in each of them the man he would become. For now, they were children like her, and they floated in a state of grace, but Aïcha understood – without being entirely aware of it – that adult life was already changing them. That work and poverty made their bodies age more quickly than hers.

Every day she followed the procession of labourers as they walked under the trees, imitating their movements while trying hard not to disturb their work. She helped them build a scarecrow with some of Amine's old clothes and fresh straw. She hung shards of broken mirrors in the branches of trees to scare away birds. For hours she would watch the owl's nest in the avocado tree or a molehill at the bottom of the garden. She was patient and silent and she learned to catch chameleons and lizards, which she hid in a box, occasionally lifting the lid for a moment to observe her prey. On a path one morning she found a tiny bird embryo, no bigger than her little finger. The creature, which wasn't even quite a creature, had a beak and claws, a skeleton so small that it was almost unreal. Aïcha lay with her cheek against the earth and watched ants running over the corpse. Just because they're small doesn't mean they're not cruel, she thought. She wished she could question the earth, ask it about all the things it had seen, the other people who'd lived here before her, those who were dead and whom she'd never known.

Precisely because she felt free, Aïcha wanted to find the limits of the domain. She'd never really known where she was allowed to go, where her family's property ended and the others' land began. Each day her energy took her a little further and she kept expecting to find a wall, a fence, a cliff, something that would tell her: 'This is where you must stop. You cannot go any further.' One afternoon she walked past the hangar where the tractor was parked. She crossed through fields of quince and olive trees, she beat a way through the tall stems of the sunflowers burned by the summer heat. She found herself in a small enclosure where nettles and other weeds grew waist-high and here, at last, she saw a whitewashed wall, about three feet high. She had been here before, a long time ago: as a little girl she'd held Mathilde's hand as her mother picked flowers and waved away midges. Then her mother had shown her the wall and said: 'That's where your father and I will be buried.' Aïcha walked through the enclosure. The scent of honey seeped from cactuses covered in prickly pears and she lay on the ground in the place where she imagined her mother's body would be buried. Was it possible that one day Mathilde would be very old, as old and wrinkled as Mouilala? Aïcha put her elbow over her eyes to shield her face from the sun and dreamed of the anatomical plates that Dragan had given them. She knew by heart the names of certain bones in Hungarian: *combcsont* for the femur, *gerinc* for the spine, *kulcscsont* for the clavicle.

* * *

During dinner one evening Amine announced that they were going to spend two days by the sea, on the beach at Mehdia. There was nothing surprising about that particular destination; it was the closest beach to Meknes, only a three-hour drive away. But Amine had always mocked Mathilde for the leisure activities she craved: picnics, forest walks, mountain hikes. People who liked having fun, he said, were lazy, good-for-nothing shirkers. That he'd organised this outing was perhaps due to Dragan, who kept urging him to stay at their cabin, and who – always close to Mathilde – saw flashes of envy in the young woman's eyes whenever he mentioned his holidays. There was no malice in that envy, only sadness; it was more like the envy of a child who sees another child cuddling a toy that she knows, with simple resignation, she will never possess. Or perhaps Amine had been driven to it by deeper feelings, a desire to be forgiven by his wife – whom he could see slowly fading here on this hill, in this world of endless work – and to bring some happiness into her life.

They left in the car at dawn. The sky was pink, and at that hour the flowers that Mathilde had planted near the entrance of the property were especially fragrant. Amine had been in a hurry to leave: he wanted to make the drive while it was still cool outside. Selma was staying at the farm. She didn't get up to wish them goodbye and Mathilde thought it was better that way. She wouldn't have been able to meet the girl's eye. Selim and Aïcha sat in the back seat. Mathilde wore her raffia hat. In a large basket she'd packed two small spades and an old bucket.

A few miles from the sea, they encountered traffic jams. Selim had thrown up, and the car smelled of his vomit: sour milk and Coca-Cola. They got lost in streets filled with holidaying families and it took them a long time to find the Palosis' cabin. On the terrace Corinne was sunbathing while Dragan, his face red and bathed in sweat, had drunk a bit too much beer. He was happy to see them and he carried Aïcha in his arms. He made her fly, and that memory – the memory of her lightness in those huge, hairy hands – would be almost as strong, almost as unbearable, as her memory of the sea. 'What?' said the doctor. 'You've never seen the sea before? Well, we have to do something about that!' He carried the little girl across the sand, but she wanted him to go more slowly. She wanted to stay on that sun-soaked terrace a little longer, eyes closed, listening to the strange, deafening sound of the sea. That was what she liked most to start with. That was what she found beautiful. That sound, like when someone rolls up a newspaper into the shape of a telescope and puts it to your ear and blows. That sound, like the breathing of someone who's deeply asleep, enjoying sweet dreams. That backwash, that tender fury, distorted and amplified by the muffled laughter of playing children, the warnings of mothers – 'Don't get too close, you might drown!' – the laments of beignet vendors as their feet burned on the hot sand. Dragan, still holding her in his arms, advanced towards the water. He put her down and Aïcha sat on the beach to take off her beige leather sandals. The sea touched her and not for an instant was she frightened. With her fingertips she tried to catch the foam that bubbled at the waves' edges. 'L'écume,' said Dragan in his strong accent, pointing at the white froth. He seemed proud that he knew the word.

The grown-ups ate lunch on the terrace. 'A fisherman came this morning to show us what he'd caught. You'll never eat anything fresher than this in your life.' The maid, who had come with them from Meknes, had prepared a salad of tomatoes and pickled carrots, and using their fingers they ate grilled sardines and a sort of white fish, long like an eel, with a firm, bland flesh. Mathilde kept fiddling with the children's plates, reducing the fish to shreds. 'Well, we don't want them to choke on a bone, do we?' she said. 'It would ruin everything.'

As a child Mathilde had been a brilliant swimmer. Her class-mates said she had the body for it. Broad shoulders, strong thighs, thick skin. She would go swimming in the Rhine even in autumn, even before the arrival of spring, and come out with violet lips and wrinkled fingers. She could hold her breath for a very long time and she liked nothing better than having her head underwater, being submerged in what was not a silence but a whistling of the depths, an absence of human agitation. Once, when she was fourteen or fifteen, she'd floated, her face half underwater like an old branch, for so long that one of her friends had dived in to rescue her. He'd thought she was dead, like those girls in romance stories who drown themselves in a river over a lost love. But Mathilde had raised her head and laughed: 'Fooled you!' The boy had got angry then. 'Now my new trousers are wet! My mother's going to kill me . . .'

Corinne put on a swimming costume and Mathilde followed her on to the beach. Further off, some families had set up large tents on the sand. They would camp there for a whole month, cooking on little terracotta canouns and washing in the public showers. Mathilde kept moving forward and when the water reached her chest she felt such happiness that she almost rushed over to Corinne and hugged her. She swam, as far as she could, diving down as deep as her lungs would permit. Occasionally she would turn around and see the little cabin getting smaller and smaller, more and more indistinct in that row of identical beach houses. Without knowing why she started waving her arms, perhaps just to greet her children, or to tell them: 'Look how far I've come.'

Selim, wearing a straw hat that was too big for his head, was digging a hole in the sand. Some other children saw this and came over to look. 'We're going to make a castle,' said one little girl. 'Mustn't forget the moat!' said a boy with three missing teeth who spoke with a lisp. Aïcha sat with them. It was funny how easy it felt to make friends when you were on the beach! Half-naked, their skin browned by the sun, they had fun together and thought of nothing but making the hole as deep as possible, until they struck water and saw a little lake form below their castle. Aïcha's hair had been uncrinkled by the sea air and she ran her hands through the pretty curls, thinking how she would have to ask Mathilde to pour salt into her bathwater when they got back to the farm.

Late that afternoon Corinne helped Mathilde wash the children. Wearing pyjamas, sweetly exhausted by hours of playing and swimming, they lay on the terrace. Aïcha felt her eyelids growing heavy, but the beauty of the view kept her awake. The sky turned red, then pink, and at last a ring of purple haloed the horizon while the sun, more incandescent than ever, was slowly swallowed up by the sea. A man came along the beach selling grilled corn, and Aïcha nibbled the cob that Dragan handed her. She wasn't hungry but she didn't feel like saying no to anything; she wanted to enjoy everything that this day had to offer. She bit into the corn and some grains got stuck between her teeth. This felt quite unpleasant and she started to cough. Before falling asleep she heard something she'd never heard before: her father's laughter, open, spontaneous, and without a care in the world.

* * *

When Aïcha woke the next morning the grown-ups were still asleep. She walked on to the terrace alone. She'd had a dream as long as those apple peels that Mathilde would sometimes make, lips pursed in concentration, intent on turning the skin of the fruit into a garland. The Palosis ate breakfast in their swimming costumes, which seemed to shock Amine. 'We live like castaways when we're here,' said Dragan, whose milky skin had turned cherry-red. 'We wear as little as possible and eat whatever the sea gives us.'

By noon it was so hot that a cloud of red, shiny dragonflies formed just above the water; the insects nosedived into the sea before gliding back up again. The sky was white, the light dazzling. Mathilde moved the parasol and the towels as close to the water as she dared, so they could enjoy the coolness of the breeze and keep an eye on the children, who never tired of splashing in the waves, digging their hands into the wet sand, watching tiny fish dart around their ankles. Amine sat down next to his wife. He took off his shirt and trousers; underneath he was wearing a pair of trunks that Dragan had lent him. The skin of his belly, back and calves was pale and there was a tan line on his bare arms. He didn't think he'd ever offered his body to the caress of the sun like this before.

Amine couldn't swim. Mouilala had always been afraid of the water and she'd forbidden her children to go near the wadi or even the well. 'The water could swallow you up,' she'd told them. But watching children plunge into the waves and small, thin, white women adjusting their swimming caps as they swam, necks straight and heads bobbing above the surface of the water, Amine thought it couldn't be that complicated. Why shouldn't he do the same thing? After all, he could run faster than most other men, ride bareback and climb a tree using only his hands.

He was about to join his children when he heard Mathilde yell. A big wave had swept away the towels and Amine's trousers. With his feet in the water he watched his trousers move back and forth on the water. The sea, like a jealous mistress, was taunting him, mocking his nudity. The children, laughing, raced to Amine's clothes and the reward that they imagined they would receive. In the end it was Mathilde who grabbed his trousers and wrung the water out. 'Come on,' said Amine, 'we should go home now.'

When they called the children, Aïcha and Selim refused to follow them. 'No!' they shouted. 'We don't want to go home.' Amine and Mathilde stood in front of them on the sand and grew angry. 'That's enough! Get out of there now. Do you want me to come in and get you?' But the children left them no choice. Mathilde dived gracefully into the waves while Amine walked in cautiously until the water came up to his armpits. Coldly furious, he reached out and grabbed his son by the hair. Selim cried out. 'Never disobey your father again, you understand me?'

On the drive home Aïcha couldn't hold back her tears. She stared at the horizon and refused to speak as her mother tried vainly to console her. She saw men in rags walking by the side of the road, their hands tied and their hair covered with dust, and she thought that they must have been rescued from some cave or hole. 'Don't look at them,' Mathilde told her.

* * *

It was the middle of the night when they got back to the farm. Mathilde carried Selim and Amine carried Aïcha. He thought she was asleep when he left her in the bed, but as he was about to close their bedroom door she asked: 'Papa, only the bad French people are being attacked, aren't they? The workers will protect the good ones, don't you think?'

Surprised, Amine sat down on her bed. He thought about it for a few seconds, head lowered and hands pressed together in front of his mouth.

'No,' he told her firmly. 'It has nothing to do with being good or bad. It has nothing to do with justice. There are good men whose farms have been burned and there are bastards who've got away scot-free. In war, goodness and badness and justice all go out the window.'

'So this is war?'

'Not really,' said Amine. And as if talking to himself he added: 'In reality, it's worse than war. Because our enemies – or the ones who are supposed to be our enemies – have lived with us for a long time. Some of them are our friends, our neighbours, our relatives. They've grown up with us and when I look at them I don't see an enemy, I see a child.'

'But are we on the side of the goodies or the baddies?'

Aïcha sat up and watched him anxiously. It struck him that he didn't know how to speak to children, that she probably didn't understand what he'd been trying to tell her.

'We,' he said, 'are like your tree: half lemon and half orange. We're not on either side.'

'And are they going to kill us too?'

'No, nothing will happen to us. I promise.' And he kissed his daughter softly on her cheek.

After quietly closing the door and walking into the hall-way, Amine thought about how the fruit of the lemange tree was inedible. Its pulp was dry and its taste so bitter that it brought tears to his eyes. And the world of men is just like the world of botany, he thought. In the end one species dominates another. One day the orange will win out over the lemon, or vice versa, and the tree will once again produce fruit that people can eat.

*   *   *

Amine felt certain that nobody would come to the farm to kill them, but he decided to make sure of it. Throughout August he slept with his rifle under the bed and he asked Mourad to do the same. The foreman helped Amine build a false bottom in the cupboard of the conjugal bedroom. They emptied it, removed the shelves and made a trapdoor to get in and out of the hiding place. 'Come here,' he told the children one day, and Selim and Aïcha obeyed.

'Go inside there.'

Selim, grinning, slid through the opening, and his sister followed him. Then Amine lowered the trapdoor and the children found themselves in total darkness. From their hiding place they could hear their father's voice, muffled, and the footsteps of the adults pacing around the room.

'If anything happens, if we're in danger, this is where you have to hide.'

Amine taught Mathilde how to handle a grenade, in case the farm was attacked while he was away. She listened with the concentration of a soldier, ready to do anything to protect her territory. A few days before this a man had come to the clinic. He was an old labourer who'd worked on the property all his life and had even known old Kadour Belhaj. When he asked to speak with her outside, under the palm tree, she imagined he must have some embarrassing condition or that he was going to ask for an advance on his wages or for one of his distant cousins to be given a job. The labourer talked about the weather, about this oppressive heat and this dry wind, which were bad for the harvests. He asked about her children and showered them with blessings. When he ran out of small talk he put his hand on Mathilde's arm and whispered: 'If I ever knock at your door, especially at night, don't open it. Even if I tell you it's an emergency, that someone is sick or needs your help, you must keep your door closed. Warn your children, tell the maid. If I come, it will be to kill you. It will be because I've ended up believing the words of those who say that if you want to go to heaven you must kill French people.' That night Mathilde picked up the rifle hidden under the bed and she walked barefoot out to the giant palm tree. In the darkness she fired against the trunk until all the ammunition was used up. The next morning, when Amine woke, he found the corpses of rats trapped in the ivy around the tree's trunk. He asked Mathilde what had happened and she shrugged. 'I couldn't stand that noise any longer. The sound of their feet as they climbed the tree was giving me nightmares.'

At the end of the month it finally happened. It was an August night, cloudless and silent. A red moon glowed between the tops of the cypresses and the children lay on the grass to watch for shooting stars. Because of the chergui they'd started eating dinner in the garden after nightfall. Green iridescent flies sizzled and died, caught in the melted wax of the candles. Dozens of bats flew from tree to tree and Aïcha touched her hair, fearing that they might make a nest in her tight curls.

The women were the first to hear the gunshots, later that night. Their ears were attuned to hearing their babies' cries, the moans of sick people, and they sat up in their beds with an ominous feeling in their chests. Mathilde ran to her children's bedroom. She carried the warm, sleep-softened bodies, whispering, 'It's okay, it's okay.' She told Tamo to hide them in the cupboard and Aïcha, still half lost in a dream, realised that the trapdoor had been closed on them and that she had to calm down her little brother. This was no time for crying or disobedience, and the two of them kept quiet. Aïcha thought about the torch that she used to catch birds. If only her father had given it to her . . .

From her hiding place she heard Tamo begging to be allowed to go to the douar to find out if her family were all right and Amine yelling: 'Everybody stay here!'

The maid went to sit in the kitchen, weeping into her elbow and startling at the slightest sound.

First there was a vast brightness, a distant explosion of violet that made a sort of hole in the night. The fire created a new horizon and it looked as though the sun was about to rise long before dawn. The bluish dazzle was followed by the orange glow of flames. For the first time in their lives, the countryside was ablaze with light at night. Their world was now a gigantic inferno and the landscape, usually so silent, was loud with the sound of gunfire and shouting, mingled with the howling of jackals, the hooting of owls.

A few miles away the first orchards were set on fire, almond trees and peach trees consumed by flames. The terrible wind brought with it the smell of woodsmoke and burned leaves, as if thousands of women had gathered to prepare a feast for demons. The yells of the labourers on the colonists' farms merged with the crackling of fire as they ran from the well to the stables, from the well to the blazing haystacks. Ashes and embers flew into the peasants' faces, burned their backs and hands, but they didn't feel the pain and kept running, buckets of water in hand. In the stables the animals were burned alive. All the goodwill in the world can't bring an end to this massacre, Amine thought. Nothing can stop them. We're trapped in the middle of the blaze, and there's no reason why we shouldn't be.

A French army tank moved through the night on to their property. Amine and Mourad, who'd been patrolling the farm since dusk, told the driver that they were ex-soldiers. The tank driver asked them if they needed help. Amine looked at the huge vehicle, the soldier's uniform, and he felt uneasy at this military presence on his land. He didn't want his labourers to see him negotiating with this man who – in their eyes – was an invader.

'No, no, everything's fine, Commander. We don't need anything. You can go on your way.' The tank moved off and Mourad stood at ease.

Under the trapdoor Selim was crying. He clung to his sister, smearing her with snot and tears, and she hissed: 'Shut up, you idiot! If the bad men hear you, they'll find us and kill us.' She put her hands over his mouth, but he wouldn't keep still. She was straining to hear the sounds in the house and especially her mother's voice, since Mathilde was the one she was most worried about. What would they do to her mother if they found her? Selim calmed down. He put his face to his sister's chest and was surprised by how slowly her heart was beating. Aïcha's lack of fear reassured him. She recited a prayer, mouth close to her brother's ear. *'Heavenly angel, my loyal and charitable guide, let me be so obedient to your wishes that I do not stray from my Lord's commandments. Holy Virgin, mother of God, my mother and patron saint, I put myself under your protection.'* And the two of them sank into sleep, soothed by the image of the angel protecting them.

Aïcha woke first. She didn't know how long she'd been asleep. Outside, all was silent. The gunfire seemed to have stopped and she wondered why nobody had come to let them out. What if they're all dead and we are the only ones left alive? she thought. With both hands she pushed against the plank above her head and climbed to her feet. Then she opened the cupboard door. Selim was lying down and when she stood up he gave a little moan. The bedroom was in darkness. Aïcha walked slowly into the hallway, feeling her way with her hands. She knew where every piece of furniture was and she was careful not to knock anything over, to make no sound. She came to the kitchen; that, too, was empty and her heart contracted. Flies buzzed over the remains of their dinner. They must have come, she thought, and taken Tamo and my parents, even Selma. In that instant the house seemed to her enormous and hostile. She imagined herself a mother to her little brother, a little girl abandoned to an extraordinary fate. Tears welled in her eyes as she told herself stories of orphans and suffering, tales that terrified her and at the same time gave her courage.

And then she heard Selma's voice, distant, quickly fading. At first Aïcha thought she must have dreamed her aunt's voice, but then it reached her ears again. She walked over to the window and there she could hear more clearly the sound of conversation. They must be on the roof, she thought, and she opened the door, relieved that they were alive and furious that they'd forgotten her. In the darkness she climbed the ladder that led to the roof terrace, and the first things she saw were the incandescent ends of the cigarettes that Amine and Mourad were smoking. The two men were sitting side by side on crates of drying almonds while their wives stood with their backs turned. Mathilde was staring at the lights of the town, just visible from their hilltop. Selma was contemplating the fire. 'It won't reach here, thank God. The hill will be spared. The wind has dropped and there'll be a storm soon.' Selma opened her arms wide, like Christ on the cross, and yelled, her voice a hoarse howl, like an echo of the jackals who'd been stirred up by the fire. Mourad threw his cigarette to the ground and roughly pulled his wife's skirt to make her sit.

Aïcha, standing on a rung of the ladder, her face just poking up over the edge of the roof, hesitated before showing herself.

Maybe she would get in trouble? Her father would tell her off for following them up to the rooftop, sticking her nose in the grown-ups' business, not knowing her place. In the distance she saw a cloud in the shape of a giant brain. It flickered and glowed, as if filled with electricity. Selma was right: it was going to rain, and the rain would save them. Her prayers had not been in vain. Aïcha's angel had kept her promises. She cautiously stepped on to the roof and walked quietly towards Mathilde, who saw her and said nothing. She pressed her daughter's head against her belly and turned her face to the dying flames.

A world was vanishing before their eyes. The colonists' houses were burning. The fire devoured the dresses of nice little girls, the chic coats of mothers. Books were reduced to ashes, as were family heirlooms brought from France and proudly exhibited to the natives. Aïcha couldn't take her eyes off this spectacle. Never had the hill seemed so beautiful to her. She could have shouted with happiness. She wanted to say something, to start laughing or dancing like those chouafas that her grandmother had told her about, who spun around until they fainted. But Aïcha didn't move. She sat next to her father and pressed her legs to her chest. Let them burn, she thought. Let them go away. Let them die.

Acknowledgements

My thanks first of all to my editor, Jean-Marie Laclavetine, without whom this book would never have been published. His trust, his friendship and his passion for literature bore me up through every page. I would also like to thank Marion Butel, whose grace and efficiency helped me steal the time I needed to write. I am extremely grateful to the historian Hassan Aourid, to Karim Boukhari and to Professors Mustapha Bencheikh and Maati Monjib, whose work inspired me and who were kind enough to enlighten me about life in Morocco in the 1950s. Thank you to Jamal Baddou for his openness and generosity. Lastly, I wish to give thanks with all my heart to my husband, Antoine, who forgives me my absences, who tenderly stands guard outside my office door and who, with every passing day, proves to me how much he loves and supports me.